Our Time

Our Time

Books, like bridges, build bonds between people, places, and possibilities.

Len DeAngelis

Our Time: "Books, like bridges, build bonds between people, places, and possibilities."

Our Time is a novel, a work of fiction. Names, characters, places, and incidents either are the product of the author's imagination or are used fictiously, and any resemblance to actual persons living or dead, businesses, companies, events, or locales is entirely coincidental.

For information about this book contact lendeangelis@verizon.net.

Class Acts
lendeangelis@verizon.net

ISBNs:
979-8-9887147-0-5 (softcover)
979-8-9887147-1-2 (eBook)
Check for Audio version availability.

Printed in the United States of America

Cover and Interior design: Len DeAngelis and 1106 Design
© Len DeAngelis, 2024

Arial, a dyslectic-friendly typeface, released in 1982 by Robin Nicholas and Patricia Saunders, is the typeface used in **Our Time**.

"May we never tire of what we feel, live, and love.
Learn the rules to play: then, explore to create more beauty."
Len DeAngelis (1942–   )

Dedication

God

Camille and Anthony
Monica, Dave, and Anabella
Celeste and Anthony
Anthony, Lisa, Jennifer, and Robert
Chickie
Doctors and their staffs

Family, Friends, Students, Readers/Listeners, and Others

Clarity, Creativity, Nature, Time, Truth, and Will

Pre-Reading Study Guide

1. What wars/conflicts occurred or are occurring during your lifetime?

2. Interview a twelve-year-old.

3. What do you remember about being that age?

4. What challenges did you face?

5. Whose passing made an impact on you, and at what age?

6. How would you describe your childhood?

7. Did you feel secure?

8. Who made a difference in your upbringing, and why?

9. Consider writing reflections on places of your youth, schools, homes, etc.

10. What qualities define a best friend, friend, acquaintance, and others?

"Nel mezzo del cammin di nostra vita
[In the middle of the road/journey of our life]
mi ritrovai in una selva oscura
[I found myself in a dark wood]
chè la diritta via era smaritta."
[Be/cause the direct path was lost.]
Dante Aligheri (1265–1321)
La Commedia

"Ask what you can do. . . ."
President John F. Kennedy, (1917–1963), 20 January 1961

"Our Time"
Our Time begins.
Prior labor dims.
Word shadows glow.
Writers will grow.
Interest may rise and fall.
Our Time awaits as do all.
-
Our Time awaits as do all.
Interest may rise and fall.
Writers will grow.
Word shadows glow.
Prior labor dims.
Our Time begins.

Contents

Characters

Alex, Lily's father, m. to Grace; brother to Alfred

Alfred, Gordon's father, m. to Vera; brother to Alex

Beau (b. 1918, m. 1934), Friederich's wife, mother of Ben and son Fred

Beau, son Fred's granddaughter

Ben (b. 1935) Friederich and Beau's elder son, brother to Fred, younger son

***Carmel** (b. 16 December 1925, d. 5 October 2017)

Cherie (b. 23 September 1954), m. Tony, PM

Cinnamon, a Cairn Terrier

Dante (b. ca 21 May-20 June 1265, d. ca 13/14 September 1321)

Dolly, cares for the children of staff; works with Zuri-Mama

***Edel/Will** (b. 23 January 1945), son of Zuri and T

***Edel**, E, daughter of Will (20 May 1995)

Fred (1938) younger son of Friederich and Beau, brother of Ben, elder son

Fred [Friederich], F (b. 1915), Friederich, German, transition officer, 1940, Guernsey; English wife Beau (b. 1918; m. 1934); two sons, Ben, age 5 (b. 1935); and Fred, 3 (b. 1938), Ben, 5 (b. 1935, m. 1960), 2 sons: (b. 1963, m. 1985); (b. 1965, m. 1990) Fred, 3 (b. 1938, wed 1968), boy, (b. 1970, m. 1993); girl, (b. 1972, m. 1994), daughter, named "Beau" (b. 1995), interested in ancestry, connects with Edel

Journal Entry 43, Will, 68, 2017;

Fred's son Fred, 79, brothers have not seen or talked to each other in 60 years.

* Indicates Journal Entry/Entries writer

***Gordon** (b. 2 August 1922–2007); Alfred; m. Lily; ship's captain, adopted by Vera and Alfred father of Willa, Will (+), Will

Gösta, 1899–1963, **SS Vega**, captain

Grace (b. 1903, d. 1983), Lily's mother, Vera's sister; husband Alex

Guion, G, nurse, substitute veterinarian, T's friend

L, silent teen, participant in writing project, Guernsey

***Lily** (b. 20 October 1923, d. 19 September 1989); m. Gordon; mother of Willa, Will (+), Will, parents Grace and Alex; m. Gordon

Mame (b. 15 September 1960); teacher; friend of Carmel and Will

PF, Palace Friend

Queen (b. 21 April 1926, d. 8 September 2022)

Ren (b. 1995), son of Japanese officer and wife; Edel's swim mate;

Robert, a student participant in the writing project, Guernsey; Edel's assistant

***T** (b. 8 April 1925, d. 19 August 2002), father of Will, formerly Edel

Tony (b. 6 May 1953), Prime Minister, m. Cherie

Vera (b. 1901, d. 1980), Gordon's mother, Grace's sister; m. Alfred

***Willa** (b. 6 February 1945), daughter of Gordon and Lily, sister of twin Will (+), and Will, formerly Edel

Will Alex Alfred (b, 6 February 1945, d. 17 February 1945), son of Gordon and Lily, brother of twin, Willa

***Will**, W (b. 23 January 1945), birth name: Edel; son of Zuri and T

***Zuri**, Z (b. 5 March 1928)

Zuri-Mama, Zuri's mother

Prologue

Guernsey . . . London . . . Paris . . . Boston . . . Newport. . . . The itinerary reads like a marquee. The order of travel to, from, and when varies. My first trip to Guernsey in 2019, to add interest to my teaching, was motivated by a book published in 2008. After returning home, opportunities surfaced, and you hold or hear the result.

On Wednesday, 6 March 2019, travel to Guernsey began from St. Pancras, a bustling London station, reflecting the polite interaction of people, shops, and refuge. Travelers were greeted by the Needle and several other sites on the train ride to Gatwick.

The delayed Aurigny flight approached a land mass. "Guernsey appears in the rectangle of window glass adjacent to my seat," I had written on a bookmark.

After landing, I followed others and boarded a bus to the center of St. Peter Port. The bus frequently mounted sidewalks, allowing vehicles to pass each other on Guernsey's narrow streets. At bus stops, the elderly and women boarded first, and several seated riders courteously rose. Many commented appreciatively at the multi-language sign of "Welcome."

Though I was unfamiliar with the short walk from the town center to St. George's Guest House, a bus transfer eased what became a frequent, enjoyable walk. After stowing the contents of a backpack and taking a swig of tea, I noticed the window view framed an expansive lack of ocean water and exposed a mud flat of boats resting on their keels, and that kindled a memory.

Juliet Ashton took Amelia Maguery's advice in **The Guernsey Literary and Potato Peel Pie Society,**© 5 May 2008, by Mary Ann Shaffer and Annie Barrows. Juliet arrived via the mailboat, thus replaying

Amelia's first visit to Guernsey as a bride. The mailboat at sunrise and visiting the other islands in the archipelago became a plan for 2020.

Before leaving for the Guernsey airport on Monday, 11 March 2019, for two days in Paris, I shared coffee at an outside table with a couple. We hushed while a man voiced his story, ending with a fist tapping his chest, a flushed face, and tear-filled eyes: "too close to the heart." The gift of his phrase of inspiration is the kernel and purpose of this work. He shared his story. His wife was politely silent and supportive, listening to the impressive details. He was born shortly after the island was liberated. His mother's pregnancy was fraught with food scarcity, anxiety, and the unknown ruling the atmosphere. How many women consider the dangers of choices, make appointments, and then abandon the possibilities? Untold stories persist, yet sharing stories enlightens. The significance of this period is reflected in many non-fictional diaries and journals. This fictional story is offered for those whose stories remain within and seek the courage of expression.

On 14 June 1940, Paris surrendered to the German forces. Hurried evacuations occurred in the Channel Islands (UK) in late June. On 28 June, 111 German bombers dropped bombs on Guernsey. The German forces occupied the Channel Islands (UK) for five years—until 9 May 1945, when the islanders were liberated.

Fiction helps polish our skills and senses to pay better attention to each other.

Blank spaces are for the Reader's notes and images.

I trust you.

Thank you.

Peace,

Len DeAngelis

Journal Entry 1, Edel, 16, 2011

Dear Reader:

This journal entry and those that follow were created for our fictional characters, of which I am one. Arranged chronologically, they represent "our time" writing this story. Please understand we often constructed journals in the present tense for imagined dialogue and to offer a sense of immediacy to the reader. There is a repetition of incidents by people involved included for perspectives. Also, we individually chose not to have our names listed as participants in this project—including Will who guided the publishing phase in the last Entry 45—supporting one among us—whom you'll meet in this first Journal Entry—who is nonbinary and never spoke, and whom we welcomed and accepted. "L" remains hesitant to those who may not be welcoming and accepting. Each of us has a signed, notarized form of proof of participation in this experience.

One's sixteenth summer: Driving permits, real jobs, Junior year. I could taste independence. The book project Dad got me into began with angst, and by September, it was out of my hands and in his as he approached self-publishing on our behalf. The night before I began classes, I read my journal entry of the summer day when participants able to attend the workshop met in Guernsey.

Monday, 25 July 2011

Because of this writing project, my Dad's birth in Guernsey, sharing his birth name, and our visits growing up . . . at sixteen, I wanted to research the location of Guernsey.

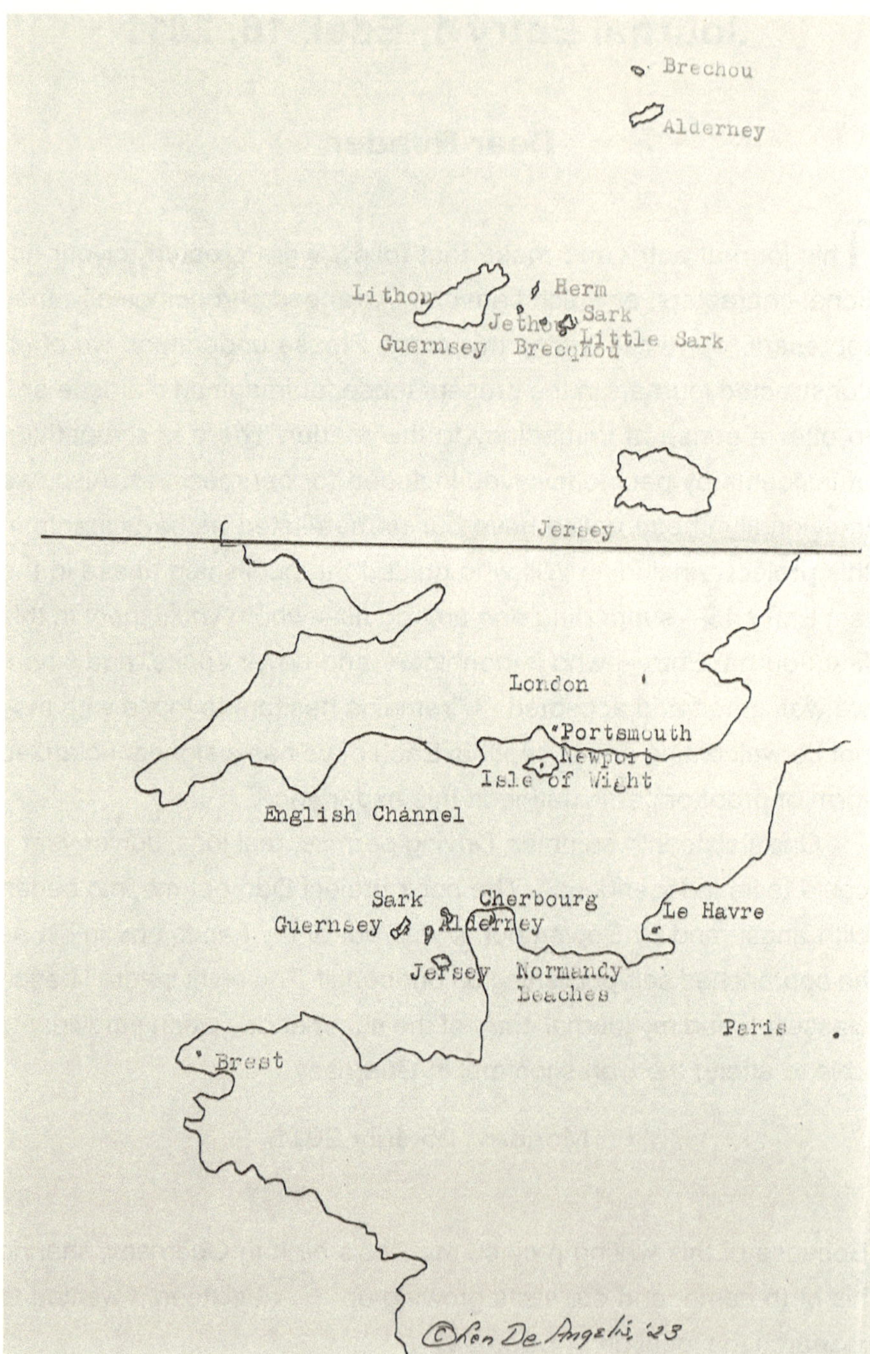
Brechou
Alderney
Lithou   Herm
Jethou   Sark
Guernsey   Brecqhou   Little Sark
Jersey
London
Portsmouth
Newport
Isle of Wight
English Channel
Sark   Cherbourg
Guernsey   Alderney   Le Havre
Jersey   Normandy
beaches
Brest   Paris
© Ron De Angelis '23

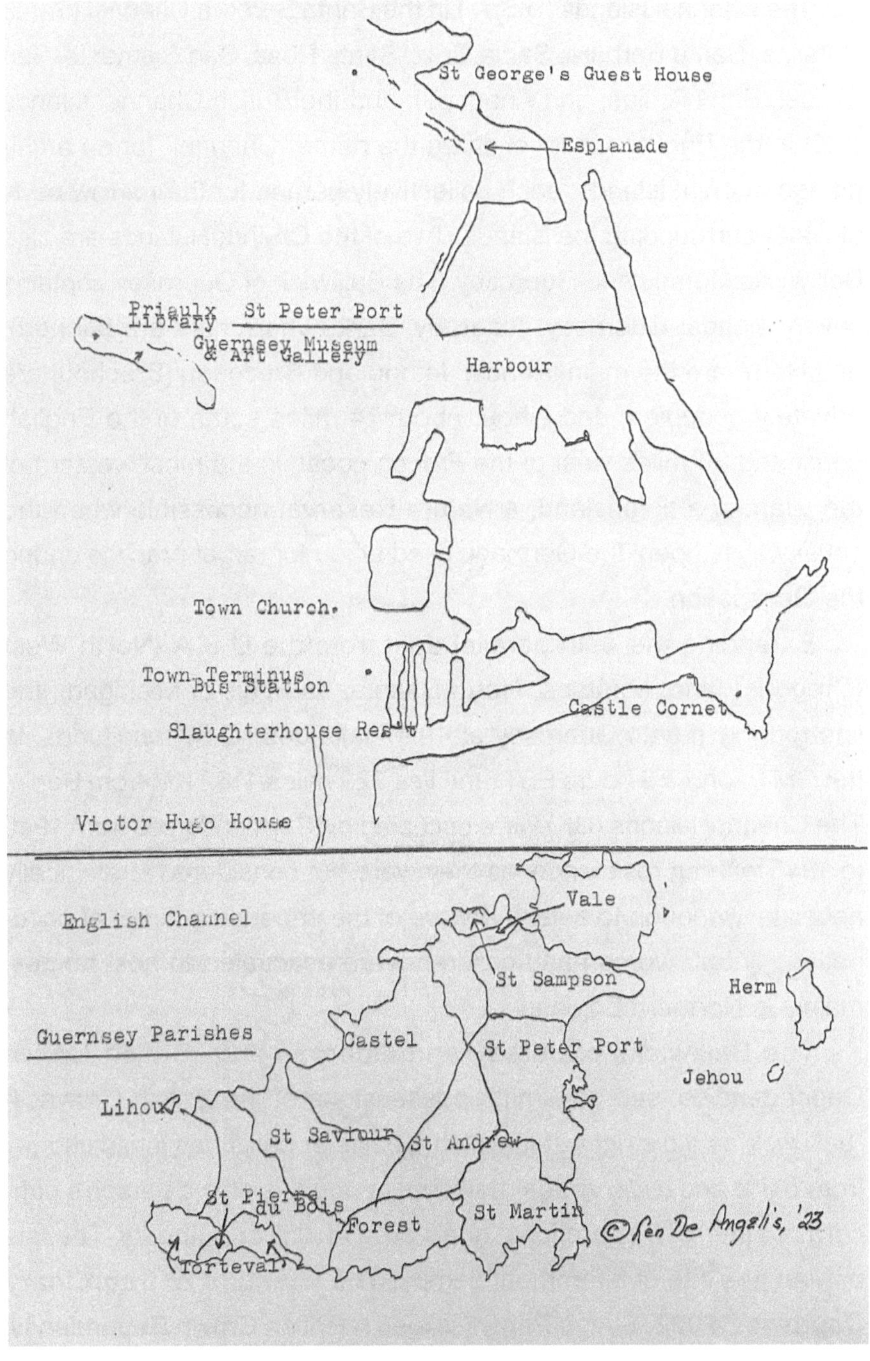
St George's Guest House
Esplanade
Priaulx Library
St Peter Port
Guernsey Museum & Art Gallery
Harbour
Town Church.
Town Terminus
Bus Station
Slaughterhouse Rest
Castle Cornet
Victor Hugo House
Vale
English Channel
St Sampson
Herm
Guernsey Parishes
Castel
St Peter Port
Jehou
Lihou
St Saviour
St Andrew
St Pierre du Bois
Forest
St Martin
Torteval
© Len De Angelis, '23

The Channel Islands (U.S.A.) in the Santa Barbara Channel (Santa Catalina, Santa Barbara, Santa Cruz, Santa Rosa, San Clemente, San Miguel, San Nicolas, and Anacopa), and the British Channel Islands (UK) in the English Channel share the name "Channel" for an archipelago of eight islands, each collectively named for the narrow body of water surrounding the islands. Two of the Channel Islands are also Bailiwicks: Jersey and Guernsey. The Bailiwick of Guernsey contains seven islands: Guernsey, Alderney, Sark (where cars are banned), and Herm are the main islands; Jethou and Brecqhou [Brechou] are privately occupied; and Lihou, about 74 miles south of the English coast and 30 miles west of the French coast, is the most western of the islands, a tidal island, a Nature Reserve, accessible when the causeway is open; the Germans used Lihou for target practice during the Occupation.

Extending the 49th parallel east from the U.S.A.-North West (Oregon, Idaho, Montana, North Dakota, and part of Michigan), the line roughly meets Guernsey at 49.47 latitudes, -2.59 longitudes, in the GMT zone, +5 hours EST, and lies 722 miles/1162 KM from Berlin. The Channel Islands (UK) were occupied by German forces from 1940 to 1945 without resistance, as they were not considered strategically necessary enough to defend. Aware of the impending threat of occupation, 17,000 women and children were evacuated to host homes, mainly in Northern England.

The Bailiwicks of Jersey and Guernsey are British Crown Dependencies, self-governing possessions of the British Crown. A "bailiwick" is a district within which a bailie or bailiff has jurisdiction—from *bailie* and *wick*, village. Bailiwick, a noun, is also a person's concern or sphere of operations, one's area of skill or authority. The Isle of Man [the site of internment camps, **The Island of Extraordinary Captives**,© 2022, Simon Parkin] is also a British Crown Dependency.

The British Monarch is the Isle of Man's head of state, represented by a Lieutenant Governor, with a Chief Minister instead of a bailiff. The Isle lies in the Irish Sea east of Belfast, Northern Ireland, and west of Whitehaven, England. These three (The Bailiwick of Jersey, The Bailiwick of Guernsey, and The Isle of Man) are British Crown Dependencies. They are part of the British Isles but not the United Kingdom. However, the identifier after Channel Islands (UK) is used.

Guernsey lies twenty-seven miles off the west coast of France and sixty miles south of London in the English Channel. During World War II, the German Forces, emboldened by having occupied other territories, took advantage of the temptation to occupy a possession of the British Crown, regardless of its status, as a step toward the capital city of London. Despite the German warning, Guernsey was not defended. The Germans landed, bombing and killing residents in Guernsey on 28 June 1940, and occupied the Channel Islands (UK) for five years. Liberation was celebrated on 9 May 1945 and every 9 May thereafter.

An ad from a writing coach appeared in a daily blurb Dad received online from "Guernsey's Goings-on," a free site to share possibilities that may interest others. The coach wanted to assemble high school-age students to write a series of Journal Entries as fictional characters in a novel about the German occupation of the Channel Islands (UK) while people who had lived through this period, 1940–1945, are still with us. Many had written non-fiction journals and diaries which we could research. Meeting and interviewing were also options.

Those able to meet and those willing to join us online from 1 July to 1 September 2011 formed the project group. The last week in July, 25–29, and the first week of August, 1–5, were reserved for live writing sessions for those able to be on Guernsey then. We met at St. George's Guest House Breakfast Room and agreed to write, edit, organize, and decide for all involved. The dates coincided with Dad's and my annual visit to Guernsey with my 83-year-old grandmother, Zuri, whose health, stamina, and appearance continued to impress. We wore name tags and introduced ourselves in a sentence, including where we were from and why we had opted to participate in this project.

Dad and Coach had swapped emails and had created a structure for the venture: Anyone who wanted to be involved had to submit three pages: a one-page journal entry writing sample of a fictional or non-fictional character; a one-paragraph or half-page list of biographical data of that character, using a first name only, and a drawing or image on the other half page; a cover sheet with the required contact information of the writer with a current photo, which could not be visible on the two accompanying pages. Dad and the Coach had tossed out submissions that did not follow directions. They kept files, assigned numbers in the upper right corner of the three pages, sent a thank-you note, and separated the cover from the two following pages. Submissions could be handwritten and mailed or electronic.

Two hundred and three submissions greeted us in stacks of ten plus three when we met on 25 July 2011. Twenty of us appeared for breakfast at St. George's. We were each to choose our top three from our stacks and then our top one. We each read our top one aloud to the group and asked for a show of hands as to "stay" or "go" based on interest and variety. Readers could resort to the other two choices if they thought them worthy of the group's attention.

After lunch, we chose a student leader and assistant, and several characters we thought would create an interesting mix. We ate outside and enjoyed the view and air. The last three submissions were for the readers who finished before the rest of us. Coach asked if any of us would mind being connected to our submissions. We all shook our heads. There were five of us, and Coach asked us to form a panel for written questions from the other 15 students in attendance. We would choose a student group leader and an assistant.

One among us, Robert, asked, "Could we hear the five pieces from the five writers who are here?"

We agreed. I was last and read my piece on Zuri.

Coach asked, "More questions?"

"Nah!" we replied.

"Can we vote on a Leader and assistant?"

I was chosen as the Leader, and my assistant was Robert, who had asked the question that had advanced us to this point.

I raised my hand. "Now what?"

The Coach said, "Are you asking them or me?"

"Both," I replied.

In an unplanned chorus, we all looked at the Coach and sang my question, "Now what?"

"In your submissions, I suggested you develop a character, a short biographical text, and a writing sample. For the next three days, work on a one-page journal entry each day for your character. In the mornings, we'll listen to each other and ask questions, if necessary, and in the afternoons, we'll try to integrate characters to see if we have a possible storyline and plot. On Friday, we'll decide from the previous three days' work how best to integrate our characters and further develop them independently or with another person's help. I'll share this online with those interested and who cannot be here. I'll ask them each for one submission by Thursday at 4:00 p.m./1600, Guernsey time."

I added, "I'm still missing something . . . I feel adrift . . . and wonder how this will pull itself together."

Several other people agreed.

Coach replied, "I thought we could wait until Friday so you could concentrate on developing your character."

"I want to know now what the larger framework is so I can make sense of what I'm writing," said another.

"Okay, try this: Decide the age of your character and the length of his/her life, and that will help determine how far back and how far forward you go and the context of your character in world events."

"What about world events and locations and their impact on characters?" asked another student.

"We can weave those together when we have a context within which to work. When the story shifts locations, we meet new people, events, and life."

"But we don't want to confuse the reader," I added, "or frustrate the reader. Allowing him/her/they to work to solve the book's 'mysteries' is okay. Most readers like that. They're not lazy just because they sit and read. Their minds are working out!"

Coach chimed in, "Right, that's refinement; let's call that *editing*. Maybe I'm oversimplifying what you're seeking, but eventually, time and chronology will give us order . . . a framework. . . ."

"Why fiction?" asked a participant.

"Research and interviewing will enhance the writing. It's summer; fiction is less academic, more imaginative, and playful."

"Sex? Drugs? Rock 'n Roll?" asked someone who'd turned around and looked for the speaker like the rest of us did; then, all eyes returned to the Coach, who looked at me.

"Would you like to talk about this without me here?" Coach asked. "I can sit outside while you, plural, hash this out."

"I'd like you to stay," I said. "Any objections?" There were none.

After some dialogue, we decided we could write about anything as long as it had a quality of respect and wasn't tawdry or something we would be ashamed to share with a family member or anyone else we respected.

"May I?" Coach asked. We nodded.

"Enjoy the writing. You may be as blunt as you like, but understand that we will edit later. This is a group effort."

"Does the group or the individual writer have the final say?" Robert smugly challenged.

"I'd like you to write with the freedom that you each will have the final say on your entries, and you will be made aware of how others feel. Let's attend to challenges as we meet them," Coach said, seeking consensus.

A silent, androgynous individual dressed in black hadn't spoken yet, and I wondered if s/he (my made-up pronoun) was a "he" or "she." S/he was wearing a name tag with a single letter, "L," and showed me a word, printed like a type font, "Memory."

"Right!" I said. "Backward and forward. Memory can help tell the story. May I share this?" S/he nodded. I did.

Coach almost ended with logistics. "Let me know how I can help; you've got many people here who can help. This is a workshop. I'll be here from 9 to 5, lunch from 12 to 1 p.m. Enjoy Guernsey. Learn about Guernsey. Plan your day."

He added, "I'd like to see you for the first and last half hours each day. You are welcome here anytime. No one is required to be here all the time. Let's see what we need, how you do, and how we integrate others. I'll guide and put Journal Entries in chronological order. We'll have to concentrate on transitions and making the work flow. See you in the morning. I swim from 7 to 8:30 a.m. if anyone wants to join me. Anyone?

"I walk at 11 a.m. and ride my bike at 2 p.m. Anyone is welcome to join me and work "out" during those times. Catch the double entendre?"

After "L" and I swapped phone numbers, I thought, Kids need other kids. I grinned to myself, recalling Zuri reminding me, only once—an admonishment almost, from her mother, "Kids are for goats. . . . Did you mean children?"

Coach held up a finger for silence and ended our session with the music of "People," and B among us began, and we joined in, "We're children. . . ."

Journal Entry 2, Zuri, 12, 1940

In June 1940 . . . days after turning twelve, I watched the boat with Zuri-Mama aboard disappear and vanish from my vision. Blip! Bling! Gone!

Numb, ashore, I patted the flattened bag under my shirt with my sewing and tatting essentials and a journal and pen I always carried. Our routine of living in London and Guernsey disappeared . . . now what? Or, "What's Next?" Mama often told me a "storyette" in British English and "storiette" in American English of twins conversing in the womb, one afraid of birth and facing the future and the other anxiously looking forward. We would change and elaborate the conversation to suit our situation, and we felt better. I can't imagine being alone, but I have to try. The Germans were coming. I was alone. I think many thoughts all jumbled together.

Guernsey's parents had one day to decide if they would evacuate the children and some adults. How long would the Germans stay? How could we adjust to the invasion? Would there be reminders that we were Occupied? A crude entry . . . with hurtful intentions. Why were Mama and I separated?

Imagine? There are things in life for which one cannot prepare. One can hope. One can pray. One can observe. Learn. Read. Write. I speak few words for two reasons: to keep my voice from causing others to question it and to reflect on the trauma of losing Zuri-Mama. I have kept language. I write. Writing offers a future.

When Zuri-Mama spoke, I took notes. Feelings, actions, and words may express emotions: love, caring. . . . What is spoken is gone with a breath. Yet the energy of expression ejaculates from the entire body. Once airborne, recorded, and expressed, who knows where words land or their effects? Energy transforms as beings are birthed. Living is a time to tend—attend, and care—just as we are treated . . . language deserves attention. Relationships epitomize the depths of mingling if we are formed from clay that may mingle us with others. Species may die in an unknown future. Writing endures.

I read, and expressive minds fall on young shoulders. Only Zuri-Mama read my words and said, "You are more than you realize." She always nodded encouragingly. She cared for and loved me. Though not seen on my pages, I free the chorus within me. Like a slice of bread in a loaf, each word, line break, pauses, images, and beauty contribute to a larger entity.

Would Mama have disguised me as a girl if I'd been a boy?

Yes.

I wonder.

No.

I wonder.

I honor my words freeing my guarded, silent voice.

Once, I asked Zuri-Mama if I were born a boy, would she have disguised me as a girl?

"No," she replied.

Zuri-Mama taught me letters, words, numbers, music, art, and tatting . . . and I continue to write in my journal.

"If the place of birth is not well known, you make it proud of yourself by sharing whatever goodness you achieve," Mama said. "And, if it is famous, like my city, London, contribute to its fame by how you live."

I have little, but I have had language since I was very young. "I Zuri, me." using the Guernésiais language form translated into English helps me connect to the land of my birth, Guernsey.

When I saw Zuri-Mama write, I said, "I write, me?" using the Guernsey *patois's* grammatical form, which I heard when we shopped.

Zuri-Mama explained a little but wanted to ensure my interest was deep even though I was young. She said, "Few people speak the language, but I find a sentence:

Oui, i dit, "Le Guernésiais est-i difficile à Pierre?" (*wee, ee dee, "leh jer-nez-yeah ehs-tee di-fi-seel a P-air?"*)

Yes, it said, "Is Guernsey-French difficult to read?"

Zuri-Mama said, "Let's make a calendar. You say, and I write?" She held a piece of paper 8 1/2 x 11 in landscape position, seven columns across, five rows down.

Number each block in pencil upper-right corner, 1–7, next row 8–15, 16–22, 23–29. Zuri-Mama said, "There, you wrote numbers! Very good."

I say, "Numbers, not words. I write words, please."

"Hmmm," Zuri-Mama said, "Time to learn letters already?"

I nod.

She smiled and placed an uppercase "I" in box nine and an uppercase "Z" for Zuri in box twenty-six. Now I understand why she asked for and collected outdated calendars at the end of every year. She hung the alphabet-like posters, low for our eye level. If anyone from a new place joined us and used a different alphabet, Zuri-Mama asked parents to give the child the family its alphabet to share in our "school" room. We all clapped and heard new words for "Please," "thank you," "name," and "age" in different languages.

She said I had "instinct," and she would not worry about me. I did not know what "instinct" meant or when I first heard her say "instinct," but she followed with a story. She would put me anywhere with spools of colored threads, and I would make combinations of colors that made Zuri-Mama smile. "I would never think to combine those two, but you make them work."

As I got older, she would be tatting pieces and ask me for a contrasting color so that one would enhance the other. Sometimes, she would give me cream and white, and I would give her turquoise and purple. I would combine the threads and show her how contrasting colors produced a more exciting piece. I played with spools, threads, and fabric. Zuri-Mama made learning interesting and fun.

She raised me as a very modest boy with a health problem, wink. So, I was quiet and lean and learned quiet activities.

"Zuri-Boy. Safer."

"We find each other," she said and winked. "Skin has no way for me to change, but gender . . . maybe. . . ."

We are cautious, and you see and feel the difference, and when you "grow up, you can see how people are treated." She always says, "You change everything for me. You are my first thought every day." She cared every day for me. "Maybe one day you will have a child; you understand better."

"So, men before women?"

She nodded.

"White before color?"

Again, nod. "We must know our place and not intrude or push, even when laws change. Prejudice is very strong. May never change, but we try, and try."

She taught me numbers, letters, and life. I was 12 when we learned the Germans were coming to Guernsey—soon after my birthday. Then, Zuri-Mama told me so many things all at once so I would know about my body. Zuri-Mama talks, and I wrote more notes.

I am slow to mature. Not all my teeth fell out as a child. No breasts yet. No period yet. Still waiting. Zuri-Mama tried to get me evacuated, but too old and not white enough. Mister tells Zuri-Mama, "He can stay on Guernsey for now. He's light-skinned. You come to London; your color here may be. . . . When this is over, I'll send for him. The future is too unpredictable to make plans at the moment."

Mama says if I stay, she stays, but Mister asks, "How could we live if you stay on Guernsey . . . ?" Mama has no answer for him . . . and no answer for us: how could we live on Guernsey with no work? Mister and Madam odd. Mama never trusts Madam. Mama said that when Madam looks at me, she looks like she is studying with a microscope. They have two daughters. Mister wanted another child, but Madam said, "No more."

When Madam is away, Mister wants Zuri-Mama. Before I was conceived, Mama said to him, "Not a good time." He insists. Zuri-Mama gave birth to me alone.

She was tall and thin, and no one knew she was pregnant. After I was born, Mama told everyone she "found" me and asked Madam if she could stay in Guernsey, and Madam said, "Oh, no. I need you in London. I am envied for the clothes you make with lace."

So, my care was deducted from Mama's wages, and we traveled between London and Guernsey for eleven years. With a hasty evacuation plan, Mister said I should stay in Guernsey, but Mama had to go to London. Mama spoke to Madam, who agreed to make room for me aboard the boat.

Mama helped Madam pack the boat with her stuff, and when I appeared, Madam sent me back to the house with a hat box and said quietly, "Do not come back. Get along." I do not turn to see Zuri-Mama but still hear her muffled pleas. I stay with "Auntie," who teaches and cares for children, and she says, "Zuri-Mama suspected this possibility and said Mister agreed to send money via T should the need arise." No one knew how long The Occupation would last. I wondered if I would ever see Mama again.

I saw children hungry at Auntie's, so I left so they could eat. T sees me in a smeuse one day when he brings food, and two days later again, in the same place, the hedges where I took shelter, at the edge of the estate above Candie Gardens, near the Priaulx Library. Children of staff were cared for in the space of a long garden shed shielded from the mansion and grounds. The slope of the land between the privet and the shed was a favorite place to sit and view the harbor that resembled a postcard.

Soon, food became an issue for both the Germans and Guernsey-ites.

Even with its temperate climate and lands of vales and hills and exquisite beauty, Guernsey could not sustain the residents *and* the invaders. The UK government decided the Channel Islands were not worth defending, and importing provisions stopped. Hunger began.

I would read, tat, and often imagine where ships were going, where they had come from, and the breeze and comfort and quiet of the space always excited my thoughts. I also watch a fenced-in space where the children play outside.

We had few supplies, but calendars, books, paper, and whatever else staff found or people donated made its way to good use. The older kids helped care for the younger ones. "Auntie" Dolly, called *La Cumata* by some and *Goombah* by others, supervised. Mama came in when her work allowed and would read or teach a skill and often said, "All I need are calendars!" Every child, including some from the mansions, was welcome. At the end of each year, we made the rounds to stores and friends, asking for outdated calendars. Mama liked the ones with pictures and large squares for the dates.

In the summer of 1940, I slept outside with my little bag with my needles, scissors, threads, and clothes, two pairs of socks, two pairs of underwear, one shirt, one pair of pants, gloves, brushes, and washcloths. I left my winter jacket for the younger children. I can make another.

Would I see Mama again? Unpredictable and abrupt changes became a reality of transition between, before, and after that lodged in

"Auntie" Dolly sketch

memory. I memorized the harbor, the land, the buildings, the weather, and the scene as if photographed. I missed Zuri-Mama. So many times, every day, I access her. *Be quiet. Be careful. Trust no one.* People remind me of who and what I am. Twelve . . . and alone. Born a girl . . . dressed as a boy. I feel Zuri-Mama's wisdom. Every day. . . . in many ways.

"Zuri-Boy, you eat?" T asked.

We called each other by our first names once a day when we first met; after that, we used just the first letter, as it helped younger kids hear the alphabet, and each letter stood for many names. Mama named me Zuri so that she could have another "Z." When I met T, we were both young; he was three years older and helped me learn letters and numbers.

I don't say anything, but my nose runs, my eyes fill when I try to nod, and he says,

"Come with me. We are friends. You help me."

I sat on the crossbar of his bicycle. He had an egg, tomato, and a roll in his pocket. I eat. Twelve years old. Life changes, but T, 15, is saving me. He says, "We help each other." I remember being alone on the pier . . . the yacht and Zuri-Mama faded from sight.

Here we are, children.

Dark, Amber light

Journal Entry 3, T, 15, 1940

Given the geographic location of Guernsey, in an archipelago of the Channel Islands, with trade winds and mild winters, the "sunniest" part of the British Isles has possibilities for self-sufficiency. Even the Germans thought it made sense and was a way to build working together.

We, in Guernsey, were dependent on many supplies from the UK.

We did not have the resources to be independent, and the status of Jersey and Guernsey as Crown Dependencies gave us the designation only one other possesses: the Isle of Man. The designation did not change the minds of the government to send us food.

I remember chuckling over why the occupiers might have considered that Isle if they were looking for a place to extend their objectives. We thought we were only heard of when Paris fell. And there we were, close by and undefended because we weren't strategically significant! Yet we were part of the German objective: the westernmost achievement of their occupation plans.

We explored food and farming; the longer the occupation lasted, the more significant the essentials would be. As time passed, I always wondered how the Prime Minister could allow us to be disregarded. As autumn became winter, what could be expected? In addition to ourselves, we had "guests"—occupiers, who confounded us at many turns. Life would have been a challenge without them, but with them, life became unreasonably burdensome.

Politically, they had objectives and forces to achieve those objectives—a reality as inhumane and unreasonable, and as much as we may disagree with them, we were living that reality. They had their jobs to do.

The means by which they got those objectives accomplished needed people with more power than we had to disagree and fight them.

Most people of Guernsey were convinced that we had to take care of ourselves and each other, and the best way to do that was to keep what we had going and whatever we had to share.

HOP E was our acronym for "Help Ourselves Program," and the "E" stood for "Eternally." We have Guernsey and Jersey cows with protein-rich milk; we have land to produce fruits, vegetables, and grain. Can land be spared?

Can we enlist help to farm? We have livestock and the sea. We have sun and wind. And most importantly, we have a sturdy stock of people who are strong in character and emotions. We can learn. We can cooperate.

We resist, but we are not foolish. We know our limitations, and the most challenging thing we had to do was break up our families. Our rationale proceeded from love.

Selfishness does not intrude on our values and well-being. My thoughts kept working on storing food and sharing what we had with each other and, possibly, our guests. Once a week, could we, as a people, one human to another, plan on bringing what can be shared, retrieving what was needed, and using a system of barter and money? How?

I imagined dividing the island into five sections and subdivided it into twenty-six quadrants. Public Works Island vehicles could transport people and products with trucks, wagons, trailers, and buses to and from St. Peter Port piers between 12 p.m. and 2 p.m./1400, Monday-Friday. The plan may have kinks and questions, but the goal is flexible, and we can make changes to improve it. The biggest challenge is getting this approved and enacted by people in Guernsey and people in power as occupiers. Those familiar with logistical elements—roads, vehicles, time, availability—could work to determine the details.

We'll let the Public Works Department work out routes and island division and invite others in the Bailiwick of Guernsey to join us as they are able.

Pickup will be where the driveway meets the public road between 9 a.m. and 11 a.m., to arrive at St. Peter Port pier, offload, and set up by noon. At 2/1400, pack up to leave by 2:15 p.m./1415.

Each household will have a two-wheel dolly and two boxes to store items.

Boxes must be strapped/secured to the dolly. Homemade products, crafts, and baked items will be collected on one table. Label the price on the front and the name on the back; the envelopes or goods may be picked up as participants leave.

There will also be a "Free" table for anyone able to help others with whatever they wish to donate for others to take immediately. This is not a refuse site.

Keep donations clean and folded; if opened, please return them as found.

Anyone may volunteer to "man" or "woman" the table in half-hour time slots.

We request that all items be as clean as possible. There will also be a table for books and other reading material to loan (if you wish the book returned, paste your name and address on the cover, please) or to own.

Questions and suggestions are welcome.

Answers will be posted on a bulletin board at the entrance, where we will publicize a schedule and route weekly and where people may sign up. Emergencies happen, but if you plan to participate and cannot, you must inform us ASAP so drivers can adjust schedules. Table assignments in St. Peter Port will be rotated for each group's participating day. Tables may be shared. Please keep prices reasonable and as exact as possible so as not to involve the need for change. Nobody has much, but we can share, barter, sell, and buy what little we have to keep ourselves going.

Even in war, we need to play. Especially in war, we need to play. Playing cards have long been entertainment, and they gained popularity during the Depression. Countries used the front—non-playing-value-identification side—to help identify aircraft or advertise places, art, and objects. The German playing cards, *Spielkarten*, had a deck of 36 and some of 32, 7–10, King, Queen, Jack, "Ace," versus the set of 52 plus jokers. German suits varied, using Acorns, Leaves, Hearts, and Bells as symbols for suits like hearts, spades, clubs, and diamonds.

Zuri and I played Cribbage regularly, sometimes several times daily, and kept track of dates, games, and scores. Zuri cut up calendars, and I remembered that the calendar was Zuri-Mama's educational basis, and we'd talk.

Zuri-Mama had a first letter of three words combination for any activity: **Easy, Learn, Play**. She could teach people how to play games or do handwork and just about anything else by starting with one Easy part of any activity, from shuffling cards to just doing a knit stitch. Then, she would add more steps. I recall the **ELP** letters actually stood for three other words that served the same purpose with a bit more accuracy, and Zuri and I took a few cribbage games, hoping those words would pop into our conversations. We did get the **L** word, Language, and the **P** word, Process, but the **E** words we discussed in depth: Zuri was sure it was "Essentials," and I said "Equipment."

We chewed over those two words, trying to explain why one was better than the other and which one Zuri-Mama actually intended. We checked journals and notes, and what worked for us was when each of us took the other's word to convince the other person of which Zuri-Mama intended, and Zuri was right—"E" was "Essentials." Fortunately, when we defined Language and Process, we agreed on the definitions within minutes. Language meant rules, and Process was how one showed someone how to do something. Then we tested ourselves by Zuri teaching me to tat, and I teaching her Cribbage, which she knew, but my challenge was teaching it to her using Guernesais, French, and German words. We knew we would not forget these conversations, as they were as close to arguing as we had ever come, and we were proud we were civil, respectful, and strong.

"Let's record these in our journal so we don't get into this discussion again?" I said with a nod.

Zuri replied, "How about we practice with Cribbage?"

Easy:
deck of playing cards
pen/pencil paper scoreboard, 121 holes, 24 groups of 5, plus 1

Learn:
cut deck, lowest dealer, 6 cards each, 2 to crib, cut deck for **scoring** each hand with a "wild card" **after** play; the alternate deal as many hands as necessary to reach 121; earn points **during** hand play and **after**; only **after** with a wild card

Play:
Ace lowest, King highest;
non-dealer first, then dealer, to 31 points or less;
15 and 31 = 2 points;
multiples of same: 2=2, 3=6, 4=12;
sequences: 3=6, 4=12, 5+ each card=5;
post play: each dealt hand as above with a wild card;
crib: for the dealer, with a wild card.

Essentials: as above, perhaps a board with holes and pegs

Language: add more agreeable rules, terms, plays, etc.

Process: watch others play; sit as a judge for disputes; correct errors after they are made; set up practice sessions to increase proficiency.

Then I asked Zuri what she thought Zuri-Mama might think of us. "She often said, 'Not all should marry, especially men. Men need to be free. Of course, when children are involved, they need to help support them and, if possible, let them know what a father is like. If he's a good friend, he's a good parent, but the government and the church . . . smother people . . . they need to let people be.'" Of our many talks and our relationship, we felt in sync with each other.

I made a scoreboard for us with 121 holes and wooden and metal pegs.

Guion—our local veterinarian, physical therapist, nurse, and friend—and I use it; and "Fred" the German liaison officer, substituted when we were otherwise occupied. If we could set an example, let's see how far Cribbage could serve civility, competition, and camaraderie. The Germans pronounced the "C" of Cribbage hard and sometimes wrote it "Kribbage."

As a language venue, flashcards and discarded file folders or cardboard, due to paper limitations, kept me and others creative. Available card decks of 2.5 x 3.5 inches could be cut in 1/2 half horizontally or vertically, and we doubled some decks that way.

The inside cardboard of tea boxes was separated at the seams, and with a reduced rectangular size, a box or two could produce a deck, and other parts could serve as a "board" before we surrendered anything to start a fire.

We used open file folders divided into four columns for the terms specific to the game: scoring while playing, scoring at the end of each game, and any other game-related term. We invited each player to create his own set of flashcards in all four languages.

The pattern of the flashcards caused a minor point of contention. I figured out the languages in each corner and the suit in the center for playing cards. I posted the numbers 1–121, plus "please" and "thank you" in each language for the "board," which helped to learn the languages.

Cribbage helped us get along and might serve as a way to endure this Occupation.

The board "holes" could be as simple as this:

ooooo ooooo ooooo ooooo ooooo ooooo ooooo ooooo ooooo

ooooo ooooo ooooo ooooo ooooo ooooo ooooo ooooo ooooo

ooooo ooooo ooooo ooooo ooooo ooooo o =121

Pieces of cardboard for the board lasted for weeks, and standard pins and nails could be used to peg.

Creating the components was possible—it was compact and worked to create positive competition and energy.

Fred supported the game, but his superior wanted to know why German—Deutsch(e)—wasn't first, in the upper left corner. "Even if we are guests, doesn't that mean we should be first?"

When I played the "alphabetical order" card in English, I was not thinking of using the word in the country's language. Yet, I saw his point and suggested we let the players choose the cards and language and remind him we did put German before Guernesais.

Fred rolled his eyes. "Vat if my superior doesn't buy it?"

I thought, then spoke: "Let's not make it a point to divide but one to help us bond. Let's leave it up to each player which order s/he'd prefer. It's not a Peace Treaty but a way for us to get along reasonably and not make politics the focus of playing."

He caught my attitude and added, "We could even do it in a different language one week a month. Let me see if I can find him in a better mood."

I added, "We need ways to work together; this is small, but the ramifications can be huge and advantageous.

Fred said, "Regardless of who wins this war, we must survive it."

We posted rules and versions in four languages.

Anyone could play anywhere, and anyone could play with anyone else. Both players had to log an entry with the date, printed names, signatures, and scores per hand, and final, and fill it with a log keeper, if one was available or in the book itself, which was accessible to all in the playing area.

At the end of the week, the top four players in each language played a game for a single winner; then, every single winner played each other. If there were none in a language, we'd go to the two second-highest-scoring players. While players played, onlookers could watch or play. Until we had more players to act as judges, "Fred" and I volunteered our services to settle disputes. Appeals and Rematches required us both to agree.

Cribbage Club has become more like Confessions Club, and I'm listening better.

Journal Entry 4, T, 15–19, 1940–1945

Like most people, I keep my journals and writings to myself, though I wonder what will happen to them.

Perhaps if I share my life and "father" and guide a child, how I grew and aged may interest someone else.

Why record my thoughts? Writing serves to help me respond to questions with temporary answers until more definitive ones find their way to me, or, more precisely, I find my way to them. I observe and keep notes on scraps of paper that deserve better order, especially my thoughts on personal subjects. I am young and maturing; between 15 and 19, I became a man in my head and eyes. I began to notice interactions differently. When we gather, sexual references grow into conversations. Men talk in phrases; they embellish, laugh, and move on. Sharing takes trust; in a family or group, any relationship between two or more, like the military, has a structure, a hierarchy.

When the company is mixed, men and women, competition exists. Each group behaves differently. Women seem friendlier toward each other; men, not so much, maybe from a fear of being labeled what one might not be. One had to be even more guarded if one was attracted to another man.

At one of our Cribbage Club meetings, the topic of circumcision surfaced. Some Germans used circumcision as a way to distinguish Jews from non-Jews. The gesture of pointing to a guy's crotch and then slicing a hand across the throat made my eyes bulge. One German officer became very uncomfortable and was teased for being fanatically modest. The talk about the subject adds another dimension when it's the difference between life and death. Terms like "cavalier" and "round head" were bandied about before health reasons and personal details came forward.

Young men, brought up by women alone, differed from boys where a man was present. I appreciated how Mister treated me. Personal experiences vary.

The casualness with which the talk topic would so often be injected with a tidbit of sex while preparing food, working on something, or walking was never extensive, just bits of expression shared, popping up like a blemish—someone may have added, reacted, or nodded. Playing Cribbage, one guy often got pissed when he had not dealt but cut a "Jack-for-his-heels," giving the dealer two points. Usually, a cut card had no value until scoring. His fist gripped, and his mouth tightened.

"I had this older relative who'd make me pay in more than points when that happened. The bastard. Sometimes, he made me pay his way even when the points were mine."

My first thought was, what happens to someone as a child gets carried for a lifetime?

One guy always apologized to others who offered painful memories of past experiences that he lugged around and had affected him since they happened and probably would forever. He seemed kind and sensitive, and one day, as I was working on one of their vehicles, I asked why he always apologized.

"No one has ever asked."

I added, "Experiences aren't always negative. Some guys wouldn't understand and might criticize people involved."

I waited.

Silence usually brought more talk, so I continued waiting.

After a few minutes, I was about to turn my attention back to the engine when he added, "I had this friend once; we'd touch ourselves when we were together, and one thing led to another . . . and I'd say, 'Easy . . . take your time.'"

"You did that on your own?"

"Well, no . . . I did after an older relative caught me looking at a magazine . . . and sat with me. 'Don't stop,' he said, 'slow down . . . enjoy it more.'

"I did . . . and he joined me . . . I appreciate his attitude to this day. . . . We'd better get on with this engine."

"You look . . . interested?" he added with a doubt.

I said, "Funny, I thought my pants were baggy enough."

He smirked and waited, so I shared a bit of my history.

"The Mister of the house has always been kind. I think my name—'T'—is a diminutive for his, and it was a way for Mom to say she named me for her favorite drink, which she loved with a splash of cream when we could get it. The letter also stands for so many other names, though that one letter is what I'm called."

I continued, "She never said he was my father, but possibilities keep increasing.

"He taught me about cleaning myself when I was just a little guy, and every week on Saturday, he'd give me a nickel if I cleaned myself every day, and when I saw him, all I would have to do was nod my head, and that was our signal, and he would always give me just a little smile.

"And I saved those nickels week after week.

"When I was seven or eight, he told me what to expect in the way of bodily changes, and as soon as they happened, I was to signal him with two nods.

"We spent time together, too.

"I'd go out in the boat with him, sailing and fishing, and he'd touch me on the shoulder, show me how to steer the boat, or grab a line, and a feeling just went through me like a current of electricity. I liked his touch.

"He was very gentle and kind.

"I never felt like he was taking advantage of me.

"When we had to make water in the boat and then toss it over the side, I would stare at him and wonder how I would grow to his size.

"When we swam, I thought the cool water would reduce my embarrassment.

"When he taught me to swim, I would get on his back, my arms on his arms, and though I could not reach his legs to kick, I would slide down and encircle his waist to try.

"He would say, 'One day, Son'—he would call me 'Son' when we were alone but 'Boy' when anyone was around."

White boys were always called "Son" by older men.

"My skin was lighter than my Mom's, and my features were finer; my hair was dark and curly but unlike hers."

"She sounds pretty," he commented and asked,

"Changes came?"

I said, "Yes, Mister told me what to expect, as informatively as possible; then he added feelings, and the whole thing overwhelmed me. I remembered how much more sense his words meant as I got older and more experienced.

"He allowed me to touch him, and it wasn't like he was asking me, because whatever he asked, I would do; he said if I wanted, I could.

"I don't usually have choices.

"It's like the military; some can choose the time to serve, but we're stuck with the events, whether we agree with them or not."

"Go on, please," he said.

"I was hesitant, but he showed me how he touched himself and what changes happened.

"I said, 'I want to.'"

"He told me what people could do for each other and how I had to be careful with women and pregnancy; just because I had the power to procreate did not mean I had to use it or risk it.

"He also mentioned men experiencing men . . . boys with boys, growing into men, marrying women, and sometimes still being attracted to men.

"Some guys are one or the other; others have a range of experiences that run from a single experience to multiple digits.

"I was fascinated."

He said, "I've always had an interest; though I married, I also enjoy men."

I commented, "Never thought about both . . . times and people change?"

"Did you both do more together?"

"Yes.

"He always asked before touching me. Every time we had the opportunity, there was something we could do, and even when something had happened before, the repetition was welcome."

"Why the smirk?" he asked.

"Well, he had a . . . 'specimen' . . . which I thought was very decent, until one day he said, pointing at me, 'You can stop growing anytime!'"

"We laughed, as I had a bit more than he. He never forced me to do anything. He told me about some things that we never did."

"And some that you did do?" he asked.

He saw my face flush.

"That's okay, no need to . . . what do you say about this engine?"

We'd been working on it while we conversed.

I said, "Try it."

He did; it turned over, and he went for a ride to be sure.

He was a big guy with a mane of silver hair and skin that darkened with a glow when exposed to the sun. Many Germans are so fair that they burn, and their hair lightens.

He probably has a mixture in his cells, but the Germans let him in their military.

His mother may have been of another nationality, or, like many children born of German fathers, the children were taken and brought up in Germany to serve Germany.

As we got to know each other better and saw each other more often, he shared a sentence that settled in me for a while:

"Finding peace in the loneliness is my eternal battle."

After a silence, I asked if I could help.

He was swarthy, and conditions had not affected his bulk yet.

Were Mussolini as tall, they'd look related.

"Fred"—he'd shortened his name, figuring so much was asked of others, the least he could do was make his name easier—he had a paternal gentleness that countered the mean quality dominant among his colleagues. Officers above and under him admired his demeanor, and he found ways to make his status and bearing work with his orders and obligations.

His hands were like ham hocks, and his fingers so unusually thick I could only imagine how many piano keys one finger hit simultaneously. His nails were always carefully manicured, healthy pink with visible half-moons and tamed cuticles with a flat, outer, curved edge where no debris ever collected.

His hands and fingers were proportionally large, even for his mass, yet contributed to his enviable masculinity. Whenever he held a pen or pencil, he sought the service of another as his diagrams and scripts were illegible, as evidenced by his signature. He carried a pair of gloves that fit to a "T" and kept the pattern for whenever he could find anyone who could sew.

"Ever have trouble getting your hands through a sleeve?" I asked once.

I could tell by the rest of his arm that they were more significant than suited his body. He made his thick fingers work, though he was self-conscious about them. He took his physical size in stride.

When I asked about writing, he related an experience where a woman used to stand over him with a rattan in hand, and every time he wrote with his left hand, the stick would strike and break.

Then he'd try with his right hand, and the forced awkwardness resulted in a script that rarely went beyond his signature, which he began slowly and then raced to the end for fear of being watched—the fear of being judged was the factor that injured and hindered him.

"I broke a lot of those rattans," he laughed.

"One day, a teacher raised it to a girl also trying to stop writing with her left hand, and she looked horrified. Fred grabbed the rattan in mid-air, snapped it into little pieces, and then offered them to the teacher, who was awestruck by the boldness.

The girl's face bore the reddened imprint of the nun's hand that slapped her because she refused to remove a bobby pin to keep her straight hair off her face for a class picture.

"Pretty free with their hands," I remarked. Then I added, "Have you ever had any instruction or tried since then?"

"When I'm alone, I often keep trying, but the fear of someone catching me doing such elementary lessons makes me stop."

"But until you get through some of those steps, you can't build on how useful writing can be."

Fred replied, "I have a good memory, so I keep things there until I can find someone to write for me, and that's worked so far.

"I'm also not very patient, and I have too much to do to fill that gap."

Whenever we met, I'd have a pen or pencil taped to a stick that was thick enough to hold comfortably, and I would space out the time by counting very slowly so he could form each letter on the paper I had lined for upper- and lower-case letters.

"I'm glad I anglicized my name to 'Fred'—fewer letters to write."

"As soon as you are comfortable with the four-letter name, let's try the full name."

I'd gradually shave the stick's thickness and kept reducing it until he noticed it one day.

"Are you doing this, or am I squeezing the implement too hard and condensing the density of the wood?"

After fessing up, I reminded him that pens and pencils may be shaped round, flat-sided, or five-sided but usually conform to standards so that hands can hold them comfortably . . . but that hands vary in size.

He held the pen alone and was so proud that he asked to keep the pencil.

He thought he might send a handwritten note to his boys, to whom he had never written, though there were weekly letters from his wife and the boys.

He also wondered if the weight of his hands would suit a typewriter since the girls taught to type kept complaining about how hard the keys had to be struck.

First, he had to learn if his fingers cleared the keys.

We talked more about his plan, which was just in the conversational stages at this point, for the offspring of the German soldiers on Guernsey; their existence was no secret. He felt some responsibility and was thinking ahead, even if it meant staying on Guernsey to find a resolution. He took notes on scrap paper he'd cut to 2x3 inches to fit into his pocket and make notes.

He seemed tireless and exhibited a sense of humor and an expression that made others feel good to see him.

I could not imagine the turmoil his insides fought.

He was the "go-to" guy, making me wonder who was *his* "go-to" guy. His clothing was always sharp, yet he'd take off his jacket and hat and pitch in with whatever needed a hand, his gesture of the man and heart within.

When we shook hands, often twice a day, he would take my right hand in his, and I would cover his right hand with my left. I always felt like I should bow or kneel as we looked at each other for a quick flash of time when our eyes met.

"Can I help?"

"Would you?"

It reminds me of being awkward with someone with whom I wanted to initiate something but never did. I didn't want to risk our friendship, and I thought making a move or suggesting more could do just that.

Usually, one can tell when an interest of that type exists; sometimes, touch or eye contact is all one needs. Aggression wasn't a strong characteristic; patience is. I'd wait; he'd wait; time passed, maybe wasted.

I phrased conversations in my head. There was only one way to know.

"I'd like to know you better; would you consider it and get back to me?"

"I will; is now too soon?" And like the pauses between notes and in poetry, a place of space versus words where each embroidered the other . . . silence enhanced time and opportunity.

Much later, my thoughts returned to the island, being self-sufficient, and feeding children.

Journal Entry 5, Zuri, 12–16, 1940–1945

T and I sleep together in his narrow bed; I face the wall; he is on his side behind me, and he holds me. In summer, he is naked; I wear a long shirt and underwear. I feel him against me and wonder if he is the man with whom Zuri-Mama said would one day be okay to share our secret. By September, everything Zuri-Mama said would happen physically happened, but I stayed Zuri-Boy, kept track of my days in my notebook, and did as Mama said: "Stay clean." My breasts are small; I think a bra could be two halves of a robin's eggshell. They stay small, but I feel a sensation when I touch them. When I place T's hand there, he says, "You boy, Zuri—these stay like this. Other parts of you will grow, like me, like when you feel me against you." I nod.

Sometimes, when he's sleeping, he wets on me. When he wakes, he says, "Sorry. One day, you understand." I remember what Zuri-Mama said. I know about men, and Zuri-Mama says that one day when love and feelings are powerful, a third person may share our secret.

T told me about one woman. He said the Lady (Madam) of his Mister saw him swimming one day and realized he was a man. When Master was away, she took T to bed. He was terrified. She said, "Just between us!"

He was not to tell anyone ever, nor would she; T was to "tend her fireplace," especially when Master was absent. One day, this will make more sense, he said.

I took notes when Mama spoke because I didn't understand everything she said, but she said it better. She told me before any-thing happened, so I knew what to expect. Now, no Mama to ask, but I know her well enough to know how she would have an answer even if I could not understand. . . . someday, answers make sense . . . if I carry a question . . . she learned from a poet . . . can't remember his name, one word . . . I leave space when I remember—Rumi. When Zuri-Mama shared her journals, I copied poems and things because they looked so nice in her script. She often found things in magazines from other countries, like the U.S.A., that the Lady has; when she tires of them, she gives them to the staff.

One she finds intact, perhaps because of the illustration of two men in a magazine, but Mama says friendship can be between men, women, or women and men, not restricted by sex, age, or relationship.

Even a relative can be a friend. When I talk with T and try to explain my view of friendship, I wonder if he understands what I mean.

I tell Mama I like words that rhyme. And, she says, you keep saying those words in your head, and you commit them to memory, and one day you understand the terms and say, "Ah, that's what it means: love!"

What I like most about friendship is it is free. Free to keep . . . free to enjoy, and free to love. T and I are friends like this.

Why do the Germans forbid radio? They always listen to the BBC to learn and speak better English. So, I will be quiet, but I listen and learn. People who get caught with a radio could go to prison or worse.

Why? Sometimes, there is music, even by German composers, or stories. I don't understand, and I don't ask, but T and I talk; I trust him, and he makes me feel comfortable.

I want more when we touch each other, and I wonder how he will take my secret. He thinks he knows about women, but I think he doesn't know—not yet.

He knows only Madam intimately in her way.

Madam, strange to me.

Over time, T made friends among the Germans, as he knew motors and used a little skiff sailboat for fishing. I painted a set of black sails, and no one saw him fishing at night. We managed food with a little greenhouse and a hidden plot of land where trees kept the ground moist, and we had mushrooms and vegetables. We never took the money for any food we shared; sometimes, we exchanged it for milk or canned goods.

Life was hard for everyone, including the Germans.

One day after I turned 15, T was so exhausted from stacking firewood and his usual work chores that he went swimming to clean up and fell asleep eating dinner. I could smell the salt on his skin. "Go to bed. I will clear here. Leave me a space." When I went to bed, his back was against the wall, and there was space for me where he usually slept. He looked shiny from the moon, naked, and a little breeze cooled our space. His leanness shadowed and glowed on his rippled muscles. He opened a hand but not an eye, and his breathing returned to a rhythmic sound.

Usually, he lulls me to sleep. Watching him. Hearing him. Touching him.

His fingers rest on me like a layer of air between them and my skin.

I moistened him . . . and myself . . . and then, he let out a stirring sound—his eyes popped open while my grip held him . . . still . . . inside me, "Shhhh . . . it's okay." After a time, he slept again and slipped out of me.

Groggy and spent, he soon muttered, "I dream? . . . did we . . . did I? What did we do?" After an hour or so, he woke me. "Zuri-Boy, did I force myself on you, into your backside? I am so—"

I smiled . . . a smirk. "T, I took you inside me, where a man can enter in moist comfort and pleasure us both—"

"But . . . you are a b b boy . . . " he said softly . . . now, with hesitation and doubt.

"Now three of us know . . . ," I began. Soon, we fell into a pattern, a routine, and one day, he asked me to marry him, saying whatever happens in these difficult times if we ever become separated, "I will find you."

Other than the strained relations I saw with Mister and Madam, I didn't know what marriage was. "I know friendship," I responded. . . .

"Can we be 'friends' . . . more formally?" His brows raised, and he nodded. Those words were our friendship vows to each other a few days later, and we carefully enjoyed being together.

Somehow, . . . an egg was fertilized.

Somehow? . . . well, we know how, but we had a way to be careful and were . . . but I suppose many others say that, too. We wondered if we should change our status, but there was no one we trusted to share that with, and any documents we'd get could be stolen, lost, or disappear.

Neither of us wanted to change our status, though we both agreed, as parents, that responsibility would be taken in conscience, and the child would always know we were the parents. Our agreement made our friendship more robust, and the child would have our love and values as well as we could provide. The child would come first, and we trusted each other with that commitment and extension of our special friendship.

Zuri-Mama once found a copy of a poem in a magazine from a man named Guest, born in Birmingham but whose family moved to the U.S. when he was six. She copied the poem for me as part of my twelfth birthday gift, and I also carry it with a cellophane cover in my journal.

Maybe this, and Ralph Waldo Emerson's words, helped me feel that a friend was the best connection between people. "A friend may well be reckoned to be the masterpiece of nature." It's a form of love that could grow . . . and maybe add a connection between friendship and morality.

Friends can enjoy each other as we do and be moral. Zuri-Mama said "moral," a word I must continue to carry until the definition—like an answer to a question—makes sense.

I also carry a card with blue lines and a red line on top, and Zuri-Mama wrote in her tiny print what lines she could fit on the front and blank back by Mr. Guest:

"Choosing a Friend," by Edgar A. Guest. Decoration by Richard J. Flanagan (1924) 1925 *Redbook* magazine. I change pronouns from he to s/he, because English needs updating!

Zuri-Mama asked me to write my own version of a poem about having and being a friend. I was stuck. I only knew Zuri-Mama as a friend. My interaction with others was limited—until T. Now I can write about friendship from a better perspective.

On 23 January 1945, Edel was born, just over 5 pounds but healthy, squirmy, and requiring warmth and feeding. I kept him swaddled to my torso, on one face-cheek or the other, close so he could breathe and have his head supported. My loose jacket served to warm and hide him.

The arrival of the **SS Vega** was in readiness in early February.

Guernsey officials and Germans lined the dock to supervise.

A Captain descended the gangplank and hurried off, and I watched for his return. The offloading began at one end of the boat, and the distribution started at the other. I felt a squirm; Edel nudged me and then settled.

Our child by children.

Journal Entry 6, Zuri, 16, 1945

The **SS Vega** visited for the second time, its trip #40, 1 February 1945, and planned to depart on 11 February. The wind began to pick up, and most of the crew worked in jeans, an array of jackets, and black woolen watch caps that so many Guernseyites wore, most with an added scarf to filter the air.

The Red Cross Ship, the **SS Vega**, derives its name from the Spanish surname **Vega**, a topographical name that means "dweller in the meadow" or "one who lives on a plain," from the Spanish word **Vega**, used to refer to a meadow, valley, or fertile plain. Captain Gösta (1899–1963) notified personnel on Guernsey that the ship was approaching St. Peter Port. The "in-port," substitute Captain, Gordon, assumed the "con"—short for "control"—for maneuvering the ship and escorted the **Vega** with tugboats into port.

Speeches of thanks were made by the Jersey Bailiff, Sir Alexander, and Victor, the Bailiff of Guernsey, who had appealed to the German authorities to allow food delivery for the civilian population.

Sparse flyers and word of mouth were our means of communication. Guernsey officials and Germans lined the dock to supervise.

Captain Gordon came down the gangplank, and, in short order, the offloading began at one end of the boat, and the distribution began at the other. T had rigged a two-wheel dolly, so Guion and I could put each box on it. "Leave it to T. Look at these . . . so clever." T rarely let any item that had a future go by.

Tires were unavailable, but T used sisal rope as tire replacements, wove the ends as close together as possible, and then secured those ends around nearby spokes.

If people needed support getting around, T used discarded bikes from which he'd remove the pedal assembly so people could walk closer to the frame for help. He installed kickstands for stability, and folks without prams to lean on found this worked. People tied parcels to the handlebars and installed boxes on the seats and wheel covers. Tires that were no longer usable for cars T adapted for footwear!

Officials had asked me to prepare a little tatted gift of a baby-size placemat, napkin, and burp bib, and I added a handkerchief for each parent with an "M" for "Mom" and a "D" for "Dad." I wrapped them in cellophane so they could be seen by German challengers who may have thought I was spying with top-secret papers or some other undermining accusation. They do have imaginations. Edel was snuggly swaddled to my chest, and I wrapped a hot-water bag around his back. I had dipped a sugar teat in diluted blackberry brandy to keep him quiet. I broke from Guion and approached Captain Gordon as he returned to the ship with a look of concern on his face and a telegram in his hand.

I took advantage of his proximity, unaware of the background I later learned.

"Our gratitude," I said. "And a little something from me for Mom and Dad when the time comes."

"Why, thank you! Her time may be sooner than expected," he added.

Mail and telephone cables were cut, yet the more expensive telegraph—unavailable for most due to cost—operated though every message in and out and was censored and prioritized. Since the **SS Vega** was under the auspices of the Red Cross, Gordon maneuvered the ship in and out of port, as Gösta was the official Captain. Though the nature of the information was personal, the censors allowed its transmission.

Classified "Emergency" and given the second highest priority: his wife was in hospital awaiting delivery earlier than expected and ended with "Come when able," which he shared with concern.

"Please, come with me; I'd like your name and address, and my wife would like to express her thanks, I'm sure."

I offered, "Please, let me hold on to the gift, as your hand is full, and you need the other to salute." I carried the parcel as a shield for Edel and followed the Captain up the gangway.

We stopped to enter my name in the log. While proceeding to his stateroom, a rogue wave hit the ship. I lost my balance and hit my forehead against the bulkhead.

Captain Gordon took my arm, and I felt a trickle of warmth going down my cheek.

"I'm fine, thanks."

He saw blood pooling along my jawline, about to drop, and pressed a handkerchief against the wound. We entered his quarters, and he sent for a medic after ordering me to lie down.

He undid my jacket, and I placed my hand on Edel's back.

"Who have we here?"

"I was keeping him warm . . . and trying not to let the Germans see him. I'm afraid for him."

"Let me put him by the stove, and Cinnamon, my Cairn terrier, will keep him company while we tend to you."

The medic came in; Captain Gordon put his finger to his lips.

I received five stitches and a bit of ice, followed by a tight bandage held in place by my hat. I began to sit up, and the blood seeped through the bandage.

"I was afraid of that," the medic said. "She should not be moved. She'll be fine soon, but that wound needs to settle and the blood to coagulate."

Gordon said, "I can't endanger the crew . . . give me a minute to think. May I have your confidence?" he asked the medic.

"Of course . . . no one knows she is not a he who could as well have been a crew member," the medic added.

"But there," the Captain said, pointing to Edel and Cinnamon.

"I can't endanger him, either. . . . Now I have three reasons to ask to go to Portsmouth . . . will the Germans buy it?"

The medic shrugged.

The Captain ordered the medic to stay with me and left to speak to Captain Gösta and then to the German officer in charge. The Captains huddled in the outer cabin, and Captain Gordon explained the additional complication of Edel and me.

The German officer had sent a copy of Gordon's request to go to Portsmouth to the high command on Guernsey, and given how things were going, the possibilities were slim.

However, a reply returned quickly: "Leave Jersey food on Guernsey. German escort to the English Channel."

"Request all military vessels allow the **SS Vega**, a Red Cross ship, to pass to Portsmouth unimpeded."

Captain Gösta's authority would resume once we were in international waters, and he added, "We could have an international incident on our hands—and our careers would be *kaput*."

Gordon said, "But we don't have much choice, and with some luck, we might be able to do this, but it could also jeopardize future food relief. If they had to leave the ship now, we might just as well put that baby into German hands. The war isn't over yet."

Gordon added, "We also have a Red Cross officer aboard, but I think we best keep this complication to ourselves . . . and do our best."

They had already sent a request to the admiralty in London to go to Portsmouth instead of the ship's home port in Portugal, as Captain Gordon's wife was in early labor, and it was not going well.

The German officer in charge agreed and took responsibility for participating in the decision, given the shortage of time, and informed others on the island who had to know.

"Would you send word to the man I was with?" I asked. "His name is Guion, big, hay-blond hair, German looking but a Guernseyman," I added.

"I'll point him out," Captain Gordon told the medic.

"You tell him," Gordon said to the medic, "and I'll go to the German officer. Come back and stay here until I return."

In my drowsiness and to keep conscious, I tried to list and listen to the English and German words being translated. The communications staff had prepared a set of 3x5 cards with words in German and English.

The sailor handling the semaphore flags was assisted by another, who shouted out letters to the sailor with the flags so time would not be lost looking at cards with unfamiliar words on them.

Another ship's officer also supervised preparation below decks and on the bridge, and someone logged every transmission to help avoid errors.

The German officer in charge was dubious but willing to risk trying.

I understood, and Captain Gösta knew a few German words, which helped also.

I learned better later about how this happened, yet I remained alert, fed Edel, and heard German words. There were some "what if" situations they tried to predict that led to some humor.

For example, what if the German reply to Head Wound was in English? "Fix Him!" over which we found some strained humor.

They decided communications between the bridge and below decks would help clarify the situation.

2 emergencies
2 Notfälle

Injured crewman
Verletzter Besatzungsmitglied

Injury?
Verletzung ?

Head Wound
Kopfwunde

Wife
Ehefrau

baby
Baby

early
früh

London . . . Portsmouth . . . please
London . . . Portsmouth . . . *bitte*

Thank you
Vielen Dan

In gratitude to the German escort, the food we would have needed if we were going to Portugal was given, but going to Portsmouth required less, and we could get foodstuffs there.

Food in life rafts
Essen in Rettungsflößen

A telegram deliverer waiting at the gangplank had a response that read, "You have permission to go to Portsmouth. The English will cease fire; request Germans do same."

"Whew!" exhaled Captain Gösta.

"I can get in and out of Portsmouth with more confidence." Looking at Captain Gordon, he said, "You can be on your way as soon as we land. I may wait until daylight."

The German officer had sent a request to the German high command but could not promise a reply before departure, and we had to leave immediately because of a break in the weather and seas.

We could not be sure when and if those conditions would persist. but the dramatic tide change in the port that Gordon remembered drawing as a child—*before* he knew about charts that contributed to his expertise—was now even more critical.

We eased into the Channel and received the reply to proceed to Portsmouth and "Advise an English and German boat to escort the **Vega** through the Channel flying white flags."

"Is the baby yours?" Captain Gordon asked.

"He . . . was given to me."

"From now on, say he is yours, or you are setting yourself up for complications you can't imagine. I know why you are saying, 'He was given to me,' but these conditions are not the conditions under which to give doubt or tempt fate.

"I'll remain on the other side of the bulkhead, write my log and journal, and continue checking on you here.

"Should you need me, rap on the bulkhead, please."

At 16:44, Captain Gösta made the log entry, "Departed St. Peter Port, Guernsey, Channel Islands, UK."

As soon as we left, I was alert and lay quiet, gazing at the porthole. As clear as anything I had ever seen, an image of a large, dark-skinned, bearded male with shoulder-length glossy hair appeared, dressed in a coarse caftan.

He sat before me; our eyes met, and he spoke, "I need you."

I didn't know what to call him or how to address him, but I felt his presence as if I'd never felt another before or since. I wondered if he was calling me to go with him.

As respectfully as possible, I replied, "So do others."

He nodded.

"You in?"

"I am."

He touched my forehead and walked through the metal bulkhead, and I noticed his sandals. Then, he vanished. Between the two of us, only ten words had been spoken. I repeat the memory in my head only and very soon adopted another purpose to my life: to His glory.

I asked if anyone had heard me speaking. Gordon said he thought I was dreaming and could not remember what I said. I was alert and awake the entire time, or so I thought.

I always notice details about people, especially hands, but I could not recall his or his feet. His walk was distinctive; he lumbered. I could not recall his facial features. I thought my injury played a part but dismissed it as more what others might say was a cause than I could ever give in to believing. I entered it into my journal without ever adding one more detail that perhaps I had forgotten. But none surfaced. I had forgotten none.

Life has gone on amidst twists and turns I could not imagine . . . and my thoughts of T persist. We have no photographs of each other, but I envision him and wonder how and when we will find each other.

How will we have changed in the interim? I will leave space for his journal entry after I describe him.

T is a slim man with short, black hair and a mixture of features and skin tones we often discussed in the wonderment of our ancestry, what percentage of our makeup may be identified, and what we may pass on. T's skin has an Asian/European glow, a tad darker than mine, exhibited by males of most species. He is six to eight inches taller than I am, and his muscles are well toned, not bulging or bulky, but visible and defined.

We often wondered if he—like most men—would show evidence of excess, but in these lean times, even mature men seem to have kept flesh close to the bone.

He always wore gloves and kept his hands clean and nails trimmed. His fingers were long and slim, and his veins protruded in warm weather, especially on the back of his hands, like a pattern of roads. His body hair was minimal, though his pubes were thick and coarse, and framed his genitals that were the darkest of his manly skin tones, and that he treated with care and daily cleanliness and shared with a satisfying gentleness. His bottom was firm, his legs nicely shaped and well-muscled. His feet were always covered and as attended to as his hands. He taught me how to keep our extremities supple to serve us better. He shaved daily, and his teeth were nearly perfectly aligned; though not bright white, they were consistently off-white. His lips were full but not excessively. His nose fit his face, and his eyes were a dark, warm brown. I noticed a grateful confidence emerging. I wondered who spoke first when he saw Guion and what they said to each other.

I hope he still attends the "Cribbage Club" on Thursdays. I liked hearing his stories without attributing the details to specific people. When the Germans began playing cards, they taught and learned other languages and numbers. Maybe that's where differences can be shared. T and I played almost every night. I remember the cards, scoreboards, and nameplates we made.

Playing . . . friends . . . children.

Journal Entry 7, T, 19, 1945

I'm writing a letter to you—more accurately, to myself—in my journal. Should I write "Dear Zuri"? I can't mail it. Writing is a way to keep track of my feelings and maybe share them with you and Edel.

What happened?

I ran to St. Peter Port Pier as soon as I was finished working on the Germans' car with a flat tire. Guion was there with two boxes from the **Vega** and was talking with a messenger who showed a message to Gordon. "Vye two?" a German soldier asked, holding two fingers. Guion was replying and pointing to me. "Here he comes. My friend had to go to the bathroom." The soldier didn't understand, so Guion quickly pointed to me and put his hand on his zipper. The soldier nodded and left.

"Zuri?" I asked, looking around furiously. The messenger had been asked to pass a message to Guion, which he did hurriedly. We read,

"Captain's guest slipped; cut forehead; stitched and 'okay' but bleeds if upright; captain taking to Portsmouth," and the messenger ran back up the gangplank just as it was lifted and the lines were loosened.

"I have to go!" I said to Guion, who held me back.

"Wait! You can't board the ship. You'll get shot. And . . . what can you do if you got aboard?" Though the messenger hurried, we wondered if he knew English and could read the message . . . what a chance the Captain took writing it . . . and how injured was Zuri. We watched the ship move from the pier toward the horizon, facing wind and water. Silence pervaded our space.

We each took our food boxes and left the pier. Guion stayed with me while we discussed the events, and I assured him I was okay. He could go home. I repeat the scene in my head involuntarily, and nothing changed. I went to tell Auntie Dolly you would not be going to help at the school. When the Germans asked, I told them you had worked in the country, on a farm, or helped with a fishing boat.

Zuri, come back soon . . . please.

The Germans are as weary as we are, and the war is not going well for them.

I am more quiet than usual.

I cannot sleep.

My nightmares seemed so natural that I awoke sweating. After a week, I dreamt I traveled to Kings Cross St. Pancras Station and walked the station all day, hoping you would appear there. Why there?

I have no idea, but it was the only station I knew. Where might you be?

I needed to do something I had not done in so long I could not remember the last time—I dreamt. Once, I even saw Zuri-Mama being pushed in a wheelchair and babbling to herself. I am beside myself with wonder, but in the back of my mind, I think you are both safer there. The war does not look good for the Germans. Who knows what the future may bring? More **Vega** visits are planned.

Guion comes to check on me often. We still play cribbage with the Germans on Thursday nights. Often, we reminisce about delivering Edel.

Sometimes, paths cross at a time most appreciated. Physically, Guion looks more German than a Guernseyman—he has height, good looks, blond, sort of hay hair, and his skin tans to a glow. He's a good man and a good friend. Maybe one day . . . who knows? I sleep a little with Edel's blanket until the smell of him disappears. I miss him. I miss you.

Remember, "I will find you"? I don't know how or when, but now I have a goal . . . for life? I will work and try to save money to send you.

Send you where? If the mail ever returns, we can write. I don't know where you are, but you will write soon? Maybe I will travel to Portsmouth one day, or you will come back . . . here?

I am so distraught, wondering, and unable to do anything or know anything more than the scene that keeps repeating in my head. I eat a little. I sleep a little. I miss you a lot. Oh, my!

The **SS Vega** made five voyages (1944–1945) to the Channel Islands.

Voyage 41, visited 6–9 March 1945, is known for delivering 9 pounds of 12-ounce parcels containing flour and yeast. We were joyful.

On a subsequent visit of the **Vega**, Gordon risked a telegram requesting I be found and wait on the pier. When the boat was secure, he walked down the gangplank, and my eyes filled.

He spoke: "It's okay. We're okay."

I was not relieved; I needed details and had many questions.

He said, "Zuri and Edel"—who, I learned, is now named "Will"—"are well."

"They live with us," and he told the story, and I could only think now I have a Will, and his Will is elsewhere—but we share our Will—and I put my hand on his. My liberation day came March 5 with news of you. Will we ever all celebrate a liberation day? I await more from you in the post when it resumes. But for now, I am so grateful and relieved that you—no one—can imagine. Friederich . . . and Guion . . . will hear. Like all children, our Will brings love, joy, and concern.

T

Hey Z,

Sometimes during the night, when I cannot sleep, and my imagi-nation keeps me awake, I think I will write or draw . . . maybe try to remember how you and Edel/Will looked, besides just saving the images in my head.

I keep working on them so I will have an image to see.

When the post resumes, that could help. You know where I am. I don't know where you are, exactly. Yet, somehow, I think you are okay. I worry and want to help, but you have resilience and make life work. You probably feel safer and think it is better for Edel/Will there than here in Guernsey.

I remember we talked about Edel/Will being in danger. There are children here, but hopefully, there are more resources there . . . , but the day-to-day routine worries me—eating, living, sleeping. You know I say, "Do the best you can," and whatever you decide is best is fine by me. Was the boat incident an accident or intentional? Not that it matters, I guess—it got you and Edel/Will away, but with the war still raging . . . anyway, time will eventually tell, and I need to keep working and stay busy to keep my mind active, and there is little choice in doing otherwise.

Peace and Love,
T

Z, me again. I must keep busy. Distraction helps . . . a lot. I think about solitude, which is okay with me. I was alone in my work, caring for the house, preparing for the owners' arrival, and opening it up for use. Thanks to you, I enjoy reading, crosswords, and journaling, but I don't want to take this life in stride or take for granted that you and Will are permanently distant from me.

The **Vega** boxes helped, but I am still working on finding a growing food cycle that might work for us and others. Remember how we talked about it when the Germans arrived? Feeding hens for eggs, planting corn . . . the German planes carried supplies and had fuel to get to Guernsey, but getting petrol is as challenging for them as it is for us, especially petrol for cars. It's as worrisome as the food supply. So many things of concern. So I am working on life here.

Cows, corn, hens, vegetables, goats, potatoes, tea leaves, (mint)-plants. . . .

It is the job of the people in power (the pips! pip-a-roos, if I remember the phrase correctly) to find a way to manage what would be a food crisis here.

We must work out a system with some community involvement, even just a few, to share the basics.

Who has cows, hens, and goats? What can we plant in our environment?

By working individually as we have, we are bound to be limited, and, as the Germans are learning, so will they. As expected, they need to be provided food, and their plans have taken a downturn. If the war is ending, then changing much may be futile, and we are hungry now!

We on Guernsey have yet to make a plan. All unexpected possibilities cannot be considered after starving. This could happen again. We need a flexible emergency plan if our future is challenged for any reason . . . maybe by a natural event. We can hope, but hope does not feed us now.

Then, there is the consideration of storing and saving food. What can we store, what can we save, and how? I need to think about this more practically and flexibly now that I have the time to do that, and it may help distract me. We have been living in a food system of patches for five years.

Yes, we did our best but could have done better, even if we had addressed options earlier. Of course, having occupiers as "guests" would have impacted our rations, but they showed unusual restraint with orders to troops regarding the **Vega** boxes.

That may be because of how their plan is working, and they may be about to reverse their goal, but whatever it is, even at this stage, discipline is remarkable. They are as hungry as we are.

Z,

When life is settled and we are liberated, will you return? When will that be? And it may be sooner rather than later. You will likely find a way to make life work, which may benefit you and Will. Guernsey is lovely; kids grow up here, but are opportunities better elsewhere? The kind of work I can do could probably support us . . . but this unpredictable unknown, both for the immediate and long-range future, makes me worry and thoughtful.

I think, too, about me joining you "there" and how much more expensive living "there" may be. Others do it, I imagine, and we would manage, too.

Could the man and family I work for here help me there? We have to wait and see, and that is a conundrum.

By myself, I allow my thoughts to drift and realize men deny themselves the warmth of other men. Sexual or asexual, the profound need exists, and many try more challenging things to fulfill the expectations of others than to learn more about themselves. Maybe it's risking being judged or guilty when the possibility is unknown. But, until it is tried or tested, one may decide to indulge in the attraction. Many don't make the time to befriend another, but how much richer could life be were the risk taken?

Guion and the guys who come to Cribbage Club are closer, sharing more, though guys generally are superficial with each other. Women trust each other more easily, keep friends, and do things together. Some of these Guernsey guys who are married are so broken. They don't feel like they can provide for their families, those with them here. And those who sent them away think they did the right thing for the kids and wonder what life will be like when and if the kids return.

Some guys are dealing with wives who are sad even if their relationship is still affectionate. For some, that affection is strained beyond reason. They nip at each other and spend too much time together, and there is so little to look forward to.

The household routine is minimal, and anger is easily accessed out of frustration. And, patience long worn is so thin, it is transparent.

We eat whatever the Germans can manage at Cribbage Club, sometimes bits of bread and whatever we can make into a spread.

Everyone is so thin. The guys look forward to playing among us and taking a little break from their routine. Some, like us, play nightly, three games, keep track of scores, read, do handwork, and try to make do. Footwear is a real challenge . . . not very much gets discarded . . . there is always a use. Someone cleverly thinks of using items in other ways.

Whatever people have, they use for themselves, and if they can share it, they barter it for something someone else has. We've become more clever and grateful to each other. I'm still trying to foster cooperation, even in small groups, to care for each other . . . with what little we have left. This could have been much better thought out, and since the government didn't—maybe they couldn't—we should take it into our own hands and execute community programs and plans.

I know you have very little with you, but do you have your flat essentials carrier with the tatting and sewing supplies, a 5.5 x 8.25 journal, and something to write with, a pen or pencil? Remember when we made journals from brown paper and whatever blank paper we could find for pages? I'll keep our journals with the trust and respect that we agreed upon and wrote on every opening page. I will read the journals we shared, especially on the food/farming we tried to implement when the occupation began. The plan seemed reasonable, and we made some headway, and the unpredictables could not be anticipated or reacted to better than we have done.

Journal Entry 8, Gordon, 22, 1945

I think back to what three guys made happen with the pressure of time, divergent interests, responsibilities, obligations, lives, and careers—what could have gone so wrong so quickly and affected so many? We decided "what the right thing to do" was and made all the other variables negligible. Nothing could compete with our objective.

Gösta, Friederich, and I stood in the small outside space of the Captain's cabin, that served as the space for the Red Cross representative, whom Gösta excused and politely asked, "May we impose on your good nature and understanding and ask you to go elsewhere?"

My concern about language eased when the German Colonel, Friederich, spoke, "I've made learning English my purpose. Please, speak slowly, and I will stop you if I hear a word I don't understand."

Zuri, Edel, and Cinnamon were on the other side of the bulkhead. There were few words. No arguments. With an eye toward the bulkhead, I laid out the predicament as best I could.

"May the **Vega** go to Portsmouth safely and as soon as possible? My wife is in unexpected early labor, and a crew member could use medical attention and the use of your cabin, where we have strung a hammock.

"We can wait in the Channel—a very few minutes—for permission, clearing us before steering right to Portsmouth or left to Lisbon. If we don't hear, we must proceed as if going to Lisbon, and I'll entrust the crew member to you, Gösta, and I will take the escort boat back to St. Peter Port."

Gösta told Friederich, "Instruct the escort-boat Captain that we will lower an inflatable life raft with the excess food we have and would need were we going directly to Lisbon.

"If we go to Portsmouth, I hope we can get supplies while overnight," Gösta said with apprehension.

I nodded.

"We will try to propel a line from the ship to the deck of the escort. The lifeboat will have a secure tarp, so even if it gets overturned, try to retrieve the food and get it aboard.

"It's not much, but *Danke!*"

"*Bitte*," Friederich replied.

We never saw each other collectively after that. Gösta and I never alluded to the incident, though we swapped the con a few more times.

I tried learning more about "Fred" when ashore on Guernsey on subsequent visits. He held a hastily delivered telegram that read, "Cease fire requested. Go to Portsmouth." I didn't know whether to believe it or wonder if others had intruded to put us in danger or if someone would not honor the Cease Fire request. The **Vega** got food and fuel overnight in Portsmouth and left early the next day.

I learned later from T that Fred had acted independently, told no one because no one needed to know, and carried a telegram reading "EMERGENCY: **Vega** to Portsmouth. Cease Fire request by all for Red Cross Ship **Vega**."

The **SS Vega** log held the data of when Gösta and I swapped the "con," but this elaboration belongs to me personally. My expertise as a maritime Captain, especially my familiarity with Portsmouth, Weymouth, and the Channel Islands, began as a child with drawings and sketches. Despite the Occupation, the ship's first visit to Guernsey on 27 December 1944 had me meet the ship after 10:40 a.m. when it was sighted. But I advised we wait for the tide change, which got the ship into St. Peter Port just after 1700 hours.

Despite offloading more than 119,000 boxes of food, I still requested we get into deeper water or risk damaging the hull . . . again on the second visit, as happened on the first visit in December, when the repair required dry-docking.

I have seen the tide recede to a point where the port is a mud flat, and some boats rest on their bottoms, with lines long enough to hold them secure when the tide is high and when the tide recedes.

When I was ignored, I returned the "con" to the Captain but remained aboard to ensure a safe departure. I suggested orders to him, and he issued them to the abrasive sound of the hull scraping the bottom like fingernails on a chalkboard. Once in deeper water, I climbed down to a tugboat and let the **Vega** proceed back to Lisbon, where I was sure the ship had to go into dry dock for repairs.

When the ship was able to return in February, my advice was respected, even to offloading the food for Jersey so the ship could depart more safely. This visit saw other complications that required action in a limited time and cooperation so that further damage would not occur. The tide issue this time helped convince all involved to decide and act without hesitation.

Fortunately, the German Colonel in charge was reasonable and had learned enough English so that time wasn't lost translating; precision to the fidelity of the language was necessary for semaphore communication.

Two issues forced a change in the plan for the ship to return to Lisbon: Lily had gone into early labor and had sent a telegram that got through with the last sentence that read, "Please, come as soon as possible." I had planned to return to London in the next day or two, but I could be there in hours if the **Vega** went from Guernsey.

Also, the guest(s)—plural to be more accurate but unbeknown to me then—I had brought aboard hit a bulkhead when a rogue wave hit the ship. The medic said the guest "crew" member could not be moved as blood continued to ooze. Should we encounter them, a hammock with a stretcher-like plank suspended from the overhead was quickly devised to accommodate rough seas.

A visit to a London hospital within hours was a better option than a week at sea and Lisbon with the possibility of returning when the ship next visited. Fortunately, the German Colonel in charge, Friederich, agreed. He was ordered to check the ship to ensure no Germans had stowed away. He took my word for that and checked a couple of staterooms to make his report credible in conscience. Though dimly lit, the injured "crew" man in the suspended bunk that held my dog Cinnamon and a swaddled bundle caused a questioning blink but not a word between us.

And though it sounds like a shopping list, what needed to happen happened. Approvals were timely, ships in the Channel were warned, and ground transportation was ordered from Portsmouth to take us to London. I was relieved to see my aide with a car and sat in front with the dog so Zuri could lie on the back seat with Edel. His quizzical look prompted me to say, "I'll explain." I did not have to return to get the ship out of the harbor to return to Lisbon, as Gösta felt confident in commanding. The tide in Guernsey threatened.

Portsmouth is closer to London, about 73 miles, 2 hours, Weymouth, 136 miles. 3.5 hours. I kept a set of cards, alphabetically using the English words, used by semaphore on my person just in case. I made them with English on one side and German on the other.

A telegram deliverer waiting at the gangplank had a response that read, "You have permission to come to Portsmouth. The English will cease-fire; request Germans do same."

"Whew!" exhaled Captain Gösta. "I can get in and out of Portsmouth with more confidence," and, looking at Captain Gordon, "You can be on your way as soon as we land. I may wait until daylight, depending on getting our stores aboard. The German officer had sent a request to the German high command that he could not promise before departure. Still, we had to leave immediately because of a break in the weather and seas. We could not be sure when and if those conditions would persist, but the dramatic tide change that I remembered drawing as a child before I learned about charts that contributed to expertise in the port was even more critical.

Gosta requested "an English and German boat to escort the **Vega** through the Channel flying white flags."

At 16:44, The captain made the log entry, "Departed St. Peter Port, Guernsey, Channel Islands, UK."

From never worrying about children to constantly worrying about children.

Gordon

Journal Entry 9, Zuri, 16, 1945

A car waited in Portsmouth; the driver handed Gordon a telegram he shared that read: "Twins! Healthy girl; struggling, but a strong-willed boy.

Love, Lily." Then he added, "You lie on the back seat with Edel. I'll sit in front with the driver."

Gordon had scribbled a note to his mother, who was watching by the sitting-room window and met us at the door of Menton House. He gave her my name, handed her the note, and tatted gifts—and then took them back to take to the hospital—and said, "She'll explain," and dashed back to the car.

She opened the door wider, glanced at the note, and said, "I'm so sorry. This all happened so unexpectedly. I'm Vera, Gordon's Mum. Please, come in. What can I offer you?"

"May I change the baby? His skin is sensitive, and though I change him often, the car's speed prevented that."

"Let me make some tea and warm some soup. I've done some preparation for my grand . . . but fear. . . . Are you too tired to talk? You must be exhausted . . . there'll be time. Do I see a nasty gash on your forehead?"

During the night, I woke up and sat in a chair to feed Edel several times.

Vera made some porridge and tea in the morning, and we chatted. She was easy to talk to—and other than Zuri-Mama, I hadn't trusted or spoken much to another woman. Gordon had sent Grace, Lily's mother, home from the hospital, and he stayed with his wife.

Vera referenced a cliché that, she said, her sister repeats ad nauseam, but I hadn't heard it before . . . something like, "Life is a ______ of coincidences," and I can't recall the missing word, but I will, ah, yes—"series," that's it. "Life is a series of coincidences."

I may be more tired than I realize. Just one of those sentences that makes perfect sense, and I wish I had phrased it. Even if I had, who could I have shared it with besides T? My head is fine, with minimal swelling and no more bleeding. This is new to me. I recall my previous times and places with Zuri-Mama, but being here, in this part of London, with the war outside, with Edel, and unaware of any options I may have, is a considerable change. The war may be making a turn, but my concern is what will happen to Edel and me.

Gordon's note asked his Mum if she could help us. Neither of us could speculate on what he was thinking. Yet, I keep hearing T saying, "Do what you think is best." That was such a help to me growing up and becoming a bit independent, but this status is different territory for me, and I have to care for not only myself but also for Edel.

Could I find Zuri-Mama? Though it has been five years, I have yet to learn whom she worked for and remember little except the family and boat.

The war continues. We all lug it around in our own way. I wonder about returning to Guernsey, now or later? I don't think it is safe to return now, not with Edel. Even considering "How would I do it?" keeps pushing me back to "Why would I do it?" Somehow, things work out as they may, and London seems a better option—anyway, we are here and need to think about the present and future.

The driver last night had to take alternate routes as debris from the bombings was a constant driving challenge.

Vera asked if she could hold Edel, and watching him being held by a stranger made me smile. His nature is quiet and trusting. He constantly moves his hands, feet, and head—he seems to take in his surroundings, and I think he feels the softness of Vera's breasts. He was good with her. We decided to wait until Gordon returned to ask what he may have thought when he wrote the note.

Gordon came home around 9 a.m., greeted us, and asked his Mum to get Grace while he cleaned up. He sat to have some tea and porridge and could not finish. "We're okay, Lily and I, and Willa." Then he paused.

"Our son, Will, is not okay. The doctor suspected twins a month ago," and he kept shaking his head . . . about a heart that might not 'be developing as it should.'

"I remember leaving her here, but can't remember why?" he asked, looking at Grace.

"A good thing, eh? She came in to help train someone for the 'Gift Shop at University College Hospital.'"

"Right, yes, indeed. We all know how Lily likes things done," Gordon added.

I learned Lily had run the shop successfully after she had completed her service as a candy striper.

"Her water broke, and the doctor was called. He got her up to the operating room and had a nurse call me, and I waited while they did the C-section. You knew about that plan?" Grace said, looking at Gordon.

Gordon replied, "Yes, we expected it but thought we'd have more time to . . . adjust to the possibility.

"They considered a relatively new surgery, horizontal versus vertical, to prevent cutting all the abdominal muscles, and they thought it would minimize the hospital stay and heal faster. But, delivering Will promptly forced the conventional surgery as it would be less strain on the baby's heart."

Gordon continued, "Imagine delivering one and a C-section for the other? . . . and it's to Will's advantage. Only God knows for how long.

Lily fed him with a bottle because they want to make sure the anesthesia is completely out of her body before she nurses . . . if she does."

His eyes were unusually rheumy.

Vera put her hand on his shoulder and asked, "Is there hope?"

"Not much. He's in ICU and being watched by nurses who rotate every half hour. There are just two boys there now. The nurses want to stay with the children, but they must rotate every half hour to not get too attached to them and, of course, to keep themselves alert.

"His heart is the size of a walnut, and though it might involve surgeries as he grows, he could leave us anytime before the final surgery, and his life will be constantly guarded.

"I want to get back there and see if I can break a few regulations. I'll keep you posted as best I can."

He had brought the tatted place mat home, and he and Lily kept the handkerchiefs and burp bib at the hospital.

"Depending on Will's condition, they will baptize the children immediately, and we had discussed names: 'Willa' and 'Will.'"

Cheerless, he walked the few blocks to the hospital with our thoughts and prayers. Lily still had a few hours before the time passed, after which she could nurse.

Vera asked my age, and our conversation continued:

"Soon, seventeen," I answered.

She shook her head and smiled. "A girl . . . and not all white . . . no matter . . . Gordon's birth mother was a young girl, poor, obedient, and white . . . she had to obey . . . sorry . . . Tell me more about you."

"What would you like to know?" I asked.

"Might I ask how you know Gordon? He hasn't found time to explain, and you both probably think it was shared by the other, but we don't know."

She smiled and listened, then asked, "I'm sorry—and I hope you won't find this insulting—but many people cannot read or write today. Can you?"

"Yes. I've read nearly every book in La Maison's library. I write and can do numbers. When the Germans began occupying homes, I boxed up Dante, Chaucer, Shakespeare, and other works for fear they would use them for target practice.

"However, they started using them for kindling. Most Germans didn't read English, so the books were useless. I cut pages out and carried them around to read while I worked."

"You speak very well. Have you had formal schooling?" Vera asked.

"No, but I helped teach the younger children of staff to read and to do crossword puzzles when we could find them. Food and other things became very scarce this past year especially. I sew and tat."

"May I see your handwriting?"

I wrote a few lines I had memorized and did some math problems.

"Your writing is beautifully neat and legible, and your figures look like typeset."

"Zuri-Mama gave me work daily; I remember learning how to hold a pencil when I was two.

"I heard her raise her voice only once—when she was on the boat, and I'd been left on the shore."

"That must be—have been—very hard," she said.

"T helped me very much . . . but Zuri-Ma—" I had to stop.

After a pause, Vera continued.

"Perhaps you can help here? Let's hear what, Gordon—" she stopped.

"I'd be grateful for any direction," I added.

"What happened to the evacuated children? Where did they go? Will they return when the war stops? Do they still take children?" I asked.

"Sorry . . . what can I do here?"

There was a knock at the door.

I went to feed Edel. The room was cool, so I asked if I could sit in the kitchen near the stove. I met Grace there.

After the sisters spoke, they looked at me and could sense my anxiety.

I don't recall picking my thumb cuticles before, but that's what I started to do. When I was younger and bit my nails, Mama scolded and stopped me by putting bandages on my fingers, but this picking was new.

"How is your head?" Grace asked.

"Comfortable, thank you. I need to change the bandage in a day or two; maybe allow some air to heal?"

They both nodded.

Knowing what they wanted to ask and not knowing how I could ask, I said softly, "Whom may I trust? And where could I look for help? How—oh, I'm rambling and thinking out loud. Sorry. I'm in a quandary—if officials get involved. And you folks have family matters to tend to as well.

"In Guernsey, I feared for his life; here, I fear for his life and how to proceed despite the bombings."

We each looked at each other and took a deep breath.

"I understand," I muttered.

Vera said, "When the children came here, no one could estimate how long they would stay, and no one thought it would last these past five years so far, and that has created its problems."

"Do people still take in children?" I asked.

"I imagine it is much harder to find foster parents now. The birth rate has declined, but it hasn't stopped. Some agencies still try to help and place and meet the challenges those services bring."

Grace added, "Remember? We thought about it when we saw the kids arrive, helped organize them, and brought them food. They couldn't eat. They were so scared and fearful."

"We both had had young children once, and though the company may be nice and a service, there was no way to know what the children brought with them any more than we could know what our eggs and sperm would give us," Vera said.

"So, we decided to help as much as we could in other ways and donate when we could to families who stepped up," Vera added.

"I think we can trust Zuri; tell her it might help," Grace suggested.

"It's not as important as it was when he was younger, and I hope he's absorbed the term historically. He knows he is loved, and I never regretted our . . . act." Vera stopped and reached for a tissue, and then continued

"Our children are married. As first cousins, that would have been risky, but they were raised together, and as teens, we wondered if the familial bond might ever turn into something more. From when he was old enough to understand, we shared with Gordon how I became his mother."

Grace added, "Both he and Lily took the term 'adoption' in stride and went on to help us keep it among ourselves as a family—we filtered sharing with a 'need to know' qualifier.

"And what do they do? Fall in love and marry! Kids!"

Grace smiled, "Though I am Lily's birth Mum, we loved them and treated them with the same love and care. Your child is named after a flower, Edel, edelweiss, and so was Lily . . . Lily of the Valley, still my favorite," and she pointed to a piece of needlepoint.

"And now they are experiencing their challenge as parents but one we share as a family, too," Grace said and shed a tear.

I looked at both.

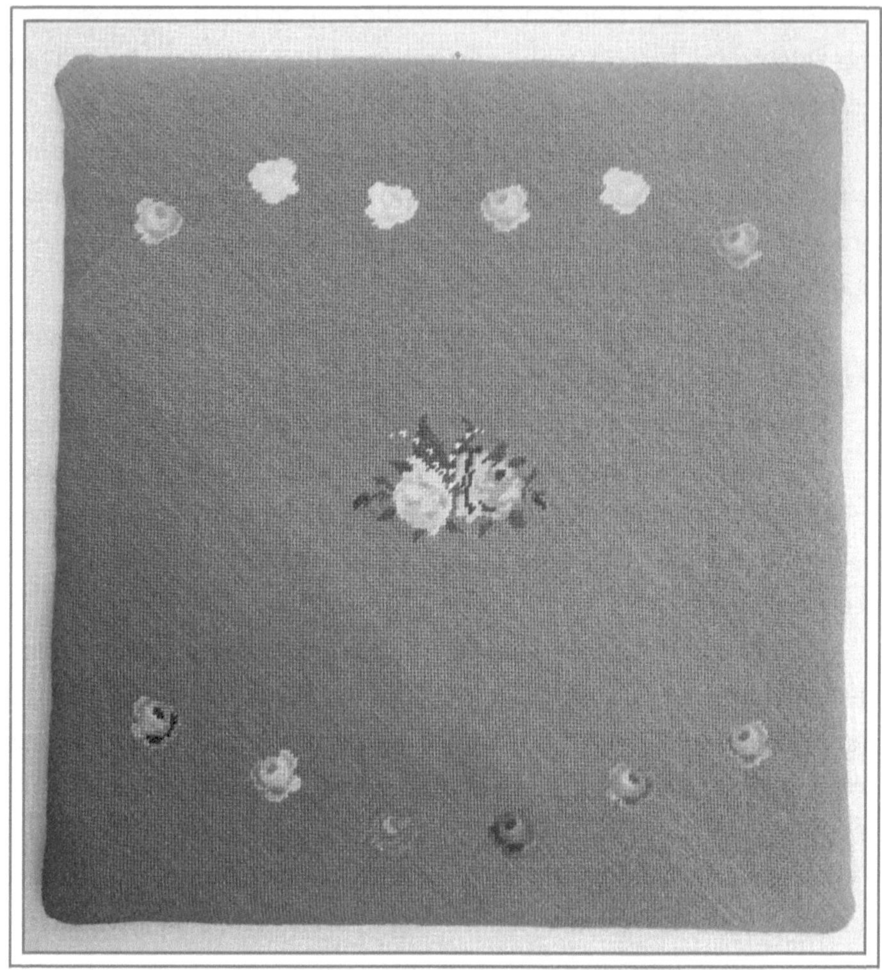

Needlepoint Lilies and Roses

We looked at Edel, and I asked Grace if she wanted to hold him.

"May I ask about their challenge?" I said.

"I'll try." Grace began. "Talk about the height of joy never matching its length, . . . the doctor had the nurses prep the stitches for a C-section while he helped deliver Willa, who seems to be healthy—a bit underweight but fine. He heard a struggle to breathe but did the

C-section, and sure enough, eased Will into this world . . . smaller but well-proportioned; Will's heart remains the concern.

"His prospects aren't good; he'll need surgeries and constant follow-ups . . . if he lives. The medical world has come a long way; it can surprise, but we want and need another for every miracle it performs."

"Oh, I'm sorry, "I said

Vera spoke. "Lily will need help with one baby and her healing, but with two, and the second one needing such care—if he can even come home. I guess that's what they are sorting out."

"My sister and I will do what we can, eh, Vera?"

"We will. We'll find ways. Not to worry."

"They're fortunate to have you both."

"Your little guy looks healthy. Did the doctor give him a good bill of health?" Grace inquired.

"Oh, he's never seen a doctor. Nor have I."

"Did you say he was given to you?" Vera asked.

"Oh, yes—sorry. Gordon said I should be truthful. . . . He's mine . . . but I consider him a gift from God. He's a miracle in so many ways.

I added, "Aren't all babies?"

There was a long pause.

"More tea?" Vera offered.

Our eyes roamed . . . seeking . . . hope?

Journal Entry 10, Zuri, 16, 1945

14 February 1945

We welcomed the date as a positive omen, but the reality of our concerns bent toward gratitude and praying. Gordon came in, and we focused on his news. No one had to ask. Vera poured tea. We waited. Edel squirmed, Grace adjusted herself, and he settled down.

"Lily is doing very well—a little discomfort—full breasts—maybe someone will need to be nursed today?

"Willa is eating well and will probably lose a bit before she starts gaining, and may even be ready to leave the hospital when Lily does.

"Will . . . " and he took a deep breath.

"Will, I'm afraid, may not leave the hospital anytime soon, and the best we can hope for is to build him up for the first surgery; even then, he may not be strong enough to endure it and may not recover sufficiently from it.

"Did I say they are both in incubators, but he is also in ICU? I can't remember what I said. If I'm repeating things, I'm sorry. My focus is Will. We can put our hands in and touch him wearing protective gear. They're trying to decide if breast milk is too heavy for him so that they may stick with a formula.

"Every move is under surveillance and undertaken with intense concern. I'll try to sleep for a bit and then return to the hospital. I can't predict when I'll come back home. I want Will to hold my finger . . . transfer whatever he needs. Whatever time he has, I want to be with him.

"I'm starting to think crazy . . . like signing them out and bringing them home, where they can feel our love and touch. I'm going to talk with the doctor, man to man."

"Go . . . rest," Grace said.

"We'll pack up some food, bring some, and meet you in the lobby," said Vera.

I ached observing a family in action.

We began making food, and I offered to make French gougères.

Gordon got up to go to the bathroom and came into the kitchen.

"Zuri. . . ."

I had not heard my name in so long.

"Would you consider coming to the hospital with me? I wonder if you'd let Lily feed Edel? She agreed to share her milk with mothers who need extra, but not many have children these days, and even fewer are in the hospital even after deliveries.

"Has Edel been to a doctor?"

"No. Of course, I'll come to the hospital with you. Sometimes, I don't think I have enough for him, and I use a sugar teat or water between feedings. I also wonder if I should change the bandage," I said, pointing to my head wound.

"Ah, yes—maybe better to have some help with that the first time. You lie down, and I'll dampen the gauze with a little warm water in case it adhered." He looked to Vera.

"Let me have a look while Grace has Edel," she said.

She washed her hands and returned with hydrogen peroxide, cotton, Vaseline, and a bandage.

Vera asked, "How long for the stitches?"

"A week to 10 days," Gordon said.

"You remember my advice about your relationship with Edel?"

"Yes—thanks. I nearly slipped. It makes sense. Thank you. I've read . . . but for actual worldly experiences . . . I'm very limited."

Gordon added, "I'll clean up a bit, and we can go in about 30 minutes."

Gordon got me through the registration process, and he and a nurse accompanied me to meet Lily; then, he left with his journal in hand.

Meeting Lily was lovely. We bonded immediately. Lily had just cleaned up a bit from a leaking breast. Willa was eating her share, and Lily wanted to be sure she'd have enough for Willa and Will, which required help lactating. Edel latched on and, for a good ten minutes, suckled eagerly.

Gordon went to Willa . . . then to Will. Lily used the burp bib I had made, and I smiled when I saw it again. We chatted. When I couldn't sleep and grew restless during the night thinking about baby Will, I wrote.

A prayer came through me. His name and his will, that invisible force within that makes him inspirational. I handed her a copy of "Will Strong," hoping it would do her and Will some good.

"Please, would you read it to me?" she asked.

"Of course," and I read:

Will Strong!

Will Strong!
That's our song;
however long it takes,
how tempting look the breaks,
investing in healing now,
helps secure a foundation know-how,
upon which he'll grow
based on the thoughts and prayers we sow.
We grasp at temptations that would delight
though what's best for him is sitting tight.
He's teaching us that "Will Strong"
is a miracle in the making, where patience belongs.

Hard as it is to wait and wait,
"things" must be right; there's no debate.
The signs look good,
Caution does what it should.
When the time is right and the healing sound,
Our gratitude and joy will continue to surround.
Trying times persist with tree holes of light,
Yet we keep our eyes on the distant sight
where some ease will balance the tension tight
where health issues align when the time is right.
Love is tough; it's lovely, too,
And loving is what we can do.

Lily was silently grateful and warmly touched my arm.
A doctor looked in and said, "May I?"

Family

He thought Edel was doing well and asked me some personal questions. I answered as well as I could.

"Eventually, your periods should return. Keep track, and come back if they are painful."

I could sense that the routine of this family had been shaken, and their priority was more critical than Edel and me, though they were welcoming and polite. I helped around Menton House as much as possible, with the few guests renting rooms.

Grace and Vera had visited the babies in the hospital and were suited up to touch Will. The staff tried breastfeeding with minimal exposure; even Lily wore a mask. Willa was taken out of the incubator and was scheduled to come home when Lily would.

Late on the afternoon of 17 February, Lily and Gordon were with Will. The time: 4:44 p.m./16:44.

Journal Entry 11, Gordon, 22, 1945

14 February 1945
17 February 1945

After introducing Zuri and Edel, Lily smiled and extended her hands to Edel. I nodded and exited, journal in hand. Tea—amidst the noise—could wait. I walked around, trying to figure out what I was looking for. I found myself in a sparse space, unlike a chapel, though a couple of needlepoint kneelers were on either side of a narrow window with a view of the sky and landscape below. A plant thrived on the sill, with a container of pens and pencils, a stack of salvaged papers with blank backs, and envelopes opened on three sides so that the empty insides were suitable for writing or sketching.

There were a few odd chairs, a couple of rockers with cushions and wide armrests, and a pair of kitchen chairs with padded seats and backs.

The door sign: "Visitors' Quiet Space. Please Keep Tidy."

There was a loo to the left, a water bubbler, and a cup dispenser on the right, above a wastebasket. I wrote and then knelt for a Man-to-God talk.

I prayed—not for anything—but for God to do what was best.

"I trust You. I will do anything for Will. I'm not giving up, and I'm not giving him up. If letting him go is his best option . . . my selfishness, preferences, and love . . . I want what's best for him. Help him . . . help me . . . help us . . . please."

I thought I had "spoken" in my head, but I heard my voice. An older man appeared at my side. I don't know if he'd been there all along or had come in after I did. While I knelt, he put a hand on my shoulder, pulled me toward him, and our eyes met. We nodded at each other, and he said, in a voice I continue to hear, "Courage." He took my hand between his two and pressed. Then he turned and left.

I thought back to my Mum and aunt suiting up to touch Will. How they peered at me when I returned from the hospital with any news. I thought of saying "Boo!" once but was sure they'd wet their knickers, so I updated them on Lily and how nicely Willa was doing, well aware of the angst over Will. I tried to vary my news and discuss Will immediately at times and later at others.

I kept repeating our efforts. "I'm afraid he may not leave the hospital anytime soon. We're trying to build him up for his first surgery and pray for a recovery. Breast milk may be too heavy for him. He would never have survived a natural birth."

Whenever I came into their space, all eyes focused on my news. No one had to ask. Vera poured tea, and eyes searched the room.

Edel squirmed in Grace's arms; she adjusted herself, and he settled down. "Lily is doing very well—a little discomfort—full breasts—maybe someone will be in need today."

I thought about the bikini cut, and I can't imagine Lily ever considering wearing a bikini. Another child? I want this one regardless of what it takes. I thought back to my prayer and "talk" with God, so He knows where I stand.

Why? Why? Why? No answer will satisfy me; that's why I keep asking. I need to grip this if I'm going to do others . . . and myself . . . any good. What's best for Will . . . I may not agree . . . I may not believe . . . but accepting for Will's sake . . . I'll try . . . it'll take a lifetime . . . best for him . . . best for him . . . not me, not us . . . him.

"And Willa is eating well and will probably lose a bit before she starts gaining but may even be ready to leave the hospital when Lily does.

"Will . . . " and I took a deep breath.

The doctor's comparison of his heart—"the size of a walnut"—I kept repeating to myself and could not imagine surgery.

I look back at my journal and see how often I said the same things.

I know where my head is . . . though others may wonder.

"I'll clean up a bit, and we can go in about 30 minutes."

Zuri needed some help with the registration process, and a nurse led us to Lily, who was getting help cleaning up a leaky breast.

Edel latched on for a good ten minutes, and I kept wishing he would guide Will, befriend him, share instinct, what a guy can do for a guy.

My despair was consuming.

I went to Willa . . . and then to Will.

Lily used the burp bib Zuri had edged with tatting and smiled when she saw it being used.

I carried mine in my pocket.

Lily's warmth and gratitude . . . let them chat . . . I quietly exited.

Lily told me Zuri had handed her a note that reads like a prayer, and we began saying it and sharing it . . . It was one of those "gifts" I knew we would always treasure.

Late on the afternoon of 17 February, Lily and I were with Will. Lily had fed him and followed with sugar water to help dilute the density of her milk. He dozed on her breast when the nurse came in to bring him back to ICU.

Will had gripped my baby finger with his hand . . . I put a finger to my lips and signaled her away amidst the silence. I felt the coolness of Will's grip and looked at Lily; she also felt Will's absence. The nurse waited until we beckoned. Behind her glasses, we saw tears staining her mask and her stomach heaving. We kissed him, held each other, and watched the nurse wheel him away, trying to get to the door and her colleagues professionally. I reminded Lily of her alteration of a phrase in a prayer that included, "Thy will be. . . ." She never included the final word, "done" and her inflection of three words sounded as if she added "Let" before "Thy will be. . . . Let Thy will be. . . ." We thanked each other and smiled in grief.

The doctor came in, touched our arms with brimming eyes, and shook his head. He asked about the "other" surgery we had agreed to and, "Have we changed our minds?"

Lily said, "If we can help another child and fam—"

I added, "—let Will's spirit prevail."

The time was 4:44 p.m./16:44.

The priest suggested holding Evensong in Will's honor and said he would wait until we appeared in the hospital chapel and that the grandmothers, Zuri and Edel, were welcome. While we waited for them to come to the hospital, we tried to adjust to a new reality. Here, briefly yet poignantly—now . . . I had this strange sensation that he was in my heart, figuratively and literally.

The priest raised his head and eyes and said, "Our Will—we treasure his shared time. May his love continue to be shared. Amen . . . and women, and children."

After the service, the priest shook everyone's hand and blessed Edel, asking, "And who have we here?"

Zuri put her hand to her mouth because Edel had not been baptized. She wondered if the name he had been given to please the Germans on Guernsey may be offensive to some in these circumstances and location, though taken from the Austrian flower, edelweiss. People and prejudices are unpredictable.

Zuri asked us to be godparents and if Edel could be named "Will."

"We'd be honored," I said, and Lily nodded, trying to smile.

Will was baptized, and Zuri was given a paper with a seal that the priest carried and listed his birth mother and father, date of birth, place, godparents, and the date. The priest recorded the data in a small notebook "To transcribe into church records."

Baby boot pencil sketch

I overheard the priest speak to Zuri. "We could use help at the vicarage in exchange for a small stipend . . . maybe room and board if you'd like to think about it," he added.

It was a restless night for everyone.

Nothing seemed to resolve itself.

In the morning, Zuri rose, cared for Will, and began preparing tea, toast, eggs, and fruit. The grandmothers and I were seated with tea. Plates were kept warm so we could serve ourselves.

We spoke among ourselves candidly.

I called Zuri over to join us.

"You're more quiet than usual," I said.

"I'm sorry," Zuri said

"Come, sit; that was a lovely gesture, giving "Edel" Will's name and having him baptized," I said.

"It felt like the natural thing to do. Thank you for accepting the gesture," Zuri said.

Vera spoke. "Pardon our preoccupation. We've felt so comfortable with you here; maybe we need to clarify our thoughts?"

"Oh?" Zuri managed softly.

"Lily will be coming home in a few days with Willa, and as much as these built-in helpers will be," I said, winking at Grace and Vera, "Lily and I think we would like you as our Nanny and general housekeeper. You and Lily can sort out duties and time off.

"We'll try to give you a couple of free hours a day. I can't be more specific, but we'll give you room and board plus 20 pounds weekly. You'll accompany us here, where we'll have more help. We had planned to return home, but even that is up for reconsideration. What do you think? Would that suit you?"

Zuri sipped water and spoke, "That's very generous. I can't think of any way to thank you for your warmth and generosity.

"Last night, the priest at the vicarage thought I might do some work for them."

"Oh, the vicarage is close by. You might be able to do some things for them, but we'd like you . . . with us. How about we meet and chat as anything and everything comes up?" Grace said. "Your primary obligation is to Gordon and Lily.

"Vera and I will take as much help as you can spare here at Menton House, and it'll give us all a chance to watch these children grow."

"It would give Lily and me time to be involved godparents," Gordon said.

"Maybe my guardian angel is at work already, or at least I like to think so, but if any 'good' from this war can be configured, perhaps the Foster Parent Plan for Evacuated Children is still in effect, and though it may be a while even after the war ends, reuniting some parents and children will take time."

Zuri asked, "Did some mothers accompany the children?"

Journal Entry 12, Zuri, age 16, 1945

18 February 1945

Vera answered, "Indeed they did. Some shared apartments with other mothers; one would work nights, and another would work days, and they cared for each other's children.

"Once the mail was stopped, help from fathers and family was impossible.

"Now there is some discussion about families here wanting to keep the children and about children not wanting to return to strangers. Everyone has a story; some stories are as sad as the war, while others are healthier and happier, but most have emotional tugs."

Gordon added, "One fellow I saw at another table having coffee the other day placed his hand over his heart and, in a whisper, said, with full eyes, "Some things are—too close to the heart. . . ."

After a few minutes, we all swallowed hard and kept quiet—even Will, aka Mr. Fidget—Gordon spoke again.

"May we agree to talk whenever anything upsets us versus letting it seethe and fester?"

We nodded.

I said, "I appreciate the facts of life you are facing and 'will' try to be helpful. Even in this challenging time, I feel welcomed and comfortable. Thank you."

All this within a household while outside a war continued, yet we had reason to believe the war's end was imminent.

After five long, wretched years.

Hearing a radio again . . . seeing newspapers in London . . . Guernsey had been isolated. A few scraps of news when the officers brought it in. If there was anything in English, I usually had to read it to the Germans; their command of English was limited to the spoken rather than the written word. Besides, no mail, and wireless sets were not allowed.

London had been pummeled, but it had a grander sense, and for the first time in a long while, I began thinking about the rest of the world, countries, and war beyond survival.

I saw a flyer from the British Museum that looked tempting.

A volunteer writing coach offered sessions beginning with the radio address made by Princess Elizabeth in 1940.

The flyer printed, "We'll be able to hear it, with all its technical imperfections, and receive a copy of the text for listeners to analyze and compare oral to aural. And, offer opinions on who wrote it, why it remains significant five years later, and our historical projections."

I asked, "Can I get some personal time for this?"

"Of course!" Lily said promptly. "I remember hearing this. We'll have more to talk about."

My thoughts remained focused on the children.

One still, two active—still, three children.

Journal Entry 13, Zuri, 16, 1945

Text copies of the address were available, and those interested in hearing the broadcast were asked to attend with comments on the impressions made after reading and listening. My hands held the words of the Princess who would one day be Queen. I liked how she pronounced "Amerika," and asked if we could hear it again; others agreed, so we did.

Princess Elizabeth's Wartime Broadcast
13 October 1940

In wishing you all "Good evening," I feel that I am speaking to friends and companions who have shared with my sister and myself many a happy Children's Hour.

Thousands of you in this country have had to leave your homes and be separated from your fathers and mothers. My sister Margaret Rose and I feel so much for you, as we know from experience what it means to be away from those we love most of all.

To you, living in new surroundings, we send a message of genuine sympathy, and at the same time, we would like to thank the kind people who have welcomed you to their homes in the country.

All of us children still at home think continually of our friends and relations who have gone overseas—who have traveled thousands of miles to find a wartime home and a kindly welcome in Canada, Australia, New Zealand, South Africa, and the United States of America.

My sister and I know quite a lot about these countries. Our father and mother have often talked to us about their visits to different parts of the world. So, it is easy for us to picture the life you are all leading and think of all the new sights you must be seeing and the adventures you must be having.

But I am sure you, too, often think of the Old Country. I know you won't forget us; it is just because we do not forget you that I want, on behalf of all the children at home, to send you our love and best wishes—to you and your kind hosts.

Before I finish, I can tell you all that we children at home are full of cheerfulness and courage. We are trying to do all we can to help our gallant sailors, soldiers, and airmen, and we are trying, too, to bear our share of the danger and sadness of war.

We know that in the end, all will be well, for God will care for us and give us victory and peace. And when peace comes, remember it will be for us, the children of today, to make the world of tomorrow a better and happier place.

My sister is by my side, and we are both going to say goodnight to you.

Come on, Margaret.

Goodnight, children.

Goodnight, and good luck to you all.

This was my first piece of writing to work with, and I had yet to learn if anyone—beyond those I live with—would be interested in my impression. I wrote this for Zuri-Mama to know what the Princess said.

The Coach asked me to read it aloud.

"I'm two years younger than the Princess, and I wonder how long she practiced to speak so well on the radio. We might consider delivery natural, yet I felt very much at ease and comfortable listening. I wish I could have heard it in 1940; I would have felt better. We did not have a radio or news and were isolated on Guernsey. I had no idea how significant the radio was and is, but it keeps us in touch with each other.

"Both the German occupiers and we were always hungry. We saw Todt slave workers who worked so hard that many died. They were never cared for, fed well, or given medical attention. I understand people here were bombed, but we had to live among them, which is a different form of suffering."

I felt like I was on the radio.

The people listening were very kind and applauded.

I felt my blood tingle.

I liked this writing session.

Journal Entry 14, T, 19, 1945

Dear Zuri,

The third visit of the **SS Vega** excited everyone, as flour and yeast were included in the parcels, and it had been a long time since real bread was part of our diets. Gordon arrived on the 5th of March to accommodate the tides and have the ship in port on the 6th. He had me found, and I waited on the pier; for a few minutes, my joy was beyond flour and yeast—he shared news of Edel—now Will—and you. I choked back tears at every word he said until he stoically shared the news of his Will and our Will.

I held his hand and felt the tears spill and dribble down my cheek, collect around my jaw, and drop onto my shirt.

I tried to speak, "It's never going to be right . . . watching our Will and seeing you—"

He stopped and turned, and I waited.

"I suppose you want them back here?" he asked.

"I'm still struggling with them being gone, hoping life will be better . . . keep us connected somehow. Options for me have been rare, but I feel like whatever I can do that is best for them is more important. There's not much here now; above all, the island's silence and serenity still hold me. Maybe what I could do here might help. . . .

"When I was young, I had to return to the city, and the noises there . . . and I . . . just didn't fit in; I always felt out of sorts, a misfit. I'm relieved Will and Z can make a life there, and I am ever grateful for your help."

We chatted about what pregnancy was like for each of us.

Each woman is different.

I shared how often we were extra hungry and the slight weight we gained we thought was from eating too little. Our chickens really helped.

How you wondered when you hadn't had your period, and when I shared that with Guion, he told me you might be pregnant, and I asked you . . . then we waited.

Next thing we know, your water breaks, and I run for Guion.

Gordon told me of Lily's morning sickness, something you avoided.

He and I must have sounded like two old men, but the sharing was unusual for guys.

He gave me your short note:

T,

We're well—don't worry or be anxious about us. I'm finding a way to make a life here. We did not plan this, and I'm trying to understand this as an opportunity, a gift.

We may decide differently when we have time to talk, but I want to see this through for now, where this takes us.

I plan to attend a writing session at the British Museum and read Princess Elizabeth's speech, which we both missed in 1940. If you can, try to read or hear it so we can discuss it.

Do you trust me to do this?

    Z

"Do you have a piece of paper and a pen or pencil?"

Gordon took out a folded telegram. I wrote on the back and asked him to deliver it.

Z,

Of course, I trust you.

Can you take photos of Will? He's 42 days old today. Maybe a hand or foot impression using cool ashes or watercolor?

I miss you both very much; you make my life exciting.

Mail will return eventually, and we'll have something else to write about.

I never thought about being a father, but holding Edel gave me chills of pleasure, realizing he depended on us—more on you, but I want what's best for him and you.

I'm trying to remember to write his new name.

I like it; he seems suited for the quality and determination of a lad carrying the name "Will."

T

Journal Entry 15, T, 15–21, 1940–1946

I'm re-reading Journal Entries I made before Gordon delivered a note from Zuri that still gives me a dry mouth.

What of our children?

What of our evacuated children?

With the defeat of the Germans and our liberation, people, feelings, and adjustments were amassed under a two-word question: Now what?

We were all affected by the war, yet we each have our own story, especially the younger ones among us, for they have longer to live in the war's aftermath.

Here is where trauma, reparations, records, generalities, and specifics deserve to be assessed and shared.

I would be among them, as would Zuri, Will, and everyone else.

On 9 May 1945, Guernsey was liberated.

A little over a month later, on 11 June, the Red Cross markings were erased from the **Vega**.

Both days were soundly toasted and celebrated.

My mind travels in many directions.

What of the Todt slave workers? Did any survive?

On Guernsey, the Germans learned hunger.

Killing people is a crime; starving them is killing them slowly.

Food affects all aspects of a being; the body eats itself in desperation.

How did denying kids dinner as a punishment or a lesson ever make sense?

Speculation absorbs time, but we have to deal with the reality of life.

War has a lifelong effect. It isn't fought just by the military.

Why do men—humans—do this to each other?

When I heard the Royal Children in a broadcast from 1940, I thought of Will. He's young and already serving a purpose, bringing love, being loved.

The princesses' parents did not evacuate them elsewhere. Some children will return to Guernsey; some will not. The adjustment for parents and children is individual and unpredictable. Each has his/her own story.

The impact will affect us for the rest of our lives.

With the forecast of an end in sight at this stage in the war, what will life be? I now understand how every day only adds to the separation anxiety.

Place will also have an impact. What about when Zuri and Will are here in Guernsey versus London? I wondered about Zuri in a writing class when she heard the address by Princess Elizabeth.

13 October 1940

Princess Elizabeth made her first public speech on 13 October 1940, with a radio address to the Commonwealth's children, many of whom lived away from home due to war. Although just fourteen, she sounded convincingly and genuinely concerned about the children. The speech may have been politically motivated and written for that reason, but she delivered a comforting speech.

"Whitehall" became a term I heard and read about more frequently.

"Whitehall" is a road in the City of Westminster, Central London, which forms the first part of the A3212 road from Trafalgar Square to Chelsea.

"Whitehall" is a metonym [substitute for something else closely associated with it . . . like "Washington" for the seat of the U.S federal government] for the British civil service and government, and as the geographic name for the surrounding area, which is commonly seen as the bastion of the British government.

So much news to catch up on with the cable being cut, and it came at me like a deluge. With time being a hodgepodge, the news lacked chronology, and though I listened, I often wondered how and where it fit.

"What's new?" took on as much significance as "What's old?"

Everyone I knew in Guernsey questioned why we weren't defended and didn't get food sooner.

Even the people who *did* know wondered about what was happening and were asking the same questions.

Evacuations again became a topic of concern in the aftermath of the act: 17,000 people were evacuated from Guernsey to London, including 5,000 students and teachers. When did the Evacuation end? Could it really ever end? Officially, World War II ended in September 1945. However, Evacuation did not officially end until March 1946, when it was felt that Britain was no longer threatened by invasion.

Unofficially, the impact of evacuations affected people ad infinitum.

Some evacuees returned. Some stayed elsewhere. Some eased back into Guernsey; most had a tough adjustment. Kids did not know the families they'd left; families did not know their kids. A five-year memory is a long time, and though memory endures as much as any life event of significance, the interruption of time and life can affect details. When that memory is a person, changes are bound to be different. And, as Peter said, some things remain " . . . close to the heart. . . ."

I found work at the Priaulx Library and, later, at the Atheneum. I wondered how and when my path would cross with Zuri and Will's. I had to believe it would, or my life would lack purpose, hope, and meaning, so I trudged on working towards an end to what I hoped was temporary.

By August, most of the children had returned. Some few "sympathizers" who had children by Germans were "guarded" for their safety.

A contingent of Germans remained to dismantle mines and defuse bombs.

What had been built in concrete remained.

The gamut of children in Guernsey now ranged from those who'd left, to those who'd stayed, boys, girls, of all ages, some who'd returned and resettled fine, some who stayed in new locations, and some newborns.

Some wrote; some did not; some talked; some did not. The span of five years away from home was a jolting event. Would parents have sent them had they known it would be that long? Damn speculation. It's hindsight and not productive. Nobody knew.

Conjecture is good for talk or tea and imagination, but history, "herstory," and fictional and nonfictional stories grow.

The few stories I know about are hardly a cross-section, as each story pattern, life, and the effect of those five years vary as individuals and perspectives. Those I write about are just a sampling. What's just as important are the stories people lived and could not be recorded or shared.

Fred's qualities were assessed early on, and the English put him in charge of cooperating with a return to life before the Occupation.

We agreed to write, and he winked and smirked at the premise.

"Maybe I'll try to call."

We missed our sons—our children.

"What will happen to you?" I asked Fred.

He raised his eyebrows and pursed his lips together.

"I hope I'll be back.

"I have an idea that might work well if I find support . . . convince others . . . maybe even an agency or organization. I've tried to keep track of every soldier who came here. I'm sure there are children of German parentage here . . . and I'd like to see what can be done for them. Maybe consciences will kick in. These islands are an excellent confined area to begin what may set an example.

"It's a long shot . . . but I'd like to serve . . . in my own way. . . . I tried while the war raged . . . the inhumanity pains me, and though I never did anything directly, I am German and in the service, and my family—"

His voice stuck in his throat.

Most kids returning to Guernsey were homesick for the host families they'd left and did not assimilate easily. Families here had little to offer. Some kids had been abused, and some who'd stayed behind in the English countryside were lost to their families here.

The trauma connected to war has enduring ramifications for all.

In August, we learned of Hiroshima and Nagasaki. The war continued on the other side of the world, and, though the information was sparse, as our Occupation ended, another began by the U.S.A. in Japan. We later learned that, from 1945 to 1952, documents about the effects of the bomb were not publicized by the U.S.A., but that did not stop individuals from sharing information.

Most guys keep private things private, such as the secret between Zuri and me. I'd had no idea she was a girl, and she managed to keep that between her and Zuri-Mama, and now Guion and me

Had she not slipped and been taken on the **Vega**, would she have openly identified as a girl here on Guernsey? But, as that never happened. It's not worth the speculation. Speculation keeps tempting.

With the BBC and the accompanying sound of Big Ben, I wonder about the post. At the same time, deliveries were being organized; the post set up a system of baskets with hanging files for each letter of the alphabet with space for an individual to stand and look through the envelopes also alphabetized within. Volunteers helped sort and keep order, as people had to prove their identity to pick up their mail. Then, some retrieved mail for others. One had to sign for them and show a note requesting mail be given to a designated person, and those were retained until the individual allowed or the designee changed. Queues moved quickly and efficiently, and I began checking as soon as we were aware of the system.

Within the week, I held a light airmail envelope with my name and the name of the house, road, and district, followed by "Guernsey, UK," and identifying numbers and letters. I kept guessing whether Zuri would use a pen or pencil, as humidity could affect ink, and pressure—and hard, or soft lead could tear the paper. She had found a typewriter at a rectory where she did some work and updated me a bit.

Maybe the nightmares will subside. All these nights of not knowing and speculating. When I tried to sleep, my mind would race, wondering where to go and what to see. Our meeting would not be accidental, but maybe I could find them. Then I thought about being just one more person in need. It sounds so crazy. Better a plan.

As soon as I started thinking of metro stations, I would jot down where and at which ones I had spent time, but my memory as a young boy was like a smeared drawing. We would meet eventually. My choice is to busy myself and contemplate our first reunion. In my mind, almost every station I'd ever been in differed from others. I wondered why Kings Cross, St. Pancras kept coming to mind.

My thoughts had no discernible pattern.

Sometimes, after five or ten other stations, it would appear again.

Sometimes, I felt like I was mixing my dreams and my reality.

In one nightmare, I ran after a woman who resembled Z physically, and it turned out to be Zuri-Mama, who was in the throes of what appeared to be what we then called "losing one's mind," and a helper was with her, provided by the family by whom she was employed, I imagined . . . or did I imagine. . . .

Now, the anxiety would have some rest or at least be replaced by the news I could not wait to read.

I resisted opening the letter and reading the contents, as I had already decided I would do it carefully, slicing the envelope with my pocket knife and extracting a thin sheet of paper headed with a date and address and an end, "Zuri" in her inked script.

I tried to smell the outline of Will's hand, and an ash image of his right foot, and my eyes filled. I treasure our correspondence and hope the images won't fade, but I am sure time will have an impact.

I shall carry this with me and re-read it many times before I tuck it away for safekeeping in my journal. I will do that now, so nothing mars the contents accidentally. They are safe. What a relief!

Edel is "Will," and he has unofficial foster parents. Zuri is making a life in London, and there is no indication of returning. Time will tell, and we will be in touch. The trauma of adjusting affects us all, some more directly, and we all have to sort out settling into the post-war, post-Occupation experiences.

Shall I continue to make a life here or start a new one in London, where I, like many others, need a place to live and work?

I reviewed my options for staying in Guernsey.

Perhaps, if I can care for myself and send Zuri and Edel—Oops!—Will—money, that would be best for now. Later—if and when an opportunity presents itself—we could try to reunite. One thing at a time. There was so much to think about.

What about Zuri and me? *We weren't officially married and had a child . . . among children.*

Journal Entry 16, Zuri, 17–19, 1945–1947

As soon as T could visit, he took the mail boat and stayed for a few autumn nights. We all got along nicely. When he saw something that needed attention, like repairing a bell or painting the hall, he asked if he could do it, and Gordon said, "We could use a handyman; think about it?"

And T replied, "When I return to visit, you can line up some work for me to do to thank you for caring for my family."

Gordon and T became "brothers."

They went to the pub together, had tea, and ran errands together, and Gordon said, "He's the closest person I've had as a brother and a male friend. My work is challenging trying to make sporadic plans. Heck, even with family, is there ever enough time? The children grow and change so fast."

Lily tried hard; the stronger her effort, the worse she felt. She didn't know what to do, and neither did anyone else.

"I'm so fortunate, and everyone is worried about me. I can't get my mind off repeating scenario after scenario. I'm not fighting it, either. I can't imagine having my Will go through surgeries and never know. I can't reconcile myself to his loss."

Vera said as she always had, "We understand . . . but we really can't understand . . . we'll never know how you feel. We pray for him and for you."

We all nodded, as we always did.

"May I?" asked T.

Lily nodded.

"Sometimes I feel a loss, too, unlike yours but similar, sort of? If I may use your word, I can't 'reconcile' myself.

"Life has changed; going back and reliving the scenario is a way of trying to find what could have been changed . . . we keep trying to find something . . . not an answer, but something to hold on to . . . and all there is . . . is . . . gratitude.

"Maybe it's normal and natural . . . and the best we can hope for is to adjust, keep losses a part of our lives, so we may live as best we can?"

Lily put a hand on T and the other on Gordon. "I'll try to remember what you said; thank you." I put a hand on T and nodded my head; I was so proud of him, my eyes filled.

Gordon rented a room for two weeks at St. George's Guest House on the Esplanade, Guernsey, the following spring. He, Lily, and Willa would go when he could get 3–4 days away. The grandmothers would take four days, as Will and I would take the rest. Once sampled, we decided a week each in the summer would be our aim.

After the children had turned two and began to talk, their playgroup/school for a couple of hours a day was a nice break for all. Willa and Will usually got along, as children their age do, yet one day, they were firmly uncommunicative on the way home. Lily waited for us at the door, and Will bounded out of the stroller and tugged her skirt.

"Can I call you 'Mum'?"

"Of course!"

He gave Willa a look that all but screamed, "See!"

I shook my head and smiled. Our family structure was different, but more and more families have unusual compositions.

While the children napped, the adults shared tea. Lily was a few minutes late and had been crying. She took a sip of tea and a bite of a dunked biscuit. If she didn't say something soon, one of us would comment, and a conversation would begin, as there was always something to discuss and comment upon.

"I'm sorry . . . I've wasted so much time . . . and may waste more time . . . and . . . I'm tired of it. Tired of being unhappy. Tired of feeling stuck. If I could make that little boy happy by saying, 'Of course!' what better reason is there to get out of this funk? I may brood, isolate, and be silent, but I must bring positive energy to this household.

"I know you'll be patient with me, but I want you to know I'm trying . . . my best . . . it's not much by anyone's standards, but it's all I've got to offer."

"Zuri, teach me to tat?"

"Mum, may I borrow that new scarf?"

"Auntie, let's go shopping for a new blouse."

"Gordon has duty tonight but expects to be home after tea tomorrow. Let's look festive and make him feel welcome!"

We all said, "Let's!" simultaneously.

Z, 1947+

Time has a way of taking flight.

The children have been walking and talking and training.

The families have meshed well, and for anyone nosey enough to ask, we say, "We're different."

The building in Cartwright Gardens, London, is a lovely family home with a small inner-city circle park, but the taxes and expenses require attention. A few long-term boarders help, and a few rooms are rented temporarily, sometimes per day, sometimes for a few weeks.

Lily and Gordon gave up their former home, which was out of the city and had a bit more greenery. Lily could not return to the planned nursery, and now there were two children and me. London is convenient for Gordon, and there is more to keep Lily busy, and we're trying to take advantage of her epiphany carefully. There are many conversations and working together, and there is more love, patience, and trust than I ever imagined there could be.

T visits.

We visit Guernsey. I don't know the source of the money or amounts, but I am careful to conserve expenses, never ask for more, and if I get a bonus, I always ask if it would be better to contribute it to the household. My tatted placemats and napkins bolster my income, and my handkerchiefs and bookmarks are always in demand.

The basement level contains the kitchen, guest dining, and washing area, outside space for a car, and a small garden area, where I try to hang clothes, though they dry well in the washing/drying/sewing area overnight.

I use a bookcase shelf in the dining room to display my items for sale, and we're talking about offering the "gift" area to others and opening it to the public, using the rear entry.

Our guests are our customers. I bought a sewing machine with a treadle, but I understand there are electric ones I may investigate.

We have a sitting room near the entrance, and in the evenings, it's comfortable to sit and talk, listen to the radio, and do handwork.

The children enjoy the space during the day and keep their toys in a chest that serves as a low table. Grace and Vera live together. Lily and Gordon have a large bedroom suite, divided into a room for Willa and one for Will. They've slept there as a treat for a few nights already, and the rooms are accessible to all. My room is down two steps, and I have easy access if either child squirms or fusses.

Long-term renters are on the next floor, and the temporary renters are on the top two levels. We do well and are nearly full every night, especially during decent weather and holidays. I've given up my room for a guest and slept in Will's room on the trundle bed occasionally. Sometimes, he sleeps on the one in my room, and Willa has rested on the one in her parents' room.

We accommodate guests. It might be our best source of income, and if and when an adjacent building comes up for sale, we could expand.

That would mean hiring help. Sometimes, we can't wash and dry sheets fast enough; then, so we use a service. I'm also thinking about opening the kitchen at four for afternoon tea. We could ask the folks who shared shelf space to sell baked and handmade goods to help with that. Perhaps make a different pastry treat or cookie daily and a martini glass of fresh fruit. . . .

I don't know what the law allows or how often sheets need to be changed; maybe Lily will supervise that aspect of our growth. Guests supported the limited offerings, and expanding would help many trying to improve life. A little extra money helps.

We opened from 14:30 to 16:30 with tea from 15:00 to 16:30 to give ourselves time to prepare and serve an evening meal from 17:00 to 19:00, for those who reserved and opted for that choice.

People who made products for sale could spare time, so they would staff sales and help "wait" on tables. Any tips were theirs. People who wanted to sell products but could not help to sell or "wait" two hours a week contributed 5% of their sales to those who could staff and do "wait" work.

Everyone contributes 5% to what we call the "house and management" for any permits or fees for which we are obligated. At the end of the year, if there is any money in excess, all who participated decide how much to contribute to "house and management" and apportion the remainder among participants.

Journal Entry 17, Zuri, 21, 1950

Will's birthday on Tuesday, 23 January 1945, is special. I remember and relive it daily for a minute or two, especially sipping afternoon tea. The ritual caps most of the day with a lull to accomplishments and preparation for the evening, including dinner, the news, and evening work. My "reward" for a journal entry. Journals give writers a place to vent.

It's been a week since Will's birthday. When he's at boarding school, I send a card, and we speak. I write before and after not to record a personal reflection on the day itself but to honor it as the most important day of my life. I've summarized the story as well as I can remember it. Every day, I review the process and give my thanks. Every day, my gratitude increases.

T running for his friend Guion, and Edel and I were doing what we did. The time leading up to his birth. The time afterward. It all happened so fast, and I want to remember everything.

While pregnant, I remember women discussing the pains and agony of childbirth. And Zuri-Mama's words about my birth and her mother's about her birth. I never imagined one could enlarge one's self to allow for the passage of a baby. By the time T returned with Guion, I was writhing a little, wincing and apologizing. I had started boiling water and gathering cloths when T left. I had never seen him so beside himself, and we often discussed the birthing plan. I wondered if I would be as Zuri-Mama said when she told me about birthing or if I'd be the anomaly in the generations of women from whom I'm descended.

T and Guion returned in less than thirty minutes, and I thought I might have to deliver the baby myself, like Zuri-Mama. Guion, a tall, blond, handsome, German-looking man, took charge, and he and T scrubbed their hands and nails. He'd brought plastic gloves, knife, scissors, needles, thread, and hats Guion had made from discarded nylons that had been washed and air dried. He knotted one end, and we each wore one.

"It's a birthday party, right?"

They put a tarp under me on the bed and rolled me left and right to even it out. He asked how I was . . . and if he could have a look. I nodded.

"This is happening pretty fast. You're dilated; I can see the head in the birth canal. T will hold a handkerchief to your face to minimize pain. You won't like the smell, but it will help."

I breathed in an acrid odor for a few breaths, then I shook my head and pushed it away into T's hand. "T, warm the cloths on the stove or in the oven, just to keep them warm, not hot." When T returned, Guion removed his leather belt and asked T to put it between my teeth so I would not damage them if I clenched too hard.

"T, cup your hands here," Guion directed. "The baby may exit with a gush; you must catch and guide it. Please don't hold it tight or push it back. I will rub the abdomen to help the muscles advance the baby."

I was okay until I felt the shoulders.

"Crowning!" Guion announced.

"It's a boy!" I said before he was out. Zuri-Mama said girls try to angle their shoulders, but most boys are like football players, and I was right. He was early and small. After he was cleaned, T put him on my tiny breast, and I felt him being nourished, and I could feel a bond growing between us. We watched him; T thanked me, and I thanked him.

Journal Entry 18, Zuri, 21, 1950

My writing group meets on Tuesdays, my chorus on Thursdays, and both from 19:00 to 21:00; these give me a social outing and an outlet for self-expression. The writing group meets in a room at the British Library near Kings Cross Station, and the chorus meets in the hall of a local church. I thought one would be a nice balance for the other, but I'm discovering how similar both are; what I am learning about myself is life-changing and exciting. I ask Lily to join me every time, and she hasn't asked me to stop asking. When she's ready, we'll be welcoming.

This week, the volunteer writing coach looked dapper, with a bow tie from the excess material of the pants' length and a fitted grey plaid suit with a thread of purple, a lavender shirt, dark purple socks, and purple oxfords polished to a gloss. We were greeted pleasantly, and the week had been particularly stressful; none of us could hide ignoring political events. We chatted before he entered, and although he greeted us individually at the door, he had some challenges getting away from the library staff organizer, who was after him to commit to more sessions.

"Did you have enough time to share your thoughts?"

We nodded.

"I'm going to alter my plan and offer you what I've termed a 'building plan,' especially after the week we've had." He handed out expired tickets, the backs of which were blank. "On your paper pads, list the three to five characteristics that got you through this stressful week. Choose one characteristic, and use a three-paragraph topic outline. Write a piece that describes, but does not name, the characteristic and 'might serve as an example to others of how this characteristic got you through the week."

"You may be as personal as you like, fiction or non-fiction, and it may take any form. Not naming the characteristic lets you see how a writer 'shows' instead of 'tells.' This may make more sense later; consider it a writing exercise. I'd like you to write a complete draft in class and hold it up for me to see before we have a fifteen-minute closing session."

One woman asked if we, the participants, could talk about this.

"Would you like me to stay or wait outside?"

"Stay!" most of us said in unison.

"What are the tickets for?"

"I can tell you now or in the final fifteen minutes wrap-up time; what's your preference?"

"Now!"

"Write the characteristic on the blank back of the ticket, and staple it to my copy of the writing. Next week, I'm scheduled to be here again; if you agree, I'd like you to bring in a copy for each of us in which you use dashes in place of the characteristic, and we will try to determine what that characteristic is. I plan to take five minutes for each of you to read your pieces and see if we can tell you the title."

One among us asked, "Why are we doing this?"

"I intended to share this later, but since you asked: Everything one writes tells you something about the writer. For every piece we write, at the very end, skip a line and write what you learned about yourself."

I learned____ about me.

"*Capisce?*"

"*Sì, Sì, grazie.*"

"A piece of writing can tell you something about the writer as the writer, and the reader might discover something about him/herself similarly."

"Were you going to tell us that in the last fifteen minutes?"

"Yes."

"Now, what will you do?"

"We'll see . . . maybe nothing. I want the room to be quiet, so I'll sit outside the door, and there'll be a chair for anyone who wants to talk to me. I'll come back at 20:45, and if you'd like any group talk, we can do it then, or you can write on. . . ."

In the last fifteen minutes, Coach returned to an earlier session to emphasize voice and added developing our voices as writers.

He said, "When did you first hear Princess Elizabeth's voice? Remember her first public address on 13 October 1940? Try to listen to it again for next week, and think about describing her voice as a speaker and a writer."

The next week, we received a list of five items and a poetry exercise.

1. Make a list of 3-5 topics responding to How to ___________________. And, Reflections on the Afterlife.

2. Collect any pieces of writing you may have saved and keep them accessible.

3. Grammar, spelling, punctuation, forms of writing, especially difficult forms, poetic forms, style, and what dictionary you use.

4. Keep track of how much time you spend writing, including non-writing times when you think about writing. Keep a supply of paper, pens, and pencils.

5. Ready for another topic? How does one earn the privilege of another's time? How would you like to go on a Treasure Hunt?

"If I may summarize our discussions, most of you find reading, interpreting, and understanding poetry to be a challenge?"

We agreed.

"Remember my offer regarding a Treasure Hunt?"

We did.

"Over the next month, try to find the poem by the American poet, Langston Hughes, born in 1902. I've rewritten it and will hand out my nineteen lines. We'll read together, aloud, and put an "x" over a word and after a line you don't understand.

"Writers often write to share. Yet, writers cannot determine how individual readers will interpret writing. Interpreting is part of the reader's responsibility. Is interpreting part of the writer's responsibility? We've talked about the voice of the Princess in her radio address in 1940. Writers have voices. How do they develop?

I will answer any questions you have weekly regarding Langston Hughes's poem if it can be answered with a 'Yes' or 'No.'"

He added,

"Most of us find the rewriting task difficult.

"How do we proceed individually to rewrite poetry, or anything else?

"When a writer writes, s/he can't predict how it will land. Writers write to share, yet how writing is interpreted depends on what the reader perceives.

"Do we all have voices?

"Does Langston Hughes project race in his writing?

"Interpretation is part of the reader's work.

"Is interpretation part of the writer's work?

"Here is my example of rewriting a Hughes's poem that I'm asking you to find."

He handed out copies, and he and we read aloud:

Thanks to Langston . . . Voices
© Len DeAngelis

All voices are heard, all voices are read,
As gifts of the living and gifts of the dead.
In our time, let's work to make life better
With words that are best, letter by letter.
Better isn't best; that's a goal from afar,
Improvement matters; acknowledge scars.
Our will can alter what can't be changed
we can free ourselves and envision range.
The skills of others grow from seeds of will,
A trait we possess even when still.
The work begins within us all.
Can we hear it as a call?
We share with others for whom we work,
Good work is that from which we never shirk.
An unsung song cannot be heard.
To some, our work may seem absurd.
A bird rehearses within its power.
How will we live? How do we flower?
Even when still, our work empowers.

"Questions?"

One participant asked, "How many lines does the Hughes poem have?"

"That's not answerable by 'Yes' or 'No.' Will you rephrase the question?"

"Does the Hughes poem have nineteen lines?"

"No, thank you."

Another asked, "Does it have less than nineteen lines?"

"Yes."

"Your poem rhymes, does his?"

"No."

"Your title has four words. Does his?"

"Yes."

"Any words or lines you don't understand?"

We shook our heads, No.

Journal Entry 19, Zuri, 22, 1951

During our first year of writing, Coach reminded us sporadically about a piece of writing for which we felt like a conduit.

"Review a piece of writing that you felt came through you, versus from you, as if a muse held your hand and directed your pen.

"If there is a story behind your story, please feel welcome to share it."

I knew that the prayer/poem for Will, which Lily carried and remains framed and visible, might have more life if I could adapt it for others.

I recited this when Will was laid to rest under protecting tree branches, near the edge of a cemetery, and by way of the prayer/poem, we stay in touch many times a day.

Four minor changes allow me to offer "Will . . . Strong,"

"Will" is a name, a verb, and a mental faculty that reflects itself in the power to choose, the force that drives us and provides us with a purpose . . . "motivation" is a synonym.

The original, for Will, is followed by the adaptation, where a reader may substitute another name.

Will . . . Strong!

Will . . . Strong!
That's our song;
however long it takes,
how tempting look the breaks.
Investing in healing now
helps secure a foundation know-how
upon which we'll grow
based on the thoughts and prayers we sow.
We grasp at temptations that would delight
though what's best for us is sitting tight.
He's teaching us that "Will . . . Strong"
is a miracle in the making, where patience belongs.
Hard as it is to wait and wait,
"things" must be right, there's no debate.
The signs look good,
Caution does what it should.
When the time is right and the healing sound,
our gratitude and joy will continue to surround us.
Trying times persist with tree holes of light,
yet we keep our eyes on the distant sight,
where some ease will balance the tension tight,
where health issues align when the time is right.
Love is tough; it's lovely, too.
And loving is what we can do.
Peace and Love,

Space to insert names: From: Will Strong!

______________ Strong!

That's our song;

however long it takes,

how tempting look the breaks.

Investing in healing now

helps secure a foundation know-how

upon which we'll grow

based on the thoughts and prayers we sow.

We grasp at temptations that would delight,

though what's best for us is sitting tight.

S/He's teaching us that "______________ Strong"

is a miracle in the making, where patience belongs.

Hard as it is to wait and wait,

"things" must be right, there's no debate.

The signs look good,

Caution does what it should.

When the time is right and the healing sound us,

our gratitude and joy will continue to surround.

Trying times persist with tree holes of light,

yet we keep our eyes on the distant sight,

where some ease will balance the tension tight,

where health issues align when the time is right.

Love is tough; it's lovely, too,

And loving is what we can do.

Peace and Love,

From:______________ To:______________

______________ Strong!

Journal Entry 20, Zuri, 27, 1956

This writing session encouraged my thoughts.

Coach began, "Remember when we began these sessions, I asked you to keep a list of topics?"

We all nodded.

Often, we have to write about things that are not our choice: school, courses, work . . . some writing that may require public sharing.

He continued, "Turn to that list, and select the topic you least want to write about. Everybody has a topic?" We did, to my surprise. He continued, "Let's see what these topics have in common and why you least want to write about them."

1. Too personal?

2. Lack of knowledge about them?

3. Create a negative emotion?

4. Lack interest?

5. How can one counteract whatever you responded to the previous four questions?

"We'll tackle #5 first. Looking back at the four questions, what would be an acceptable antonym for the keywords? Add those below."

1. impersonal

2. learn, awareness

3. positive emotion or at least one with a better balance

4. interesting

"For this exercise, list the topic you least want to write about, and write one sentence that addresses each of the four keywords and their counteracting words that help clarify how you will prepare yourself to write on this topic. You are not being asked to write on the topic but to explain how you will prepare yourself to do something you do not want to do. We are all faced with such challenges. Spend the session writing about preparing to write/do something you prefer not to write or do, and we'll listen to everyone this session and next."

If this were a contest with a monetary prize and getting my piece published, I'd have the "will" to work on responding. "Will" is the only word of three in my topic of "Invisibles"—"Soul" and "Conscience" being the other two. No one ever asked me what I think about soul and conscience, and I don't know enough about them to write. I've seen "Will" as a motivating force is often exhibited as determination, which may be admirable but can also be used for evil or revenge. One needs to approach this *en garde*! In this trinity, "Will" is the jewel. Often, it is preceded with an adjective: "Free" Will. My "will" is free of "Free," as I prefer it to shine simply stated: Will.

Journal Entry 21, Zuri, 31, 1959

Writing Sessions.

Topics.

Notes from sessions.

When the coach uses "you," I perk up. Is he talking to me directly? I'd better listen and take notes! An early writing session dealt with keeping track of topics. Topics come and inspire unexpectedly—and may flee unless they are recorded. The exercise of recording can become obsessive. Find what is practical and works. A separate notebook? Most writing projects have a shelf life: an assignment, a short story, a novel, a shopping list, et cetera. Keeping topics in a proper place requires discipline and routine.

I always carry something to write on and something with which to write.

It's not easy to do when I swim or get an idea while showering, driving, or while attention is elsewhere, and I'm trying to look attentive and interested. My mind focuses and wanders simultaneously. How many good ideas and words are lost unless jotted down?

Noting everything is impossible; it is cluttering, and it defeats creativity. Make time to keep, or dismiss, a topic.

If something had merit once, is it worth keeping, and when might it be explored further? A unique phrase can affect an entire piece. When, where, and what were the circumstances? The more he spoke, the more I wrote. Something about him kept my attention beyond the information. There was a connection I could not place. And then I thought . . . he reminded me of Zuri-Mama. She spoke, I wrote . . . not always, but as I aged and grew, I wrote and listened more, . . . and then she was gone.

Whenever I think of her, I try to find more details in my memories, I wonder how she learned yet had so little formal training. "Listen," she would say, "Speak like you hear other educated people speak; I will not accept an alternative. Life is a series of choices and often 'things' one can't control."

"I oversimplify, but 'mark my words,'" a phrase I remember him saying verbatim. As much as I was attentive to him, I wondered how Mama learned what she knew and passed it on to us.

She watched.

She listened.

She imitated.

She had standards.

She had a demeanor.

She often said, "I choose to be happy. I choose to act educated.

"Your penmanship is better than mine because you began earlier to write every day. I did not have that opportunity. I still practice writing every day."

I remember Zuri-Mama commenting on my creativity, putting threads together for tatting. I had kept a journal but have matured and experienced some life; I wonder about expressing myself and sharing it.

She was interesting—always something new.

Zuri-Mama never bored me.

And T, The Inexhaustible Man-Friend.

Time, patience, interest . . . love?

His qualities ignited my trust and my response.

Qualities I admire:

Energy.

Simplicity.

Will.

Do I express them?

Coach asks us to make carbon copies of our finished work to share, keep drafts to see how writing develops, and revise our work, especially reading aloud to ourselves and others.

Topics, possibilities, ideas—whatever term covers the inspiration or deserves a place. Thus far, I've incorporated them in my journal with an asterisk preceding them. The following "Possibilities" have asterisks since I began this session at the British Museum with this Writing "Coach."

Some may be developed here or in later Journal Entries.

1. Dialogue on public transportation.

2. Write a poem as another version of a prior piece.

3. Write (3x5 card) about a characteristic without naming it, and see if others can guess it. Place the answer on the back.

4. When did you first hear the Queen's voice?

5. Listen to her first public address on 13 October 1940. React.

6. What's new?

7. What's old?

8. Why wasn't Guernsey defended?

9. Why didn't we get food earlier?

10. Whitehall

11. Recipes

12. Directions

13. Who, What, Where, When, Why, and How

14. Listening

15. Reading

16. Hearing

17. Interpreting

18. Sharing

19. Forms, style, grammar, spelling, punctuation, vocabulary

20. Afterlife

21. A piece that writes itself [Will Strong]

22. Time

23. Our Invisibilities: Soul, Conscience, Will

24. Writer versus author

25. Never underestimate_________[anyone/anything].

26. Crafts? Tatting.

27. Roles

28. Resiliency

29. Dreampanion [versus companion]

30. List words that may not go together, but interpret them with that goal and see what happens.

31. Or, using the word "purpose" as the magnet, select a word from five: Grief, Health, Resiliency, Work, Income. Write about that word. Let the mystery unfold.

32. Story behind "Finding a book."

33. Words, races, scaffolding

34. A Favorite Toy

35. Musing about more time with another . . . T for me.

36. How we see things before and after cataract surgery is the difference between before and after truth, or seeing things one way and allowing a perspective 180 degrees from the original. How do we discuss topics with people holding opposing views?

37. Political leaders do not act alone.

38. What of people explaining their danger before their rise?

39. The UK had internment camps on the Isle of Man.

40. The UK's behavior before WWII toward Jews was shameful. Agree or disagree and substantiate your position in a paragraph.

41. Create 5 examples of an oxymoron, a figure of speech that combines contradictory words with opposing meanings, like "old news," "deafening silence," or "organized chaos." Express each in a sentence and explain how they serve or disserve your expression.

42. What legacies are we leaving to our progeny? Groups to which we belong with or without choice.

43. Caucasians pride themselves on what good things they have done for civilization, shared medically or philanthropically, etc., but the shame of what they have done to others pales compared to the damage they have done. Good can not balance shame. The balance is not a contest. Facing one's history

should motivate people and countries to rectify the past, not be stuck in that past.

44. Why separate children from parents?

45. "Enemy Aliens" was popular after World War I and especially after World War II. Why? Meaning?

46. Creativity.

47. The greatest sin? Taking advantage of another.

48. The second sin? Selfishness

49. ____

50. ____

Resiliency/Purpose:

What factors help us assess events, and what are the impacts of those events on us?

Memories take us backward and forward and are seen through a veil of the unknown, wherein hovers anxiety, apprehension, and wonder.

Where and how we find resiliency is worth sharing.

Using the human body as a metaphor assesses where resiliency "stands" and the individual and the event. The myriad of variables above the "feet," represented by the cells of a body above those feet, is better left to the speculation of others.

Back to the feet: if we replace "the events" with the word "challenges," the individual remains the constant variable.

Among those that rate challenges from minimum to severe, there will always be those that will shake one to the core: being blindsided, the unexpected, the unimaginable, the un-expressible. We live through them and "see" how from the vantage point of memory . . . perhaps. We cannot prepare for them.

We can enlist qualities that help: prayer, faith, support, discussion, friends, etc.

Often, we dash to the apparent threat to the physical and dismiss the mental-health threats; though they may not be evident as quickly as the physical, their effect may last longer. With us are the qualities we project, the opportunities we find, that bloom into view and endure in their limited time of beauty by memory, record, and example.

There is more to this.

Journal Entry 22, Will, 14–15, 1959–1960

"Zuri!" I yelled into the phone after she had wished me a Happy 15th Birthday. Though it was a Saturday, and I was at boarding school, we could take calls on a birthday, and I expected my family would somehow find a way. T had already called while I was at breakfast and was due in the pool. That left Mum and Dad, separately, if Dad was away, and Willa, depending on when she could find time in her day. "Fifteen!" Zuri reminded me. "It's so hard to believe!" That's how old "T" was when he took Zuri under his care. I can barely care for myself. "I'll get back on the phone after Mum and Dad, and we can talk songs if you have time."

Zuri knew of my interest in U.S.A. songs and told me the top three for the week:

"Running Bear"
Johnny Preston

"El Paso"
Marty Robbins

"Why?"
Frankie Avalon

"Aw," I replied. "Please, keep an eye on Avalon. You know how much I like him." I thought Avalon was smooth and his voice silky. He carried himself with humble confidence and always seemed as surprised at fans as they were at him. When I saw his photo, I could see why fans screamed for him, but I liked his humility even more; he brushed attention aside and made others feel his words came from his heart, not just the throat and the head. He was genuine.

I was surprised that all the songs were about love; maybe that was the most challenging emotion in the U.S.A. It made me think about love for family and love beyond family. Here I was with four parents, and some kids had none. "Thank you, thank you," was all I could blurt out to Mum and Dad.

At every opportunity, I thanked them for what they'd taken on, and I could not imagine what life would have been like without them.

Somehow, this "family" made life work.

They provided room and board for as long as we needed it, and once Zuri could contribute a little toward the household; they agreed to pay my school expenses for as long as necessary. I am beyond fortunate.

T sends what he can. I spoke with him earlier, and he always tried to be early and avoid running the risk of missing me. Today, I asked about spending some break time with him and maybe some weeks in summer to learn Guernésais.

He said, "My life is simple, and I don't have much to offer; you'd be roughing it . . . are you sure you're up for it? I can't compete with what you have or may be accustomed to."

"We'll manage," I replied. "Don't change anything for me. Let me fend for myself. I'll even bring a sleeping bag!" I had to develop flexibility, and worldliness deserved my attention. "I'll try to earn my expenses and not intrude much on your lifestyle."

Willa and I got along better than most sisters and brothers. When she asked, with a great sigh of relief, if we were going to repeat what her Mum and Dad did—marry!—I replied, "I don't think that's likely."

She looked at me and nodded. "Have you talked with Dad?"

"Oh, yes, some time ago . . . you know him . . . always ahead of the curve," I answered.

He showed me how to clean myself when I was just out of nappies, and he kept checking with me, and every once in a while, he'd remind me about things I might hear from the older boys and friends, and he somehow filled me in on those details before older boys and friends had a chance.

I always knew about changes, discretion, privacy, modesty, and choice. "Choice" was the word he kept returning to every time we got serious, and I needed to know about life.

The federal law establishes the age of 12 as the minimum age of consent, while the age at which there are no restrictions for consensual sexual activities is 18 (sex with someone 12–18 is not illegal per se but can still be open to prosecution under certain circumstances). Children protected in UK 1889, age of consent 16; US, 1980. Incest: sexual intercourse between those forbidden to marry. I wondered about the prejudices laws fostered.

My buddies at school helped me celebrate my birthday. They say if I continue to be cool, at the end of the year, girls, and maybe other alternatives . . . that sounded ominous, but I did not pry. To be honest, I'm scared. And afraid. I am anxious to try girls, but what Dad says about being careful, not trusting condoms, and not knowing what she'll do or what could happen if I don't use a condom. Dad also suggested that I say my beliefs support waiting and leave it at that. Even some of my friends ask about my attitude and comfort, and all I can say is, "My Dad," and they ask if they could talk with him or get in on our next conversation.

Kids, like parents, are all different, and some of us feel more adrift than others, especially regarding sex. We wonder what lies beyond this awakening, how some guys make a big deal out of sex, and how others seem to take it in stride. It's new and essential, but no need to let it consume me.

It's not everything I am. It'll have its attention, I hope.

We have to get on with everything else, too. Yet now, everything seems to have a sexual connection. I get teased about my name: "Is Will short for Willy? Were you named for a body part?"

Dad said, "Tell them, 'The only thing it is short for is what you got. Is that why you ask?'"

I say, "Will means 'determination.'

"If you have something to say about that . . . maybe it's too 'long' for your vocabulary!"

That usually pisses a guy off enough that he'll leave me alone, or maybe he feels I could get to him with words he lacks?

Many guys have sisters at the girls' school, so word gets around about how brothers perform and with whom.

Ugh.

I trust Willa and don't want to know with whom she may experience anything that personal.

Guys have already teased me by saying, "She's good. Too bad you can't have her as I have."

I know they're fibbing.

Willa and I have a solid relationship, and I'm not sure she'd tell me if and when she had sex with any guy I know.

I told her I might tell her when it happens to me, but not with whom, and she nodded.

She might be told by someone else, but it won't be me, and I'll ask whomever I have sex with to keep it between us, but I can't control another person.

All the complications kill whatever drive I have, but I suppose one day it'll happen . . . maybe; nothing demands I participate, though life is hell for the guy who stays a virgin.

I trust very few others a bit more, and that feeling of trust excites me. When I fantasize, it's a guy-related thing. I've felt girls up, and I like the softness and the reaction of touching them, Of course, at my age, I could get an erection watching two dogs go at it. So, I'm unsure if I'm hetero, bi, or gay.

Someday, I guess, this will all be taken in stride, and discussing such a massive thing as sex will not be shared or discussed as much as in a locker room.

Some older guys already handle themselves maturely, aren't super modest, but take what they have in stride, have confidence, and don't horse around as much, fake "grabbing," or snapping towels. Hence, we younger ones look up to them and get winks now and then, making me feel cool and accepted.

I have reports to keep track of and book journal entries to make.

Z is usually right about keeping a running journal for these things; I've had some benefits already. I want to stay on top of these things.

I swim and play tennis; I'm trying to push bike riding, and I think I might start working out. I could use a little definition, and it'll burn up some energy that might be pulling at me elsewhere. I have friends who aren't as lucky and some who are luckier but take it for granted, and I'm always grateful and humble about what has come my way.

I'm looking forward to time with T and studying the language used on Guernsey, besides English, as I don't know him well. Time will give us the opportunity.

When we go to Guernsey in the summer for a few weeks, he comes into our lives more, but I'd also like more time between us.

After the family summer stay in Guernsey, I might stay an extra week with T and revisit him for one of the weeks we get off for December and January, just before I turn 16—coincidentally '61—how weird is that?

How T manages to find work and live life borders on ingenuity; every time I'm aware of another example, I shake my head and wonder if my name was his! He's determined to make life work—he has a Will—and I guess he and Z decided for him not to move to London and find work and provide a place to live and keep us fed and clothed. It could have worked. But it was too risky for him to try and then learn otherwise. What would that have meant for Z and me? His concern for us was more substantial than risking our status and good fortune. What if Z and me—I like the rhyme—went back to Guernsey?

He is the original Mr. Go-To. If something needs repair, he can do it—from cars to toasters. He is the epitome of an Organized Man. What he does not know, he learns. He'd find someone who knows what he wants to know and learns and improves on the basics. After the war, tourism became a possibility for more people for whom the larger houses were not wanted or needed—and many could not afford them. Yet, guesthouses became the envy of resources, and private homes with a room to spare took in guests.

Some owners installed bathrooms in the homes and let guests use them, while the outback privy became a valuable part of ownership.

T took work at St. George's on the Esplanade and devised a workshop, bedroom, and laundry—in a space that housed the burner that always needed attention—off the breakfast room adjacent to the kitchen. He also took janitorial work at the Priaulx Library. He kept a bike and a spare, which I enjoyed, especially in summer.

December 1960: he walks to the library or rides up a hill, which makes me gasp every time I try. I usually walk the bike up the last 50 feet, and he goes past me, saying, "See you there!" The library has some enviable material on language, and I use it quite a bit, but I want to hear the language among the people. I took the bus to more remote areas or wherever meetings were held so the language could be used and heard. We play cribbage, listen to the radio, and I don't miss our TV in London.

T borrowed a mattress from one of the rooms and slid it under his bed.

"If you get too cold, we have more blankets, and you could always share with me, though it'd be a tad tight."

I reminded him that I'd brought a sleeping bag as well.

We wear nightshirts from a pattern Z had designed that was practical, comfortable, and easy to access body parts using the loo. I wondered why and when men's standard wear became pants—kilts aside—and women's were skirts. Summer nightshirts were lightweight, sleeveless, had pockets, and ended at mid-thigh, covered, and comfortable. Winter fabric was flannel with sleeves that didn't need buttoning and a triangular hood that lays flat above the shoulder blades until pulled onto the head for warmth. At school, we wore "jammies"; some guys wear underwear, and some don't.

One night, I am cold. He offered to swap my mattress for his bed, but I think one or the other of us would still be chilly.

"Can we try sharing yours?" I ask.

"Sure.

"I'll sleep outside because I have to use the loo at night, and I don't suppose you're at that stage yet?"

"No, I still wet the bed!"

We both couldn't stop laughing.

We talked more during the night in bed than usual, and it was a night I knew I'd remember. I felt the warmth of his body and how close we are to each other. I imagine how he and Z slept, and I often wonder when he still thought and acted as if she were a he. On Guernsey, Z was a "he," and I know Guion knew, yet they kept my birth among themselves, and I guess the Germans never heard me as an infant, and if they ever did, T planned to say, "Ah, Z is listening to the forbidden radio," which he never had to do.

The house's walls were solid, and Z and T would put a mattress over the door "to keep the heat in." I asked many questions, playing detective, comparing notes between what I had heard from Dad and Z, and what T said, awaiting a flaw. Whenever Dad said, "Any questions?" I was usually so wide-eyed at what he said that I didn't dare ask for more. But T, whom I saw infrequently, made me feel less formal and more comfortable, and my trust was easier, maybe more natural. Maybe I took T for granted?

I love my Dad and admire him—as do my friends—but T, in his own way, makes me often wonder what daily life would have been like if Z and T and I had been a family that lived together. I asked if he had ever thought about marrying someone. Does he have anyone special in his life?

"You mean, am I intimate with anyone?"

"Oh, no!!!" I blurted out as fast as I could, embarrassed as hell.

He waits.

Very slowly . . . and softly, I say, "I guess . . . that's . . . exactly . . . what I mean."

He waits.

"I know it is not my business and very personal, and I'm sorry for being so clumsy about this . . . I'm still trying to figure all this out for myself."

"What do you have questions about?"

I wait.

He waits.

"What if I want to be touched sexually by someone?" I finally utter comfortably.

T says, "And, there's the corollary to that: what if you want to touch someone . . . sexually?"

I wait . . . and add, "Yeah . . . that, too."

I could have asked Dad, but I didn't . . . .

Talking to T was like talking to an older friend who'd had experiences I hadn't had yet.

"You and your friends talk about sex much?" he asked.

"Oh, Gawd!" I said.

"No!

Then I weakly added, "Only all the time!"

He said, "Hmmm . . . that sounds fairly common among boys your age, especially if they think no one is listening . . . go on, please."

T looks like this could give him time to think about "how" to say what he wants.

His sentence confirms my expectations.

"I'm thinking about how to answer you," T said.

"How to go on and try to get this right without fouling it up, so I wish I said something better.

"Okay, look—I'm going to work my way through this . . . just know my intent may be better than my expression.

"I love you, Will, and you are loved by people who care about you and guide you.

"Some kids never have even one person with whom they feel comfortable."

"Z had a Mum until she was 12," I said.

T replied, "There was never a Dad—though I could share my speculations sometime.

"Then, Z and I had each other.

"Then, there was you . . . for a very little while, we were physically together . . . and what matters is you, first and foremost."

T said, "If I stop . . . like now . . . I'm thinking.

"If I ramble, I'm stumbling and thinking out loud. This may feel like an hour, but I bet it only takes minutes.

"I'm trying to say, 'You're young, Will, and you have the rest of your life to wrestle with decisions and temptations.'"

Pause. "I understand the novelty and feelings surfacing, and I know patience is difficult . . . but maybe slowing down and appreciating the process might help?"

"What works now may work for a while . . . you may want more . . . yet looking for an answer for life is a little premature. Take your time. Explore. It's okay. You must be careful and consider the consequences; there is no simple answer.

"Either way, it's okay.

"We're all different. Even you.

"That's the essential part of all this. You accept yourself at all stages.

"Z and I made our life work. We're friends. No label or descriptor could be more accurate."

I add, "You have male friends, too . . . whom you trust?" Though I want to ask more, I don't. It isn't my business; it might intrude on his privacy or comfort.

I say, "If I could find a friend like you, I hope we wouldn't 'muck up' our friendship."

"If you compromise and listen to each other patiently, you and your friend or friends will be fine."

After a while, we yawn.

T said, "Let's get some sleep and let this rest, too."

"I love you, T."

We hug.

I turn and face the wall; he holds me, man to man.

I feel a warmth and trust between us that I hope to find with another someday.

With only a couple of years of school left, I began thinking about university. Despite the respected colleges and universities in the

UK, I want to know if I could get my yen for the U.S. either out of my system or so invade my system that I make a life there. Colleges and universities in the U.S. are better respected; education there, even if I return to the UK, could be advantageous. Language wouldn't be a problem; perhaps my accent would be a novelty, especially when trying out for dramatic roles or school plays. I propose the idea to my four parents.

"I'm wondering about attending university in the States."

They all look at each other and nod like words they had expected.

"I'm wondering if I can find a school with a reasonable tuition, not far from an airport, so I could fly home at least during winter break and certainly for summer."

"Would you board at school or try to find a place to live if the school does not have . . . dormitories, I think they call them?" Mum says.

I responded, "Well, we have time to do some research.

"Maybe this could be a family project?"

Dad spoke "I wonder if we can put an ad in the newspaper or get some newspapers with ads to see what options we could have?"

"Or maybe there is some kind of a housing office/boarding office?" Z asks.

"Any chance each of you would explore your question, and let's see what we can come up with?" I proposed.

They all agree.

Z adds, "Does this rule out considering a university here in case this fails to materialize?"

"Not at all," I answered, adding, "I plan on applying here as well."

"Is Willa in on this venture?" Mum asked.

"We've talked about it. She knows my interest, but I would not risk speaking for her."

"Wise Man!" Dad adds with a grin.

"We have discussed it in some depth, but I think she mentioned wanting to start here for two years and then consider pre-med, maybe in the States.

"Do you remember our conversation over tea, Z?"

"That's about my recollection. And, it is easy enough to get an update."

"She should be part of a plan."

Mum suggests that next time she calls, "Let's see where she stands on this topic so we can do our research for one or both, as the same considerations would contribute to an educated decision."

Dad adds, "How about we each do some work on one topic at a time, come up with a 'suggested' possibility, and then consider other topics?"

Mum and Z agree.

"The ultimate decision is yours," Dad adds, focusing on me, "and I feel kind of lucky we're working on this jointly and you've asked for our help."

"Well, I know this will cost a fair sum, and I'm willing to do what I can to keep costs reasonable and work and pay for what I can," I say, and add,

"I have no expectations. I have friends who will get the boot once they reach 18 and finish school. They'll be on their own. I could be, too."

Mm said, "You've done so much more than we—Z, T, I—could imagine."

I responded, "I'm 'willing' to consider whatever you suggest."

"I'm not taking anything for granted, nor do I expect my bills to be our bills."

Mom reminds me that her dad and dad's dad left a little money for Mum and Dad to "play with" to build the coffers for prospective progeny education funds.

"Still, two is more expensive, and you have every respectful right to use it entirely for Willa," Z says.

"We couldn't," Mum adds.

And simultaneously, Dad says, "We wouldn't. Let's pool whatever you and T can contribute, use it to pay for what we can, and see how far that takes us."

"For both Willa and Will?" Z adds; "that's a question and a statement."

"T and I would be happy to contribute to both."

"At some point, we may not have enough, but let's cross that bridge when we come to it," Dad adds.

Mum stands.

"All of our lives have been enriched by each other. Let's have tea."

She and Z go into the kitchen, and I hug Dad and hope I can control my feelings.

I have this sensation inside that makes me shiver and tingle.

Journal Entry 23, Zuri, 34, 1962

As we welcomed the New Year, I thought of Zuri-Mama every time we changed calendars and how she based what she taught on outdated—useless to some—discarded aids to learning. I checked January 23 and February 6, both on Tuesdays this year. Our children will be seventeen.

Despite celebrating Willa's birthday, there was always her twin. Though absent, we came to celebrate the births of all three and perform an act of kindness on 17 February, a Saturday this year, the day our first Will journeyed beyond us.

When my thirty-member chorus met on the second of January, the new rector sent his housekeeper/cook/live-in staff member to inform the director that the music selections had to be entirely religious and that

"Secular music would not be welcome inside the church."

Even Christmas carols would be sung outside when parishioners entered and exited. Instruments would be the piano, violins, harps, and not guitars.

"The radio in my room must be low enough not to be heard," she added.

Lily often substituted for the pianist; we buzzed about a new group.

"We can call ourselves 'The Rebels,'" an elderly man said.

Lily often played piano in the hospital's atrium for practice and entertainment during visiting hours.

"Could we practice there?"

I said, "How about a metro station with a piano? St. Pancras has one."

Since we couldn't rehearse in the church, we spent the time strategizing.

More members reacted: "What about music?"

"This was my only outing . . . my sister stays with . . . " she sobbed.

"I work outside for the city and look forward to this all week," a man said.

After a long silence, many of us shrugged our shoulders, and we began to gather our belongings and put on our coats.

Finally, Lily and I chatted, and she said, "Wait, I have to check with the hospital, but if each of you helps, we can do something together. Give your contact info to Zuri, and she'll give each of us a task."

On February 17, "We Healers" sang selections from **Guys and Dolls** and **West Side Story**; we sang "If I Had a Hammer" a cappella and ended with dancing the Twist, The Mashed Potato, and the Watusi to the radio in the hospital's atrium; donations benefited the gift shop.

Journal Entry 24, Will, 17, 1962

When Z spoke with T, he asked if I knew what I wanted to do.

"Good question," we agreed, as I had always thought about my reply. "Be a father!" I exclaimed, laughing. When I was a kid—three or four—that was my answer, and again, that response brought a smile to adult faces. I didn't understand the amusement of Mum's friends when one asked, though I wondered why Mum blushed and laughed too, injecting, "He only knows what he should for his age—at least Gordon keeps saying that!"

When I spoke with T, he asked what age group I enjoyed working with and if routine and repetition bored me. My volunteer work in London's Italian quarter gave me an other layer of understanding of community. I enjoyed the household age span and picked up a few words of Italian. T suggested I post an ad in local newspapers in cities with Italian districts and see what responses are offered.

"And, any narrowing down on professions?" T kept asking.

"I don't like being bored and want to make enough money to live comfortably. Money isn't a considerable objective; I want to cover my expenses.

"Z has helped me become frugal and careful, so my forecast regarding money., would be 'spend after acquiring, not before'— except for a large expense like a house. Borrowing involves interest, which pains me, but I'll work extra and hope to pay a mortgage off earlier."

T kept asking, "What about a car? Would that be worth borrowing for?"

"Maybe, but I'd try my luck with secondhand cars until I saved enough for a new one and try to live so earnings and expenses balance.

"It'll be a juggle, but I'm 17, almost officially close to an adult, and I'll have to juggle many options, so I'm thinking in those directions and hoping I won't get tempted otherwise."

"The U.S.A. is pretty big, and many kids have cars, but I wonder if public transportation is possible, negating the need or want for a car?"

"Are you narrowing down any areas yet?"

"Boston and New York. I'm thinking more about what I might like to do.

"I asked one of my teachers how he decided to teach, and he said he was asked what profession presents material and then may refer to it, but usually it takes a year until it is the focus again.

"Even doctors repeat operations; medicine is a more extended preparation, and doctors can become specialists, and the money is better. He said the money can be difficult, especially with a family, but sometimes part-time work helps. It's tiring, but the work satisfies.

"I like kids.

"Some try to be obnoxious and a pain, but they usually have legitimate reasons, and when they can't resolve the issues, they see themselves as the cause, probably because that's the easiest answer. That's where another adult helps."

I could almost see T's smile.

"Hey, Almost Adult—any response to ads?"

"Yeah! I almost forgot!

"One guy wrote that his brother called him 'Pro' for Professor, and it caught on. He's retired and decided to return to his roots, the North End, Boston, Massachusetts, and he bought a building on Hull Street. He's looking to help a kid with room and board in return for keeping the building clean and in shape, shoveling in winter, and earning a few dollars in spending money. I wrote back."

"That sounds promising!"

"Well, you may think my admiration for the President had an impact . . . and maybe it did."

T said, "He's got lots of fans. What is it that draws you?"

After a longer-than-usual pause, I said, "Energy."

T's eyes opened wider, and he waited.

"He has many attributes: looks, money, culture, and a lovely wife. . . ."

"True," T said and paused.

"But despite so many challenges too, especially health, that we don't know much about, he exudes an energy that attracts people . . . even those who may disagree with his politics.

"Anyway, my feelings have substance, not just fluff."

"So, I'm leaning toward Boston, Massachusetts—if I ever learn how to spell that state!"

"Lots of schools to choose from?"

"I'm checking now. I don't want to waste money on applications . . . so I am trying two, maybe three, and one here in the UK."

I applied to Boston College and State College at Boston, in the States.

In late February or early March, Mum left a message for me to call home:

"All is well; I just thought you'd like to know a letter arrived for you from Boston College."

After swim practice, I called. "I suppose I could have you open it." She was quiet; I could almost hear her heart beating over the phone.

"Could we meet this weekend? You drive up, or I can try to come home?"

"Of course. You have too much to do. Would you like lunch or dinner? Can your grandmothers come? They'd love to go for a ride."

"Hmmm, that's quite an audience, but I wouldn't deny them regardless of the contents."

"You're sure? Dad and I and Z can come alone if you prefer."

I waited for them at the driveway entrance to the school. They were already in the back seat, so I walked alongside the car. Though the sun was intense at midday, the wind kept alerting us to the temperature. Mum handed the letter to Dad, who gave it to me while he parked the car.

I used the depressor on my fingernail clippers to slit the envelope open. I put my hand to my mouth, and my throat tightened. I swallowed hard, looked at them in the car, and nodded, "Yes! I got in!"

The doors flew open, and hugs and good wishes surrounded me.

Dad stood off to the side and let the ladies have their way, and I walked over to him for a longer-than-usual tight hug.

"When do you have to let them know?" he asked.

"Oh, I didn't get that far . . . let's see . . . three weeks, and they want a check to hold the space . . . and being international, remember mail, et cetera."

Over lunch, we talked about my other application, for which I wanted to wait, as the cost for a state school is considerably less, but the competition is high.

"And we also have Willa to think about," I added.

Dad countered, "That's our worry, not yours."

"We'll do the best we can, eh, Dad?" Mum said.

"And, Z and T will contribute to the educational pot," I added.

Z was quiet until we looked at her.

"I'm . . . I don't know what to say. I'm so proud of you, of us. Who could have imagined?"

We all nodded.

"Can we put in a call to T?" Grandma Grace injected.

Within a week and a half, Boston State, a shorter version of the more formal name, had sent me a letter, and this time Z called to notify me.

Rather than repeat the first performance, I asked her to open and read it to us.

"'Congratulations, we invite you to be part of the class of 1966. Kindly respond with a deposit to hold your place within three weeks . . . don't forget mail, etc.' Have you given it much thought?"

"What do you think? It's all I've been thinking about . . . and I've decided. This is a more manageable tuition should anything happen. I feel more comfortable going to Boston State.

"And, if I'm lucky enough to get into BC for grad school for a year, that'll be a little easier on everyone."

"You're sure?"

"I am. I've thought about it, and that's what I'd like to do. Would you share it with Mum and Dad and ask them to send the deposit to Boston State ASAP?

"I've started a thank-you note to BC and will send it from here."

"Keep a copy for your files."

"I knew you'd say that!"

"And, thanks. I have learned some things like that . . . to keep my 'britches fitting,' if I may quote you and T."

We laughed.

Z said, "I've never had opportunities like this. I've been lucky, in many respects, and I'm very grateful for all the help I—we—have gotten . . . but I see what could have happened when I pass women in train stations holding babies, which pierces me to the core.

"I buy them food or something to drink, and most accept it gratefully."

"I remember you would have Willa and me deliver food and drink in train stations while you waited off to the side to keep an eye on us."

"Now for a place to live," I said, adding, "I don't think Boston State has dorms. I've been writing to Pro; he sounds like a working option. He sent photos and a map of Boston, so I think it could work. I think I'll go a few weeks early to get the living conditions under my belt before school starts . . . and, if it doesn't work out, I'll have a little time to find an alternative."

Zuri said, "Seeing you go off to school has been happening for many years, and it still tugs at my heart . . . but going to another country . . . well, it is your life, and you will live it."

"It's all our lives . . . and we'll all live it . . . and Willa's, too."

Zuri agreed, "Indeed."

"How lucky we are, eh?" I said.

After I finished secondary school, I went to Guernsey alone for a few days to spend some time with T before the rest of the family arrived. I took the mailboat, inspired by the Channel waters; arriving as the sun set was like animating a painting.

Often, the clouds compete, or the winds are too strong for comfort, but this time felt like I'd made the right decision.

I wrote some notes in my journal on my impression and took my time leaving the boat.

T kept bobbing his head, looking for me; then he nodded, and I knew he understood my delay. I like spending time with him. I learn so much. He's clever and exciting, and we enjoy each other's company.

My Dad is a swell guy, too, but he's spread a little thinner with my Mum, sister, and grandparents.

We enjoy each other's company, and sometimes he—and Mum, too—get a look when they stare at me a little longer than usual, and I can see what they're thinking, wondering how their birth child would have grown.

Z accompanied Willa and me back to London in early August to prepare us both for university. Willa spent time with her girlfriends, and Z and I had time to ourselves.

I couldn't relieve Z's anxiety about going to the United States. She's had an English perception I term "pride and prejudice" as the two outstanding characteristics of the U.S.A. She also feels there's a difference between people there as individuals versus people collectively.

"It's a different country, Will. You'll manage okay; you're young, but as soon as you open your mouth, you'll be "foreign," not one of them, and some have an unusual lack of being civil, it seems.

"I hope I'm wrong, I'd like to be; some of this is direct experience with tourists and hotel guests and what I've seen. They settle right in, don't act like guests, and don't exude politeness and courtesy—certainly, a generality that's more common than not.

"And intuition based on a feeling I have from news and newspapers and those with whom I've had direct contact."

Then, she changed the subject while thinking softly, "There's a difference between being a guest and a host . . . I don't think they . . . ."

"Are you excited about meeting Pro and assessing your living arrangements?"

"Oh, yes. He'll meet me at Logan—the Boston International Airport. I arrive in the afternoon, and . . . we'll go from there, I guess."

Sleeping on the flight didn't happen.

It was daylight extended.

Reading didn't keep my interest as much as the body of water below and the occasional ship.

I went through customs with my two bags, a backpack, and saw Pro waiting. We had swapped photos.

He looked comfortable and casually classy in an open-ironed shirt, shorts, and tennis shoes.

"Gotten some sun, have you?" I said.

"Oh, it comes easily; give you a hand?"

"I'm pretty well balanced with two bags."

"I can take your backpack. The car is in the lot. Are the bags hefty?"

His late-model four-door Ford was cleaned and polished, and the chrome glistened.

I thought I'd test his sense of humor. "I see a mark on a whitewall tire."

"I'm forever hitting curbs. A little cleanser will do the job."

"That part of my duties?"

"If you like! Hungry?"

"Not really. Anxious."

"I thought we could ride through the city, and I'd show you a few places.

"Then, I reconsidered and figured you've been cooped up all day and might prefer a walk?"

He dropped me and the bags on the sidewalk of 12 Hull Street and gave me the key to the apartment while he parked the car.

There looked to be no open spots on the street, and he had a permanent place in a building at the bottom of Commercial and Prince Streets.

There was a cozy, teapot, and a Pyrex glass pot with a pouring spout. I set to making tea.

He knocked on the door before coming in and saying, "Oh, good! I hope you like it strong?"

I gave one nod and added, "With a slug of milk. You?"

"Yes.

"When I'm out, I order light cream. To celebrate your arrival, I bought us a small container. Is 'Cheerio' an appropriate welcome?

"Have you looked around yet?"

I hadn't.

"Not much, basically three rooms on the 'stoop,' as we call it here."

His bedroom was the front room with two windows that faced the street. In the front corner of the room near a window was a raised platform at which I squinted, and he noticed.

"That's headroom to exit from the cellar, just below; take barrels out, coal in.

"There are sides of adjoining apartment houses surrounding the courtyard, in the back, which is our outside space, though it borders on number 10, next door, and a building facing Sheafe Street.

"The fire escapes, which most use for plants, have never been used by people, but we have to have them, and they get inspected infrequently. I own the courtyard and pay the taxes on it.

"It has to remain empty, so I see to that. Rarely does someone have an animal and will use it in inclement weather, but the caveat is if it's not cleaned up—including soapy water and the stiff-bristled broom by the door—there is no future use.

"No need for odors to rise; too many people live here to be inconsiderate."

The kitchen had a door to enter from the hallway and separated the front room from the back room and the adjoining bathroom. The kitchen had a large double porcelain sink with windows overlooking the courtyard and a high sky.

"That's where women would wash clothes on one side and rinse on the other. Some bathed children, and adults have stood in a container and given themselves a 'French Bath.'

"We have a washing machine—each floor has a day—and a dryer, which I discourage. We have a clothesline system for each floor and wooden devices we also call 'dryers' near the washer in the boiler room.

"There are four floors. Families rent the top two floors, and indi-viduals or couples rent the second floor. No noise, no loud devices, like radios or TVs or Victrola phonographs.

"We—you and I—use the tiny front single bedroom on the second floor for closet space, as it can be entered from the hall and closed off from the rest of the apartment when it is rented.

"The other three rooms are laid out like this: front, kitchen, back, and bathroom. The 3rd and 4th floors have 'crappers' in the hall.

"I have rugs and padding on the second floor and encourage all to take off street shoes and wear slippers in the house."

I looked at my shoes. "Oops! I brought slippers."

"I make exceptions. I'm flexible, I like to think."

I wondered.

"I've not done this before, and I hope the experience will be positive for both.

"I'm an active guy and keep busy, and when I learned of the limited living space for students and some schools that don't have any at all, I decided I could try to extend hospitality."

"The occupants are responsible for their hallway and the descending stairs. Swept daily and a piney soap wash on weekends.

"We have the vestibule and exit/entrance, which everyone uses, so we contribute and are responsible for clearing stairs and sidewalk when it snows."

I was going to ask if this was his definition of ". . . flexible . . ." but decided I'd better wait; maybe he had a test for me when he finished.

He paused.

"Is the back room mine?"

"I thought you'd rather it, as it is quieter, though darker; I'd reconsider, as I use the bathroom during the night . . . though come to think of it, I could use a 'guzunder'—I think that's Australian for port-a-potty, but I like using the word ever since I learned it."

"I don't think you'll wake me; let's see. I've been rooming with mates, so sharing with one should be easier."

"I've also thought about you on the second floor if things get tight here. The beds are a bit of a hybrid I came up with, and with a little help from a basic woodworking course at the Industrial School on North Bennet Street. Let me show you."

"Let me run to the WC!" He said while moving briskly and adding, "Meet me in my room."

He had made a frame that held two single 38x74.6 inches twin mattresses; the bottom one, though not a box spring, had a purpose. The back, which leaned against the wall, supported the back, and with two pillows behind the mattress where it met the bottom one, it allowed one seated to lean back comfortably. If pulled out, it could be a double bed.

It was high enough, so boxes for "sox" (Was this how I'd have to spell "socks" if I lived in Boston?), underwear, and tee shirts slid under, with side space for shoes. One side support had a shellacked-finish rectangle with a leg that swiveled out for support for desk use.

"I've been using mine since spring to be sure it worked before building the second one."

It required dropping the top mattress onto the bottom one, repositioning the pillows, and unrolling the blanket. The sheets served as mattress covers. It reminded me so much of Guernsey and T, as did he in some ways.

"I'd luv for you to meet T," I said and elaborated briefly on the connection, which he accepted with a welcoming gesture.

"That would be my pleasure! Maybe we could figure out a way to host?"

"How tired are you? Care to walk?

"You can unpack while I make dinner?"

We climbed the hill, and I saw Copp's Hill Cemetery and the water view of the **USS Constitution**. We walked down the other end of

Hull Street, a hill that passed the Brink's Building. We took a left onto Commercial Street, passed the factory structure where he had a parking space on the corner of Prince Street, and headed to North Station. We took the train for one stop, got off at Haymarket Square, and walked home. He had a schedule and map of the transit routes that were like London's tube system, but I didn't comment on the comparison.

"Salmon and green beans for dinner? I got a fresh loaf of Italian bread, and you can decide how we can have that. Depending on how the wind blows, you'll wake to the aroma of fresh bread now and then. Your towels and 'things in general' will be on the left since you have an "L" in your name, and mine will be on the right since. . . .

"I usually shower before dinner, after I've earned it by exercising. See what suits you and when hot water isn't short.

"Here's a copy of the Transit lines you may find helpful," Pro said.

The next day, we took "The T," which stood for Transit—I couldn't wait to tell T one more thing his letter stood for—to 625 Huntington Avenue, walked around the Fenway, Harvard Medical, Mrs. Jack Gardner's Palace, also known as the Isabella Stewart Gardner Museum, The Museum of Fine Arts, and Northeastern University; then we took the T back to North Station, walked up the hill and down to 12 Hull Street. The area was making sense, and I was getting my bearings.

We bought eggplant parmesan sandwiches for lunch and ate them at a park facing Hanover Street, with stone benches adjacent to the Eliot School, where we could see the back of the Old North Church, "One if by land, two if by sea." The front side faced Hull Street, where tourists took photos year-round, adding to the space-sharing history's welcome congestion.

"Want a little time for yourself?" Pro asked.

"I hadn't thought about that. You want to take a little time off as a Virgil?"

"You know of Dante?" he asked.

"Not much, but wasn't Virgil Dante's guide?"

"One of them. We can talk about the other two sometime."

I held up the map and key, waved, crossed Hanover Street, and tried assessing the other half of the North End that had an identity of its own. I found one of the many coffee shops and got in line.

"Tea, please."

"Here or to go?"

As I was about to answer, one of the clusters of three guys behind me stuck out his little finger and mimicked me.

I was about to react but figured I didn't need to make a skirmish.

"Here, please."

I wish I had said, "To go," but now I felt stuck with my reply.

As I added milk to a heavy white mug, the mouth behind me opened . . . again, "It's 'tea, please!'"

This time, I did turn, and one of the other two was embarrassed and rolled his eyes at the third, who just shook his head.

"We're sorry for our friend; he's buying and thinks that entitles him to belittle—"

"Hey, you can buy your own! The guy sounds like a faggot."

Then I piped up, "I bet you don't know what a faggot is."

One of the other guys said, "He doesn't, but we do. It's a bunch of sticks, and why he—"

Mr. Mouth interrupted again, moving his shoulders, projecting one side and then the other, running a finger over an eyebrow, and then speaking.

"A Brownnose that does what?"

"Look." I halted the talk and, glaring at Mr. Mouth, continued, "I'm not from here. I have a name, and your lack of manners is unwelcome."

As Mr. Mouth started to say, "Well, listen to you—" one of the trio said, "Come sit with us."

And, looking at Mr. Mouth, his friend added, "You can come too, if you shut up."

"You could come to see how people should treat other people," the other of the trio said.

We spent about 10 to 15 minutes having our beverages and making conversation.

They were close to my age and had gone to high school together but were off to other lives soon thereafter.

Mr. Mouth hadn't said a word.

"Say it!" the shorter guy said, looking at him.

"Sorry . . . my friends put up with me, and I never seem to learn, and I try to be funny and fit in, and it turns to shit because these guys don't let me get away with anything."

"Because someday, somebody's going to kick your ass! We're your friends—at the moment. You keep embarrassing us, and you'll fly solo." Capisce?

"You come here often for . . . tea? I'm Nick," the shorter guy said, introducing the other guy as Ernie and Mr. Mouth as Gus.

They held up their mugs in a welcome toast, and we parted, shaking hands and agreeing to meet here again.

Gus hung back while Nick and Ernie exited. "You look like you wanted to say something." I stated.

"Oh? I didn't realize it was that obvious," he said.

"Please. . . ." I encouraged and added,

"You pay for everything?"

He nodded. "All the time. Usually. Always been that way."

I thought to myself, *Is this worth saying?*

"I'm new here and hesitate to interfere . . . but . . . they are your audience."

He squinted. "I think I get what you're trying to say. I need to think about it more, and it'll dawn."

"Thanks." I managed.

"Catch ya." And he was gone.

22 November 1963

Numb.

The cliché "Life changes in an instant" applies best to my feelings, and I wondered how long they would last.

A lifetime?

Quiet.

When the news interrupted classes, we all looked at each other.

Sophomore, American History, the woman prof who epitomized control and knowledge and whose classes mesmerized us with details, turned toward the blackboard behind her with a tissue, ever so briefly, and then back to us.

"I'm sorry. Maybe the best thing we can do in his honor is wrap up this class. If anyone needs/wants to leave now, you are welcome to do so without any ramifications. To those who wish to remain, I could probably finish in 15 to 20 minutes."

Students shuffled in the corridors, but the usual noise was absent.

"Here we are studying history and making it," she added.

When she concluded, as was our custom, she exited first while we got ourselves together.

Today, we stood, eyes brimming, and choked out a collective "Thank you."

Friday afternoon.

Pro and I walked to Garden Court Street, where Rose Kennedy was born.

Pro broke the silence: "My parents and I lived at number 10 when I was born."

"And when was that?" I asked.

"1925," he injected and went on.

"And Rose Fitzgerald Kennedy wore the same toast-colored gown to the Inaugural Ball as she wore when presented to the Court of St. James," I added.

At 73, she had lost a third child and was adamant about shielding the news from her mother, who shared the President's middle name.

We spent the weekend listening, reading, and watching the news and TV, as repetitious as it was, including the murder of the alleged assassin on TV, followed by a day of National Mourning on Monday, the day of the funeral.

How events unfolded stymies imagination, but the dignity so characteristic of Jackie pervaded the cold sunny day.

Journal Entry 25, Zuri, 38, 1966

Writing Exercises, continued!

Dialogue

How does Coach find these topics? A mimeograph purple print hand out of directions read:

Select one quotation, and write a series of sentences that tell a brief story that serves as the lesson for the quotation. I will provide three quotations, or you may provide your own. For those whom the exercise may intimidate, cut out pieces from a newspaper or magazine that demonstrate the rules of using quotations: singles, doubles, punctuation, titles, style sheets, languages, variations of marks and rules, etc.

How do rules and symbols differ in other countries? If you are familiar with another language or are descended from another country, you may use that country and its language as an example for this assignment.

1. "And you believed them?" "I did." or "I did not." or both?

2. "I want the script!"

3. Two friends (males, females, one of each gender): One friend: "Aren't you afraid of being hurt by him?"

4. The other friend: "I don't know him well enough to be hurt by him."

5. "'Tis by no means the least of life's rules: to let things alone."
   —BALTHASAR GRACIAN

We agreed on number 5 as our in-class example.

Coach spoke, "Let's set a scene where two workshop participants meet for coffee/tea; one agrees with the statement's sentiment, and the other does not.

"You may work on this individually or be one of the two people and converse now for 15 minutes.

"Record or imagine the scene; continue the dialogue, and identify the characters by any name, age, sex, description, and relationship to each other. The descriptions need not be part of the scene but may be a prelude for the benefit of the readers.

We paired up.

After 15 minutes, we reassembled.

"Is the exercise enriched by details of the speakers? How much could you use versus how little can be enough?"

"Speaker 1, pro-male/female?

"Speaker 2, anti-female/male?

Another handout had an example:

Two Guys

"What's new?" John, one of my locker mates, asked.

I answered.

John asked, "And you believed them?"

I trusted John, and no one else was in the space to overhear me

share my experience of losing 75% of my life savings.

How about the other side?

Cops go to the pool, where he swims, and arrest him.

Eventually, the bank proves fraud.

I am musing about more T time.

Next Writing Class Topic: Directions

"How to do something, short demo, samples, an activity has a life of its own."

Peanut butter sandwich example.

1. Put the peanut butter on the bread.
   The coach takes the jar and holds it on the loaf of bread. We laugh. We get it.
   I think I'll try explaining tatting—simply.

2. Writing a Script

The coach came in with the setting and line of a conversation: "I want the script!" The observer is dining alone at an adjacent table against a wall. Assignment? Write, essentially, a One-Act Play of Family Dynamics. The dinner conversants speak their lines and freeze while the "I," a waiter, and an observer speak off to the side.

What caused the outburst?

What "script" would you provide?

Before moving on, we spend a few minutes on the personal rewards of reading and writing by being reminded of what we learn about ourselves by writing . . . and what our writing tells readers about us.

Journal Entry 26, Will, 21, 1966

I decided on the title of my thesis: "The Range of the Truth of Fiction."

Although the title sounds like an oxymoron, fiction creates its truths in many formats: novel, play, short story, and poem—indeed, any piece of writing or art. Facts, labeled non-fiction, are facts upon which we base beliefs and actions. Facts may be proved. Are they convincing?

How does what one believes to be facts become the reverse of what others believe to be facts? Do the twains meet? How does vocabulary affect facts? How does fiction present its facts when interpretation can alter beliefs to the extent that readers/viewers/listeners/writers/and commentators give opposing perceptions?

As firmly as I am convinced that the range of fiction serves more powerfully than facts, another may refute my presentation with arguments and data that show a preference for non-fiction.

Perhaps for another degree, I will take the opposing position for the sake of exercise and a good exploration that serves both my *and* the public's quest for truth.

Periodically, I return to the beginning of my thesis and attempt to rewrite it to make it clearer and more practical. I remember my childhood when Zuri would meet Willa and me at school and take us home.

We would play for a while; then, before tea, Zuri would have us practice penmanship and cursive writing with and without lines so that Willa excelled in cursive writing and I in printing.

Zuri would say, "Presentation; make it look like it came from a typewriter.

"Will we always practice writing and printing?" Willa asked.

"Oh, no! This is the only time you have to practice, and you will write and print the rest of your lives, so every time you do, it will be practice, but others will envy how precise you make the letters.

"Remember when you learned your name and would fit the letters into squares in which there were dates?"

"Yes!" and Zuri saved them all.

"May we have tea?"

Our teas were always comfortable but formal. Real china, cloth napkins, and Zuri would make something special. Willa wore a necklace. I wore a tie, not tied yet, but I was practicing.

Whenever we had an assignment to write, Zuri would try to make it fit or connect somehow to what we had done before, and that link offered a depth that motivated us to complete the assignment . . . usually.

"Why are we doing this?" I asked.

"Willa, can you help?" Zuri asked.

"When we go to university and write papers for degrees, everything we've done before contributes."

"Do you know what you want to be yet?" Zuri asked.

"No. I'm still thinking," Willa said.

Zuri asked, "You still want to be a baby doctor?"

"Yes."

I asked, "How can you do that? You're a girl."

"That's how she's going to do it—*because* she is a girl—and girls can do anything," Zuri added.

"Can boys have babies?" Willa asked.

That always made me turn red, and I asked if I could be excused.

Babies made me think of why I called Zuri "Zuri." Because everybody did. I called Mum "Mum," because Willa did. Zuri was my biological Mum, but it would be confusing to call her Mum too, so we agreed on Zuri.

Whenever we were alone, Zuri always reminded me, "Remember, you're special," and winked and patted my shoulder. "An extraordinary young man."

Grad School at BC brought challenges: a thesis was one, and studies were more concentrated and independent. At this point, most of the profs considered one knew how to learn and teach oneself; increasing the work put the onus on us. Many worked jobs, some were married, and the division of time needed support.

A couple of guys and I decided to get together since we shared courses to re-inject the study-group concept I had practiced as an undergrad and put most of the responsibility on me. I didn't have more time. I just spent my time differently, more on studying, and often, these two guys could barely stay awake once they sat down. They were stringing the courses out over years, and I wanted my work done this academic year. I wanted to sample other parts of life.

In the four courses I took, we were in one class together and each of them in one other of mine; I had one class without them—but I still made two extra copies of my typed notes via carbon paper, which helped when we studied for finals, as well as when classmates were absent.

Interestingly enough, their parents would host a dinner or two or three, especially during exam time, which helped us study and sleep, and the history the parents had lived through enlivened the conversations. Much like those of Z and T, Americans and Italians, and Americans and Iranians, of which my classmate A was one, and M was the other.

All of which I incorporated into my thesis because although there were few printed resources, the interviews' and anonymity I was able to offer gave them a comfort level from which to share, made my orals lively, and got me a verbal offer to consider staying on for a Ph.D.—for which I was grateful, but declined.

I needed a break. I wanted to do something different, something more worldly than academic experience. My family left it up to me.

A's parents grew up in Iran, and though the political differences between the U.S. and Iran seemed cordial, they had the potential to be a challenge, and there were factions within Iran that were strong enough to be a force.

Both of A's parents took in refugee Jewish children, and claimed them as their own to protect them, and kept carefully hidden memories they recorded so that these kids would not forget their history. The kids accepted this as most of them had no papers yet and were old enough to remember their families, names, places, and incidents, and once presented with the reasons why they had to take the Iranian family name and be assimilated into its culture, even temporarily, it was better than risking their lives.

Most kids whose families took in children were amazingly welcoming, saying, "What if our parents had more of us?"

That seemed generous until I recalled a quote from Thomas Hardy that I try to forget about an eight-year-old who killed two of his siblings and himself and left a note with something like "There were 2 many of us."

It still chills me.

There were enough children in Tehran to play together and attend schools together. Parents knew the tension and danger they were giving their families and realized the dangers these children would otherwise face. Only time might allow one to share the truth or be buried with a secret.

M's parents and family's challenge was similar to what the Japanese encountered after Japan bombed Pearl Harbor, and almost 3,000 lives were lost. Japanese-Americans and Japanese immigrants were placed in Immigration/Detention Camps, and most lost everything for which they had worked.

The Japanese camps were not publicized, but their existence was less a secret politically than humanly. A sense of "deserved" seemed to hover the veil over a prejudice that challenged a culture where young people felt so strongly about the Emperor that they would become Kamikaze pilots.

This intense loyalty and stubbornness of the culture prevented surrender. They elongated the wars and retaliation so that it took not one but two atomic bombs to convince the Emperor that his people would consider death an honor and that the entire empire and culture could be sacrificed for that tenacity.

The Emperor agreed to reason, which was surprising and necessary if Japan and its people were to have a future, even one with unconditional surrender, which the new U.S. President, Harry S Truman, became familiar with and implemented decisively. Earlier in the war, the U.S. was at war with Italy in Europe.

I learned that between 1941 and 1943, 600,000 Italians had to register as political enemies. They were placed in Immigration Camps, guilty until proven innocent, as opposed to the reverse, on which their adopted country prided itself on the lines engraved on the Statue of Liberty, "Give me your tired, your poor, your hungry yearning to be free." Many registered and wrote letters of their experiences, some of which families kept but many of which families and friends destroyed for fear of governmental reaction or retaliation in some form of retribution.

Prejudice, fear, and intimidation were strong among individuals and governments. Would this ever become public? Secrets were kept—like pregnancy in a single, unmarried woman. If she later married, the entire "secret" was honored and buried, like some parts of history.

Journal Entry 27, Zuri, 42–52, 1970s–1980s

I do like a good newspaper with an image and a story to accompany my morning tea and start the day. Add listening to a solid British accent—especially the BBC, with depth and research emphasizing truth and an attempt to shroud opinion, though the selection of adjectives often colors reporting, I learn by listening carefully. The radio is company; the interviews and programming allow me to stay active and work, versus the passive state I allow myself at dinner and beyond.

The British Museum posted a notice entitled "**Stories**." Adults are welcome to attend a writing, art, and oral-expression program to rebound what we have experienced. Guest facilitators have volunteered.

"Participants" may register (name, contact information, health issues, emergency contact information) at any time and attend as time allows.

"Dates the cards, available at the desk, when one enters, and, on the rear side, print the name you wish to be called. The facilitator will pick them up at the end of each session. All participation is voluntary, and we request respect for differing views. By signing below, you agree to contribute to decorum. Thursdays, 1900–2100."

It sounded like an evening out with a purpose, and though attendance was voluntary, some, like me, were there weekly. Businesses provided paper, writing implements, and art supplies as a contribution to the community, and we were welcome to take them as needed.

I thought about what Zuri-Mama did for children and felt this was an adult version. In one session, the facilitator was late, called to forewarn us, and asked us not to leave. S/he suggested we discuss and write about "How to _______." We were to make a list, narrow it down to the top five, then three, then one, until s/he arrives. I couldn't decide between preparing food and tatting.

"Coach," as he preferred to be called, arrived with a stash of energy and humor: "You know my paying job makes life happen!" His attire: bow tie and coordinated colors, looked as fresh as they probably did that morning. We had about 40 minutes, so he asked what two choices we had discussed. I thought: *He heard me before I spoke! I'm not alone.*

The assignment has challenges as part of its core. "Keep the list. You never know when one of the other topics rises to the top. Write the first sentence. Those of you with two, write the first sentence for each; take 3–5 minutes, and make any changes you like. Read your sentence aloud to yourself. Make changes. How many have two top-ics? Read the second topic sentence aloud to yourself." Three of us did. "Does that help you narrow your choices? Please read your sen-tence to us. If you would like a comment, ask, and if anyone is willing to comment, raise a hand and let the reader select one." Then he got us thinking about images and choices. "Would you like an image to accompany your writing? Black and white/color? Drawing, photo, size? Caption? Who do you think would read what you wrote? Who do you think would not read it? M/F, age. Don't forget prisoners, the religious, and teenagers. Questions?

Wouldn't the topic take care of readers? "Perhaps. Let's use our-selves and survey the group. Back to topic, eh? Interest is the key," he said, but it's not the reader's job as much as it is the writer's. Fixing a flat tire: "Did anyone choose that?" No one did. Bait the reader in the first sentence. Try it now. We read our boring sentences.

"Don't forget an essential element—maybe two crucial elements: humor and mystery. Try writing that first sentence again."

One participant asked, "A flat tire on what—a bicycle, a car, a truck?"

"Your choice. The more you think ahead, the more 'fun' and engaging the writing can be, but if you overthink, you won't get to the writing. Plunge in; write for ten minutes, and we'll use the last ten minutes to listen."

Most couldn't get far, and few opted to read even one sentence, so he guided us with more prompts.

"Think of someone in a situation like a flat tire. Who?"

A few people came to mind, and as soon as someone said, "A nun," Coach asked, "In or out of habit?"

"They always wear habits when they are out," someone added.

"So, a nun on a bike," and we smirked.

"There is humor, an event, and a character.

"We know a nun walking a bike with a flat tire will get help. This one is independent . . . let's hear what you come up with next week.

"And work on your directions to do something, please."

I worked on the nun now and then, as we were all eager to hear how she made out. What sounded best was a hodgepodge between fact and fiction. The nun had seen where sisal rope was used in place of an inner tube, and rubber and spare parts, like tubes, were mainly patches. Strong sisal rope could be wrapped around the rim of the tires and secured by weaving the two ends together.

The pockets of her habit were large and held many things: gum, candies, pliers, screwdriver, wrench, patches, tatting supplies, scissors, needles, and thread, but no air pump and no sisal rope. Hmmmmm.

The tire had to come off; she used the wrench and the pliers handle to work the tire's edges from the rim. The tube inside had many patches, and any one of them could have let air escape.

However, she wore a softer rope as part of her habit.

She undid the knots on her ropes, wrapped them over the tube twice around the rim, and secured the result with tatting thread and a large-eyed needle. Then she worked the tire back onto the rim with the pliers handle on each of the two edges of the tire.

Off she rode, her habit blowing in the wind. How she explained her dishevelment to Mother Superior either got her booted out of the order or they assigned her to the laundry for penance. How about the dialogue of that conversation for another time?

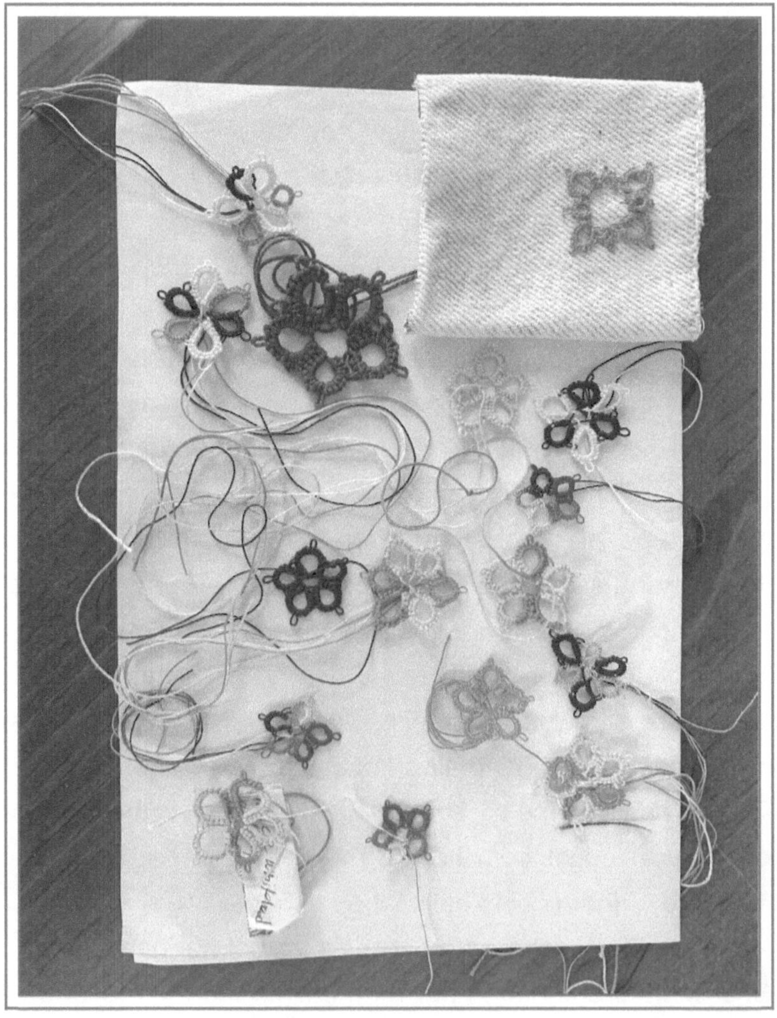

Pieces of Tatted Lace

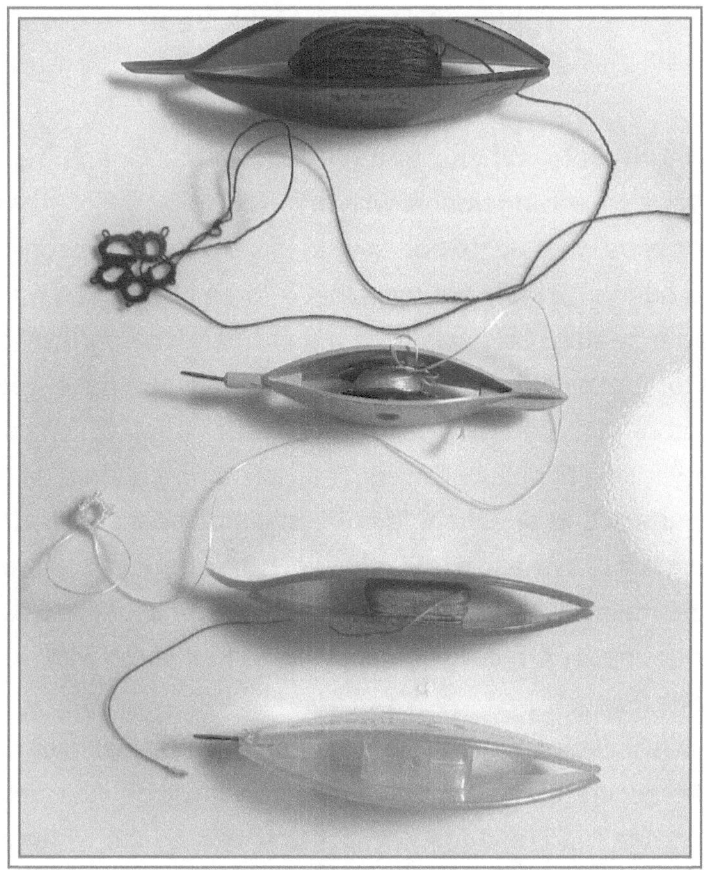

Tatting shuttles; thread

Top: large purple plastic shuttle with wound thread, plastic tip, and a tatted piece.

Next: gray plastic shuttle, metal tip, bobbin insert with wound thread.

Next: smaller plastic, wound thread, ready to tat.

Bottom: plastic, empty shuttle, metal tip, centerpiece with a hole for tatting thread to be inserted and held in one hand while winding the tatting thread from a spool or other supply resource with the other hand.

The pointed tips are helpful in un-knotting a thread.

Tatting: A Way to Make Lace

I'm having trouble. When I brought it up to the Coach, he asked, "How many are having trouble with the 'How to __________' writing?" Several hands went up. "Good time to talk. How many people sew?" Then he added, "By hand or machine?" Three people had machines. One had a treadle. One was from a salesman who agreed to return once after the initial sale and delivery, and one purchase was made from a store that offered house calls once for a fee or a package of three anytime schedules allowed. They all came with manuals, some with a pattern and direction: female, male, or household. "Did they have diagrams? Were they clear? Was this a step-by-step process?" When the men yawned, he asked if any had ever assembled a model of a car or boat or furniture and appliances that come with manuals? Same questions.

"This is technical writing. No plot or characters, just information. It has to be accurate; one cannot predict how it will be interpreted. Not everyone can read, and few can comprehend as the writer intends. The more one tries this writing on others, the clearer the writing may become. Bring photos or magazine ads on your topic, and let's work on this. Also, in the meantime, try to think of a brief personal story that might help other readers see themselves stymied and upon whom your directions can improve."

Knitting and crocheting have been credited to men at sea making patterned water-resilient sweaters using wool containing the natural oil of sheep and goats. Often, when boats sunk and sweaters washed ashore, the pattern helped identify where sailors were from and con-tributed to learning the fate of the voyage. Tatting produces handmade lace and is a decorative addition that enhances fabric.

I implemented Zuri-Mama's "Easy, Learn, Play" and "Essentials, Language, Process."

Easy: shuttle, thread, low numbers are thicker, high are finer; needle, scissors for cutting thread. Tatting may also be done with a needle. Directions here are for the shuttle only.

Learn: insert the thread into the drilled hole in the centerpiece of the shuttle that holds the top and bottom in place, and wrap the thread in a circular motion. The tail of the thread can be held in place by a thumb and finger on the bottom of the shuttle, creating tension while winding. Cut from the source. This tail end is worked to form loops called "stitches" by forming a triangle from the thread held by the thumb and index finger extended to go around the middle finger and back to the thumb and index finger.

Two half-hitch stitches = one whole hitch stitch—like 2 tires on an axle

1. where the shuttle goes **under** the taut line and returns **over** the taut line between the taut line and the shuttle thread; and,

2. where the shuttle goes **over** the taut thread and returns **under** the taut line and the shuttle thread.

Together, 2 half-hitch stitches equals one whole stitch. The tension of the thread forms a taut line to hold the stitches in place.

Play: wrap thread onto the shuttlecock, practice alternating one over, one under for **20 whole stitches**; (20) under (20) over = **20**

whole stitches. Stitches should be tight enough to surround the thread on which they are placed and loose enough to slide when the tail end pulls together the first stitch and last stitch. Thread tension is critical.

Essentials: shuttle, thread, needle, scissors.

Language: *barchetta* in Italian is a "little boat" that resembles a tatting shuttlecock. *Chiacchierino*—tatting in Italian—is "a little chat," which people do while tatting. The French call tatting *frivolité*, close to English "frivolity."

Chains are a series of stitches. *Picots* are loops larger than stitches that separate a specific number of stitches, like 20, for added interest and a lacey look.

Process: follow the directions of others, or create one's own design for pieces on handkerchiefs, placemats, napkins, bookmarks, etc.

Since tatting is compact, several men attempted the craft and expanded our offerings at Menton House, where crafters earned a little money and got some business exposure.

One of the women who liked working with wood helped make shuttlecocks in the war's aftermath. Plastic might have potential, and metals had long been favored.

Hardwood could be made into a handsome, smooth finish with a sharp point for working out thread knots or a visible error in the design. Its portability and easy access make it attractive to many.

My background story about tatting became a discussion. One of the participants corresponded via letters with family members a fair distance apart. She offered to ask her sixteen-year-old godchild if she would share our projects with classmates and get their reactions to our writing. This might help them bridge a generational gap and provide us with a response to understanding and clarifying our directions.

The young girls choose to whom they would correspond based on their interests, and if there were male-oriented topics, they knew boys who would also help. I took photos and agreed to forward a shuttle, thread with a choice of color(s)—and a bookmark as a gift with a piece of tatting on one side and a quotation on the other side with my name and contact information. I also opted to send stamps. I received a note thanking me for the writing, the bookmark, and the pink, purple, and off-white threads.

The note included a line we found applied to many adults: "Please understand, I have not successfully done crafts like this one.

"I've tried knitting, crocheting, embroidery, and even sewing with prospects of getting a machine of my own, but the results have all been trashed. I'm hoping there might be something to redeem my lack of success. Are you patient?"

Signed: Cherie

Tatting took visits and required being shown and imitating. Doing as little as ten stitches a day helps one remember the process. Cherie mastered the tension challenge in making the half-hitch stitches: too tight, and the half-hitch would not slide to close; too loose, and the half-hitch formed a gap like a picot. Her patience took concentration, but once she passed the frustration, she continued to make bookmarks for gifts, and our correspondence led to visits and a warm friendship. My concern was what could be forgotten with gaps between projects and how diagrams and words could be improved.

I made wedding handkerchiefs in 1980 when she and her boyfriend Tony married, which they always sported for formal events. As their family grew, each child received a baby ensemble similar to the ones I'd made for Will, Gordon, and Lily. I got to tell them about Baby Will and how my child was baptized, and one of the fastest pieces I worked on was a baby set for Willa so she wouldn't feel left out.

A Palace Friend (PF) remarked on the handkerchiefs and asked Cherie to ask her source, me, to make wedding handkerchiefs for gifts with the initials "C" for him and "D" for her for the event on 29 July 1981.

I was a guest of Tony and Cherie's at a Tea for C and D, and I brought the handkerchiefs and left them with a lady-in-waiting before meeting the Queen.

The next day, a driver in a Rolls delivered a handwritten thank-you note requesting instructions for a "Palace Friend" to tat. The driver waited for my response and said I would be contacted for an agreeable meeting time, and he would be my driver. I made a diagram with fingering positions to review when I was not there. I agreed not to deny nor confirm any questions regarding identification, which I understood and respected.

Journal Entry 28, Will, 25–35, 1970s–1980s

After graduating from Boston State in 1966 and Boston College in 1968, I wondered if my opportunities would have been as productive in the UK. Would my motivation have been as strong? In the U.S.A., I was on my own and free; my only limitations and obligations were self-imposed. Was that maturity?

I continually marvel at Z, who, without a formal education, guided Willa and me to write papers that connected somehow so that, as we aged and wrote more required papers following the same objective, when it came time to consider a thesis, both fiction *and* non-fiction held my attention and interest. I'll continue to vacillate between them, and arguing with myself is as healthy as arguing with anyone else. 1968 was an Annus Horribilis, with the assassinations of Robert F. Kennedy and Martin L. King and the accidental death of Thomas Merton. I considered how a country abundant in opportunity could also be abundant in violence.

My skin color was woody, varying between oak and teak. I tanned well, and my features caused questions. I saw how prejudice thrived, and guns were ever-present.

Home began to worry me, and Z caught a little break between rearing Willa and me before caring for my grandmothers. Vera, Gordon's Mum, died in 1979. Grace, Lily's Mum, died in 1980.

My concern for my Mum and Dad grew stronger as I began teaching, and Willa was in London, though her relationship with Mum wasn't as strong as mine. In 1989, Mum, born on 20 October 1923, died at 66 years of age and left letters for us. Dad floundered about. He never knew his biological Dad and always wondered about the Mum who gave him up.

Vera talked with the girl who bore him. Did either tell the truth or change it for his benefit? This was a question he carried all his life.

Z always said he looked at the sketch of the dog Cinnamon in a silver frame frequently, wondering about the little girl and if she ever became an orphan. We were never sure of the dog's age because she, too, was adopted.

I wonder how T's love for us was stable, solid, and persistent, and mine and Z's—were steady, prosperous, and natural for him.

Pro and I kept in touch; we'd alternate meeting for lunch or dinner once or twice a month. I'd often go to Boston for a concert, play, or lecture and stay with him. He didn't rent out my space after I left. He wanted me to feel it was always there when I wanted or needed it. He liked visiting Rhode Island; the drive was unlike Boston traffic, and he liked the Jazz Festival and always brought a welcomed crusty loaf of Italian bread.

He once said I was the son he wished he could have fathered. I blushed, speechless, and nodded.

In his day, the best a single male could hope for to guide a non-biological child was The Big Brother Program, where he volunteered for years. He and the boys assigned to him keep in touch sporadically. He supported and connected with a couple of young boys, some of whom shared stories about connections with the clergy that made his eyes wide and frightened him about risking his reputation, whatever the truth may be. The headlines and attention never competed with an apology if the charge was an error or given the space the charge was given to correct the wrong if it was wrong.

"What if they are telling the truth?" We took sides for the sake of conversation and debate.

Him: "What if they are exaggerating and/or lying?"

Me: "Would adults take advantage of kids?"

Him: "Why would the victims not say something sooner?"

Me: "Who'd believe them, and what kind of stigma would be part of the rest of their lives?"

I thought about the servicemen who were quiet after serving and turned to alcohol or drugs. Thanks to Vietnam Veterans, PTSD became a diagnosis for all to find a connection. We discussed being a Dad, something we both wanted and, despite our age gap, was remote or off the charts. We never ran out of topics to discuss.

Journal Entry 29, Zuri, 52–62, 1980s–1990s

Afterlife/early draft

The luxury of thinking of the future, life after death, aka the Afterlife, was stimulated when the writing Coach offered a summary of Dante's life. Considering the depth, intensity, and expression with which Dante approached, accepted, and defied adversity, challenged humanity, and created a cross-section of humanity; he astounds and interests me.

I was also impressed with these words from Albert Schweitzer (died 1965): "I don't know what your destiny will be, but one thing I do know: the only ones who will be happy are those who have sought and found how to serve."

Could someone construe those words to apply them to a race?

If one is Caucasian or religious, the words could be massaged to some acting masterly and supremely and to find the rationale in those words to doing "God's work" by putting others into a servile capacity.

"Afterlife" final draft

Coach's presentation on Dante's despair highlighted continued interest and readership more than 700 years after his death, making him unique. His misfortunes—exile and excommunication—motivated him to write *La Commedia* (written c. 1308–1320). Though most literary works were then written in Latin, during his lifetime (1265–1321), he chose to write in vernacular Italian and to favor an eleven-syllables-per-line rhyme scheme called *terza rima*.

Lacking a religious upbringing and too busy living, I hadn't given the Afterlife much thought. I was interested in what Dante had written, even with so many translations from the original. My awareness and attempt to read fell short, and I hope to return to the work one day and approach it as we did in our first class with Hughes' poem, writing Dante's words in our words.

We practiced with the first tercet, three lines, and a sentence, though we relied on available English translations. The coach added more background information: In 1555, Boccaccio added **Divina** to the title, by which it has since been known. The absence of a third word in the title fits Dante's obsession with structure. However, it also demonstrates his respect for all readers to insert an adjective of the reader's choice, not just Boccaccio's. I like **La Commedia Humana**, The Human Comedy. If Dante wanted a three-word title, he'd have chosen it.

Three canticles, the concept of the Trinity—a three-word title would have been in that line, but he did not want it, and who is anyone else to rewrite Dante's work? Though no manuscript exists in Dante's hand, an "original" manuscript is preserved at the Biblioteca Nazionale in Firenze, Italia. Perhaps the monks of the Ravenna Monastery, where Dante's remains are, made a copy?

Dante, via the Coach, made me wonder about my views of life after life.

Dante had Virgil; we had the writing Coach, which made some sense to me. After questions and thoughts, two possibilities surfaced: Nothing and Transition.

For those who don't believe in an Afterlife, "Nothing" writes itself: perhaps by not mentioning it, Dante expressed himself as much by what he left out as by what he included. Transitioning from life to death is virtually instantaneous; I wanted to put that under a microscope of thought as the first experience of the dead—being judged and going somewhere.

Dante solidified previous thoughts on **Purgatorio** as he sought a gray area between two extremes: **Inferno** and **Paradiso**. The prelude to **Paradiso**, pre-**Paradiso**, the "not-so-fast-eventually **Paradiso**," was **Purgatorio**.

And, again, I oversimplified so I could focus on my thoughts of an "Afterlife." Dante placed people directly into **Inferno**, just as a few people went directly to **Paradiso**; **Purgatorio** would give Dante that gray middle space between two extremes. The word **Purgatorio** had been present, yet no one depicted it as well as Dante.

The Church that exiled him eventually adopted his perception and incorporated it, with its theology making his view its view, heightening the service Dante provided to Catholicism.

Despite what people thought while they lived, there was a chance, when newly dead, for some to reconsider the reality of death versus speculation.

This possibility was based on two factors of living:

1. advantage taken of other(s)

2. One's legacy: what we leave behind, including our impact on the planet and people, and how we made life for others better and worse.

In my interpretation, from the moment we are born, five "dead" souls watch our living and record the data on the following:

1. advantage

2. planet

3. people

4. better

5. worse

The souls would present their lists to us when we were newly dead. We could challenge the data. We were beginning Eternity, so there was time.

If one lived to be 99, one slept approximately 33 years; 66 years were lived, and Eternity provided the time for one to accept or reject the data entirely or in part. In other words, we sleep approximately eight hours daily; and are awake approximately sixteen hours per day.

One could dispute, but that did not change—though it could delay—the Eventual Eternity, and one was also slow in knowing where one was going. One of the benefits we all experienced was being reunited with those we knew and wanted to know and being able to meet and greet those still living.

This would be an experience for all. People were endowed with a *Star Trek*-quality regarding travel.

Even though *Star Trek* was first broadcast in the UK on the BBC One on July 12, 1969, with the episode "Where No Man Has Gone Before," repeats were rare, and VHS tapes were expensive and difficult to get ahold of after the show was canceled.

Eventually, all the living would die, and if one were in **Inferno**, time away for meeting and greeting the newly dead would expire in time. At the same time, those in **Purgatorio** and **Paradiso** would continue with their progeny and those interested in ancestry.

Some who may not have remorse or the patience to deal with their particular version of **Purgatorio** or who prefer to go to **Inferno** directly had that possibility.

For one remorseful and willing to accept punishment, the family and friends of the injured, indeed all affected by "being taken advantage of" by them, was to be lived by the newly deceased one's "new lifetime," for which Eternity existed.

Once those punishment times were completed, **Inferno**, more intense punishment, and punishment more suited to the sin remained a possibility.

God was the final judge. Though God could be responsible for creating people who lacked the power to avoid the temptation to take advantage of another, God said, "You were given a conscience to deal with Earthly temptations, and even in the afterlife, we have choices."

God was God, and the individual was dead, with the possibility of an afterlife or nothing.

God spoke: "You may watch what goes on here, for as long as you like, until you decide."

"If you decide 'Nothing,' press a button, and there you'll be. Should you decide on Purgatory, you see what you will experience, and you can change your mind and choose 'Nothing' at any time."

Z's Purgatorio:

God: "Your senses as you knew them would be assaulted. There is neither food nor drink, and you will be constantly thirsty and hungry. You may be blind and deaf to be reminded of what you did not hear, see, appreciate, or understand while living.

"There is constant noise and wind. The temperature alternates between Arctic cold and desert heat hourly. You will live and feel through every day and night of punishment.

"You will constantly itch everywhere.

"And at this end, there may be **Inferno**, where you would be with others like you. You choose to act on Earth; here, you also have choices: Go or No . . . No is the beginning of Nothing.

"You have alternatives.

"The hourly time here and on Earth is the same . . . only you'll be living the lifetimes of others affected by one individual at a time.

"Once you live through the punishment, there is an equal period of rehabilitation, serving others, and living as an example here of what you were not while you were living."

You: "May I talk with anyone there or who has gone through it?"

God: "There is no need. We may meet when your time here, in *Purgatorio*, is lived."

You: "And I may go to *Inferno* now or later and be with others like me and suffer with them?"

God: "You understand? *Capisce?*"

God left.

I believe there is an Afterlife. The choice may be deserved agony or nothing. We have more to learn; this opportunity is fraught with negativity as I could not imagine seeing what I saw . . . what I envisioned. . . . If I deserve punishment, I'll take it . . . I heard "may meet." I could change my mind and choose "No" at anytime, and selecting "No" now means there is no recourse.

I chose "Go."

Journal Entry 30, Will, 44
(Lily, 66, Willa, 44,), 1989

Dad asked Willa to explore Mum's papers, among which she found a packet of handwritten letters. Willa promised not to discard anything without checking with Dad, who asked Willa to distribute the letters. We all grinned at each other, assuming Mum's traits of order and direction would be evident. Dad also shared a bit of Mum's letter to him. Mum felt less "exciting" for him than he deserved, and she hoped he would eventually free himself to enjoy someone else after her passing. Dad said he always found Mum interesting, and "exciting" did not fit her personality; "subtly exciting" was as close as we could get his description, and even that bordered on a blush. "'Exciting' is tiring and requires energy all the time," he said. He also shared how her broken heart never healed enough to live fully, and wanting to be with "her" Will would be agreeable to her at the first opportunity.

Mum kept scrapbooks of articles and photos. We all read her favorite book, **My Ántonia**, by Willa Cather. In one of her last readings of the book, Mum rediscovered how the last few pages impressed her as a student and how that impression evolved to its current status and marveled at Cather's forecasting ramifications she probably hoped for but did not predict. Still, the interpretation of Jim being a gay man gives her words foresight.

"Gay," a 12th-century word meaning "full of joy and mirth," acquired a sexual component in the 1960s, referring to gay men who liked other men, dressed interestingly and colorfully, and maybe exuded the comfort and discomfort of being themselves.

Mum's birth and death dates: 20 October 1923; d. 19 September 1989, a month shy of 66; she left letters, as I've stated, and visitors were asked to read Zuri's prayer. "Each reading offers a new insight," she had said and died holding the paper Zuri had given her as Dad recited the prayer.

She had mused about having a conversation with Willa. She and Dad worried Willa would be a concern if she married. English laws were what they were and favored the male heir. They could not know whom Willa might love and/or marry. Willa had a head of her own and certainly raised some brows, becoming a female doctor. Willa promised Dad that while Zuri lived, she would be respected and welcome to stay at Menton House.

What if Dad married? Mum wanted him to marry again and wrote a letter to Gordon's next wife. We shared the generalities of our letters, and Zuri was very quiet. She put her hands out to Willa and Gordon. "Lily and I were like sisters . . . when she brought this up between us, I thought it premature and better to leave Gordon to act freely and best not to mention it to anyone, as it might seem like a request afterlife, which some honor even if contrary to his/her own wishes and feelings. "Gordon and I are friends. Our friendship may get more intense with our loss. Life is unpredictable . . . what Willa and Will decide when their time comes to do so, I will not challenge."

I added my two cents: "Willa may be assured of my cooperation and advice if she seeks it, and I will support whatever decision she makes and do my best to ensure her decision without compensation." In Mum's letter to Zuri, she expressed her blessing if Zuri were Dad's choice and if Zuri accepted.

We turned to the scrapbook section on Willa Cather. **My Ántonia** is about a Bohemian family, friendship, love, and immigration. In this early-20th-century novel, Cather provides a biographical narrative of Ántonia Shimerda, a character based upon Annie Pavelka, a childhood friend of Cather's Ántonia.

Newspapers ran weekly columns on public and private schools, subject to space, editing, and news. London Collegiate School, an independent school in Edgware, England, is about 35 minutes, 12.5 miles from Kings Cross Station, boasting about 1000 students; no-boarding facilities headlined this story on its front page with a photo and continued inside.

First Woman Accepts Academic Award

The prestigious private/public [American/English] London Collegiate School awarded the coveted and highly competitive Academic Award, for the first time in its history, to a woman, Lily. . . .

Students are aware of the contest requiring the writing, presentation (reading), and public copy, which will be published in the Sunday edition magazine section.

Standing erect and slim with an unbroken smile, Lily wore a white suit with an "A" shaped skirt hemmed below the knees and carried a single calla lily during the graduation ceremony. Students wrote about their favorite books.

What singled out Miss Lily's efforts was her application of the book's appeal spanning academic disciplines, including a foreign language.

After writing the paper in English, Miss Lily translated her paper into French for her final exam. "I made a friend of the character. My own boring, planned, programmed education paled compared to the immigrant child who made a life in a new country.

"The author, a woman, chose a male character to narrate the story. The friendship he (Jim), the narrator, and Á shared was never formalized by marriage yet maintained itself throughout their lives." I connected that friendship to living as Z and T have and being friends as the most important of relationships.

Over tea one day, Dad read part of a journal entry of Mum's to me because I was mentioned. He asked me to keep it to myself before destroying it.

"I wanted to consult Willa, but my familiarity with my mother and aunt didn't continue between Willa and me. We've never had words; she's always been respectful and dutiful, but there was never a friendship many parents feel with adult children. Thankfully, Gordon and I feel a special "friendship" with Will.

"Zuri and I are like sisters.

"I've left letters and asked Gordon to destroy my journals. I've used them to put my feelings someplace and not lug them around, so they weigh me down. I've been fortunate and hope Gordon can find some of the excitement he deserves that I lack. Our relationship was solid but expected and routine.

"The energy I believe a woman contributes to a family and home drained out of me, and as sensible as I try to be, the sadness and loss of my Will and my will are elsewhere, and at the first opportunity when God calls, I'm ready.

"I want Willa to realize she was always enough and has made a name for herself and us in medicine; that took courage. She hasn't married . . . yet, but she might, and hopefully to a man with a family, so she has progeny to fulfill her life. I want her to be happy.

"Zuri has been a role model in so many respects.

"Gordon and I wondered if Willa would challenge our estate wishes as the blood child but hesitated to ask as she might interpret our question as challenging. She and Will have always exhibited sibling compatibility.

"Will has assured us that, should a challenge ever surface, there would be none; whatever Willa preferred, he'd support. We never did anything formal about our relationship. Love governed our acts—I include all in 'our.' He has gained from us more than we could have wished and often wondered what life would have been otherwise, but we left that to the imagination.

"We were always as grateful as he. He hasn't married, and if his choices differ from expectations, we support and love him. We often touch hands to demonstrate support and love."

Journal Entry 31, Gordon, 77, 1990s

Lately, I find solace in taking my afternoon tea and scanning the collection of photos on the piano. They no longer get dusted daily, yet I recall additional details when focusing on one longer than the others.

Most are in black and white, and shades of gray in silver frames.

I smile every time I think of my aide who met Zuri, Edel, and me with a car and kept suppressing his smirk.

I apologized for getting him up and active at that time of night or day, and rattled on for a while, as he'd look at me, nod, and say, "Yes, sir," every so often; then he'd look ahead or turn slightly so I wouldn't see his face. The traffic was light, and he sped carefully.

"Captain, Sir, with all due respect, please understand . . . I'm not being disrespectful, but you are precise and predictable . . . and here you are with a dog at your feet and a woman and baby on the aft seat, and you're going home to your wife who may have delivered a child . . . am I making any sense?"

"Too much sense, I'm afraid."

Cinnamon . . . The **SS Vega** . . .

I remember researching the ship's name and making an entry in my journal. The Spanish surname "**Vega**" is a topographical name that means "dweller in the meadow" or "one who lives on a plain," from the Spanish word **Vega**, which refers to a meadow, valley, or fertile plain. Ported in Lisbon, she had to have her bottom scraped and needed repair after the first visit; to prevent a second occurrence, I took the ship into port, where I met Zuri and took her and Edel/Will to Portsmouth during the war, with a dog named Cinnamon. A local tugboat met us; Capt. Gösta took the "con," short for "control," and my aide was waiting with a car. The next day, Gösta took the ship to Lisbon.

I first met the **Vega's** Captain Gösta (1899–1963) when he notified personnel on Guernsey that the ship was approaching St. Peter Port.

I assumed the "con," for maneuvering the ship and escorted the **Vega** with tugboats into port. Arrival was in readiness. Guernsey officials and Germans lined the dock to supervise. The Guernsey Bailiff, Victor, and the Bailiff of Jersey, Sir Alexander, made a speech of thanks.

I remember the Red Cross markings were erased on 11 June 1945.

And the terrier Cinnamon, who never left my side.

I saved the little girl's letters, some with tear stains. She said that when she didn't write back, it was because her father could not afford stamps, which I then included in my letters.

Her father added a line in one: "She reads and keeps every one of your letters."

I had left pregnant Lily with her mother and aunt at the London home we named Menton House, after the French resort city near Nice, which we visited in summer when Lily and I were children.

I hustled to St. Pancras Station to take the tube to Weymouth to meet a boat and wend my way to report to the **Vega**, which had yet to make its planned second trip to the Channel Islands.

"Taking the con," control of the ship, in the place of the captain, especially at this time, awaiting my first child, was a tough decision.

Yet my knowledge and service were essential in a port as tricky as St. Peter Port, and, as well as I knew it . . . I was learning. . . . I was learning the meaning of duty and service. I'd have been conscience-plagued to do otherwise.

I'm reminded that I thought I'd be back in time for the birth, get a few extra days at home, and convince Lily it was the right decision. Like many wives, she worried when I was away, as the return was always dubious.

There was a collection of people outside the station and about fifteen dogs on leashes held by authorities. I imagined this was one more of those awful times when families could no longer care for pets, and they were collected at various sites where local people were invited to come and adopt for the duration of the war with the possibility of returning or retaining when some semblance of "normalcy" returned.

A little girl, about five, in a frosty-green quilted jacket, held her father's hand. Two tracks of tears lined her cheeks and dripped from her jaw to her jacket as she tried to be stoic. Her father muttered, "This is not a good idea; please, let's go." He tried to tug her away, but she said, "Not yet! You said we could wait until someone takes her . . . away. I'm not going."

"Luv, you're five; you've been through enough loss; please don't add to it. I can barely take care of you alone."

The apricot Cairn terrier kept bobbing her head left and right, and the volunteer holding the leash sucked back the mucus about to fall from his nose.

"Ten minutes!" someone with authority called.

"If you can care for one of these loved animals, please help. They don't need much food and will give you great comfort and company.

"Come closer; take a look."

A few people took a step. Some left a husband or wife and then stepped back to report the animal's friendliness.

The Cairn stood there, and when she opened her mouth and let her tongue out, there was a gap where an incisor should have been.

I began to pass, and the little girl broke my heart every time I looked back.

I turned toward her, and our eyes met.

I thought of all the reasons I couldn't, and I'm sure she understood. Then her mouth began to pucker, and she whimpered ever so mildly, looking up at her father, who kept shaking his head.

Then at me.

I approached the dad, "Tough, eh?"

"You have no idea."

"May I talk to her?"

He nodded.

I tried making sense, and she heard every word I said, but she would have none. I tried to distract her while they started whisking the animals into a van. If it were the last look, she wanted as much time as she could freeze into her memory. She knew, without being reminded, of the animal's fate.

I asked her the animal's name.

"Cin, Cinny," she said, barely able to say her name. "It's short for 'Cinnamon.'"

"May I pet her?" I asked.

She asked her father, "Just one more time?"

He shook his head, and she managed to break away and run toward the dog.

Dumbfounded and exasperated, her father raised his hands, "Aw, Mate—can you help?"

I ran after the little girl. Now, kneeling on the pavement, embracing the animal. I took the leash from the volunteer, gave it to the little girl, and walked her back to her dad.

"Would a little money help?" I said to him.

He shook his head.

"I can't have someone come to the house and care for the animal while we're away during the day. I don't want to . . . it's not a choice I'd wish on anyone . . . and she'll never understand . . . or forgive me.

"I've been giving up some of my food—"

I knelt beside the little girl and took a card from my billfold.

"This is my contact information. You hold this and write to me every week or two, and I will write back and tell you how Cinnamon is doing.

Okay?"

"We'll be going on an adventure. I'm a captain; sometimes captains can have a pet in their quarters. She'll be warm, and I'll arrange some food for her. Write and tell me what she likes, okay?"

The little girl smiled and smudged her cheeks.

"She likes everything. And she likes being warm. You can nap with her; she'll like that."

"And when I return, you can visit as often as you like, okay?"

I stood; her father winked and pointed to the van.

I bent down, holding the dog, and the little girl hugged us both tightly with strength I could only imagine.

Then her father picked her up; she put her head on his shoulder and watched us through teary eyes, a smile, and a wave before we lost sight of each other.

I walked past the van, my bag slung over my shoulder and the dog in my arm.

Zuri always says, "No relationship is stronger than friendship."

My health generally remained well, and when ashore, I took advantage of more exercise, especially swimming, and now work out with 20-pound hand weights.

On a Tuesday evening, just as the year was about to end, I felt dizzy.

I tried to isolate the feelings, but they didn't last very long, and though this was new for me, my concern was more serious than disregarding it as just something new.

The following morning, there were a couple of reminders, but nothing stayed long enough or diminished my routine, so I swam 65 laps.

On Wednesday, I couldn't wait to get off the phone and get to the bathroom while eating dinner.

All I could think about was Vesuvius in eruption. Once, I had sailed into the port of Naples and woke early to see the day bring the image into view. Here was this silent purple triangular mass, and I wondered about its potential as my core began giving unusual signals. Now I felt it.

After a busy few minutes, I found a break in its demands and rang Zuri, and asked her to get the car and transport me to the ER. I had never vomited in my adult life . . . not since I was single digits old, maybe 6 or 8 . . . I couldn't remember exactly. But I did remember the urge being involuntary and projectile, which brought a correction to my memory.

Once, when I was sixteen and sitting in the rear of a new car, my Dad was driving and smoking a cigar.

When I complained about the odor, he shook his head, looked at my mother, and said, "Suck it up! Be a man."

I looked at Mum, who shrugged her shoulders, knowing we had no choice. "Peace at any price" was her mantra.

I tried to get the window down as fast as I could turn the handle and managed about halfway before a gush exited into the window well and over the door, and I could barely hear my Mum say, "Pull over!"

Here I was again, almost 60 years later. The ER kept me for what eventually turned into an overnight, and now I carry meds for dizziness and nausea. As strangely as it approached, it left begrudgingly. I weaned myself off the medications as they gave me headaches and drowsiness, and I couldn't drive.

Yet when clarity began to wedge into this prison of fog, I felt like my body was being pulled back into the grip of vertigo; as I expected to land the next step, it would exert a very temporary hold.

The doctor also prescribed helpful exercises and said to keep track of every incident and keep him posted. I get twinges now and then, but nothing like the first onset. I have heard some limiting life stories from others who cannot get out of bed or work for days.

Journal Entry 32, Will, 48, 1993

Several years after I started teaching, Carmel joined our staff, and I opted to be her "Buddy," one of the few programs the school committee and the union supported as soon as it was proposed. The "Buddy" staff program was an informal attempt to welcome new people, whether one was an aide, a professional, or any other part of the service corps. The program meant sharing coffee and casually familiarizing the newly hired with the policies and idiosyncrasies of our community.

Soon, students imitated adults and began being "buddies" with new students, kids helping other kids, which always made us smile.

Carmel was a bit older, and we clicked immediately, though she, as the school nurse, was an entity to herself. She met with other school nurses in the district, and had volunteer doctor access.

When Mame joined us in 1990 as a thirty-year-old divorcee look-ing for a fresh start, Carmel and I were her "Buddies." The three of us developed an enviable friendship that included eating out, museums, performances, and trips. I learned the circumstances of Carmel's status during the first coffee we shared with Mame.

Carmel mentioned that she was a widow but never elaborated. She wore a wedding band most days, and when not in uniform and dressed for a social event, she added her diamond engagement ring.

Mame asked about our age and families. On hearing of Carmel being a widow, Mame asked when Carmel had lost her husband.

"Just weeks before I started here."

I was stunned.

"I didn't know that," I injected.

"You never asked, and I was grateful you didn't. I never thought it mattered, and I was trying to take a deep breath and begin what I expected the rest of my life would be. I'm glad you were so supportive and I was so convincing. A widow was an identity I was not yet ready to define myself.

"My husband was a bit older than I was, and I knew he was gone as soon I went into the den after hearing the plate and utensils fall to the floor. I called his name; he didn't answer, which was so unlike him.

"I rushed in, opened his shirt, tried some compressions, and called the fire department, who arrived in minutes . . . to this day, I keep thinking, 'All this education and I couldn't save—I'm okay . . . it still gets to me. Working, this school, and people,'" she winked. "These kids . . . I'm okay."

Looking at me, Mame asked, "And you're single?" Carmel winked again, this time at Mame, and looked to me for an okay. I nodded, and Carmel pulled her over and said nothing I could hear, and Mame nodded, "Thank God . . . I thought I'd have to fend you off, too!"

We laughed.

Mame was a striking woman, the definition of a classic: tall, slim, gracious, stylish, feminine, and confidently humble.

"Have you given up on men?" Carmel asked.

"Not entirely. I think boyfriends are still possible.

"You?"

"Oh . . . I'm older, but I could never imagine anyone like my H. I've gone on a few dates, but none I'd encourage beyond platonic.

"Are you feeling left out?" Carmel added, eyeing me.

"Just entertaining myself listening and observing," I replied.

"You have to watch this guy; he's easy to love.

"He's sweet . . . I try to help foster and adopt children," followed by another wink.

Women have friendship down to a science. They have an innate trust between and among them that men could learn from, but men fear the accusation of being sexually attracted to each other, to which Carmel says, "So what?"

And Mame added a word, "So friggin' what?"

As soon as she walked into the cafeteria, where we met that morning, she caught my eye and ear. I heard her stilettos on the recently waxed floor that had been buffed to a gleam. I was sure anyone else would slip on "their" ass in nothing flat, but she click-clacked in, placed her chocolate-chip cookies on the table, and looked around.

"I bet you don't eat any of those," I said.

"Oh, you'd lose that bet . . . I eat everything . . . carefully and with a limit. My downfall is chips! Even after a nice meal, I get home, limit myself to three, and let them melt in my mouth like communion wafers!"

"I'm Will."

"I'm Mame . . . I'm looking for a guy named Will and . . . Caramel?"

"Carmel . . . she'll be right back. Parents met her outside and asked about their kid. We saved you a seat with us if you like. I told Carmel we'd meet you here when you came in. The opening program takes about a half hour; then we break for coffee and chat, go to our buildings, and meet as a group and then by department. Do you know where you're assigned?"

"Here, I think. Home Economics."

"Here's Carmel."

"Hey, sorry . . . nervous parents . . . catch me up."

To Mame she said, "Ah, yes, welcome! Home Ec, right? Your rooms are next to my office space. Our academic friend here shares his wisdom on the second floor, but we share our planning periods and lunches as much as possible. Sometimes we don't see each other for days. Welcome, welcome. Bedlam Begins!"

Over the past four years, our friendship has intensified. Carmel remains twenty years older and so much wiser. I'm approaching fifty, and Mame is a stunning thirty-four. I imagine she'll be stunning her entire life. She'll work at it and make it seem as casual as breathing.

During our first meeting, Mame shared that her birthday was in mid-September, so Carmel and I asked if we could take her to dinner.

None of us drink alcohol, though Carmel sips champagne to toast a bride and groom as if she were at a New Year's celebration. She said she enjoyed a scotch on the rocks occasionally but only ordered it at a cocktail party, and I never saw her finish one.

I always felt I had to be alert if a student called for a ride, as I promised them I would deal with their parents later. But I asked they not ever ride with anyone they thought had been drinking, and I would take calls any time and drive them home, no questions.

Mame said alcohol was the cause of her divorce, and she worried that the gene could be passed on. The guy she married had agreed before marriage to be a stay-at-home dad if she got pregnant, which she wanted to be. Yet, she had a consuming fear of newborns and wanted her husband available in case she was frozen in fright and endangered the baby. She was willing to get up and tend to the child in the middle of the night. Still, even then, the discomfort and anxiety were things she doubted she could ever adjust to. And, being the breadwinner and having work that provided health insurance, she thought having one child could be a possibility.

Her husband agreed, but his at-home time was too convenient to slide back into behavior he hadn't planned, and Mame did not want to jeopardize a child, so they divorced before there was a third being to worry about. "I'd still like the experience of carrying and delivering a child," she said, "Maybe someday . . . though my bio clock is ticking."

"Would you be a surrogate?" Carmel asked.

"Probably not. Too business-like. Knowing I had a child out there with no possibility of rescuing if trouble came to him or her makes no good sense to me."

Carmel had asked me about a surrogate. I worried that the mother might change her mind after delivery, and I might be more like a substitute father, paying child support but not having the paternal experience I wanted.

"What about a partner and pursuing adoption?" Carmel asked.

"A partner complicates the issue. What if we split and I was challenged for custody?" I answered.

"That could happen even if you were married," Mame added.

"Right. I think a lawyer could help set up a plan."

"What if love came to you after the child was born?" Mame asked.

"Kid first, if that was accepted. I can't imagine loving anyone more than the child and would not compromise my duties as a father."

"What if the child had special needs?"

"Still, my priority, and even more so, as it would be lifelong and even after my life, that care was necessary and had to be provided, maybe with my pension or state services. A lawyer and I need to explore that more. I keep attending to this; laws and people change.

"I keep paying my lawyer, who always says, 'You ever think of marrying a woman and going about this as most people do?'"

"And my reply is, as T always said, 'If there is a hard way to do something—no pun intended—you'll find it!'"

After discussing books, movies, and current events, this topic piqued our interest, yet we knew when to give it a rest.

I valued their opinions, and no possible conception had been discussed with such preliminary possibilities. The love and trust among the three of us grew as time passed. We each had an independent relationship with the other two that I always compared to baguettes in a diamond friendship ring. We each valued our independence and enjoyed our own lives as well. An enviable, healthy balance kept our garden thriving.

On a vacation lunch break in the spring of 1993, Mame asked, "Have you had sex with a woman?"

I didn't answer immediately but wondered why she asked.

We practiced a policy of not answering a question if it made us uncomfortable.

"Why do you ask?" I asked.

"I wondered if you'd given any thought to direct insemination versus 'artificial.'"

"Hmmm, I haven't ruled it out; I think that's probably a possibility . . . between the woman and me. I've purposely avoided the experience, wondering if I did have sex with a woman, she might have a child of mine whom I might never know about. So, I think the best way to be sure is not to, and if I ever did have a child, I could assure him or her that s/he is my only offspring."

"You know I'd like the experience of carrying and delivering a child and my traumatic fear of babies."

I nodded.

"And being a surrogate is only a part of the experience."

"Right . . . and I've never asked you to elaborate on what the other 2/3s are because . . . well, I guess you'd share when you are ready; if asked, you'd have a choice of answers, and I did not want to intrude on your privacy."

"Are you interested in my reply?" Mame asked.

"Of course."

"I've had this conversation with my ex, and a few days ago, I asked Carmel to role-play this conversation with me so I could review what I would be comfortable saying."

She paused and smirked.

"You know her well enough to know what she said, and she asked if I had anyone in mind."

Pause . . . long pause.

"You didn't answer her question, but you smirked and didn't need to answer."

Pause.

I continued "Excuse me, I'm old-fashioned. As much as I'm a fan of equal rights and equal pay, girls can ask for dates as well as guys can . . . holding a door or just being polite . . . I'm not apologizing for how I was raised . . . but in a possibility like this . . . I finally asked a female lawyer friend to put our—hers and mine—conversations in some sort of order so that I could share this as a start. I don't sweat but am perspiring, and I hope this doesn't sound rehearsed. Still with me? You haven't gotten up and left."

"You'd have heard my heels, *n'est pas?* Mame said.

"So, copy for me, copy for you," I said, handing Mame a folder. "We can read this together, alone, or with the lawyer. Your call."

"Would you like dessert? Coffee or tea?" The waitress asked, filling our water glasses.

I said, "Please, give us ten minutes before bringing one chocolate lava cake, vanilla ice cream, whipped cream, and two forks.

"One cappuccino for the lady and a double espresso for me in a mug, and fill the rest of the cup with whipped cream."

"Oooooo, may I join you?" the waitress asked.

"Ten minutes."

We each read for 3–5 minutes; I made a note.

"You've given this some thought," Mame said.

She held up her water glass; we toasted "to proceed" and sipped.

"It should be 'right' from the very beginning. And, the kid is the priority—ad infinitum," I added.

"That's new and different for me . . . given that we aren't married and don't plan to be."

"I'm trying to be careful, not clinical, and this is new and different for me as well . . . to be honest . . . probably in more ways than I ever considered; but if there's any possibility . . . I don't want either of us to lose a chance to explore . . . and . . . eventually enjoy an experience with comfort and . . . may I add pleasure?" My mouth was dry.

Mame put her hand on mine, "Shhh, you don't need to say more. I'm not looking for a proposal or marriage. As odd as all this may be . . . it feels right. Whatever other 'what ifs' come up, I expect we'll be civil enough to address?"

"Kid is the priority," I repeated. "Would you like to meet with the lawyer separately or together?"

"I'll give her a call," Mame said.

The waitress pre-divided the lava cake and smiled as she placed them before us.

"Where's yours?" I asked.

She patted herself and added, "I'm going to watch you enjoy this from over there, and I may ask a question with your permission when I return."

I placed my card on the tray.

"My birthday, once-a-year dessert, and now the second time before a year is up!" Mame announced.

"I'm hoping you or Carmel change your birthday preferences, for variety's sake!!

"Two cannoli in two months works for me! I luv it, but oh, the work I must do!"

Journal Entry 33, Will, 49, 1994

I asked Mame two questions over lunch in June:, "Is there a timeline? Number of attempts?"

She said, "Yes, more for me than you.

"Men can parent into old age; women are best by 34-ish delivering by 35, which might still be classified as risky, so we take the next year or so to fine-tune and draw up the necessary paperwork—then three attempts if that's okay with you: One "A" month begets the other, August to April; September begets May, October "breeds" June.

"First, at my place; second, your plan and surprise; and if necessary, a third, if we wish. If it doesn't happen by then, we might have to consider other options, maybe artificial insemination?" I raise my eyebrows while listening.

"I'm very regular. I've kept a log since I started at age 13, and every 27/28 days and the 12–14 after my last period are best for conception. You know all this?"

I nod. "I try to remain sensitive to my female students and ensure my boys understand hormones and possibilities. Carmel gives me a hand with this and what parents may object to. She also attends my sessions just in case I'm challenged."

"Have you been?"

"Once. A boy's parents did not want him informed, and he wanted to be. I use an audiotape presentation. I invited them to attend with or without their son. They came before classes one day."

"So his classmates will know, and he won't?" they asked.

"If that's your choice."

"But the other kids will tell him."

"I can't stop what kids share. I monitor this responsibly and help them understand biological processes before what they don't know might have consequences for them and others. I encourage them to talk to their parents and explain that parents may be as uncomfortable as they are, so be patient with each other."

Mame said, "He attended."

"He did. And he stayed later and said proudly and loudly, 'I have a girlfriend, and she has a boyfriend . . . me.'"

To myself, I said, "Shit, too late."

The kid added, "Is it true she can get pregnant without . . . you know?"

Mame said, "Okay, back to us? We can always change our minds, no reason needed."

We toasted to the process of sipping the cool last dregs of our coffee. The waitress returned my card, and I added more to the tip for the extra dessert attention.

I asked the waitress, "You had a question?"

"How often do you indulge in desserts? You're both in enviable shape."

Mame replied, "Birthdays, maybe nibbles on holidays, rarely a cookie if homemade. I am tempted every night, but I end meals with a piece of fruit and have a daily exercise regimen—genes are not in my favor."

The waitress asked, "Will you be back for her birthday?"

Mame said, "Hmm, that's a few months away; let me check my calendar . . . September 15, 1994, Thursday, lunch or dinner?"

"School day; dinner, 5:30 p.m.?"

"You have a plan?" I asked.

"I always have a plan, but it falls apart, and I return to bad habits because they're easy . . . and I overindulge," the waitress replied.

Mame said, "Take my card. We can talk about this. I'll share a few suggestions; let's see if we can make a difference."

Her eyes filled. "Really? You think it's possible?"

"I do," Mame replied.

"We do!" I added.

In the parking lot, Mame mentioned the benefits of conversations.

I suggested we consider emails to give each other time to think of responses and keep a record for the child as to how and why we proceeded, and we could edit it later and decide when to share which ones with the child's age, without being clinical.

Mame said, "Let's rest with this between us, let it settle in our heads with the 'proceed' option, and go from there."

I said, "Let's make a list and try to prioritize topics." I got a look.

"Hmmm, I think I should shut up." Then I smirked before adding, "What about Carmel?"

"She's already aware. Remember, she discreetly played matchmaker, in general terms, and I'd rather share her as we do now, and what goes on between her and me—and you and her—remains between two of us or among the three of us," Mame said.

I said, "If she's uncomfortable with this actually happening, we have other friends and resources, and we can refer to ourselves with others in very general terms, 'I have a friend . . . '"

Mame asked, "What about marriage?"

I tried to clarify. "Between us, or if we marry others?"

"Are you asking me in a parking lot?"

"Ahh, no, hmm, just thinking ahead to options and possibilities," I said.

Mame said, "Hmm, I hadn't thought about others, but let's email and see if we can decide for us as individuals and as a couple, each of us with another. Kid first. And let's try not to complicate this any more than we have to."

"Kid first."

"Thank you," Mame said.

"Thank you," I rejoined. "This is something we're doing for each other and the kid. Let me know when you are ready to email, and let's send them simultaneously. Thus, we aren't affected by each other's statements, and we see how close we are to agreeing if we do and proceeding! Or, don't open mine until after you end yours."

Mame said, "We already decided not to marry, which makes the legalities easier now than later. If we change our minds later, we'll see."

I said, "I couldn't think of anything but marriage to compare to your selflessness, and although there may be many advantages, I don't trust myself to give marriage what it takes to endure, even if there were a time limit, like after the kid graduated high school.

"Others? Very doubtful; our agreement is like a pre-marital caveat; anyone who disagreed wouldn't get a second date. We are free to do as we like. Our minds could change, but why spoil a friendship with an obligatory marriage?"

Mame said, "Flattering, but no, thanks."

"Kid is the priority and the best reason for not marrying."

"If I were the custodial parent and needed child support, the courts should still give me that option, married or not, right? Regarding others: very doubtful; once was enough—why tempt fate again?"

I asked, "What about living together with someone?"

Mame said, "Not for me. I want my bedroom and toilet. Look at your birth parents."

I said, "Death and incapacitation demand attention, and as the kid is the priority, and I am the single (meaning "only" and unmarried) custodial parent, in the event of my death or incapacitation, my choice would be for you to take the responsibility and custody of the child until adulthood, and my resources are to serve the child first. Should you die or become incapacitated, Willa and Carmel will make decisions for the child.

"Depending on the child's age, his or her preferences will be included in decisions, and my sister Willa and friend Carmel will be consulted. At the age of 12 and after that, give or take a reasonable adjustment, the child's preferences have more consideration.

"Should the child have a friend whose parents wish to offer a home, kindly explore their backgrounds, resources, and intentions and decide accordingly.

"My estate and resources are for the child's well-being and what is least traumatic, least disruptive, and most conducive to a continuation of life during an unexpected disruption. At eighteen, the child will decide for herself/himself, and it is hoped to be receptive to the counsel of any of the individuals above.

"I wish that they supervise the use of whatever resources remain and that education remains the focus. Should there be financial advantages to investing the resources, a qualified and experienced professional should be consulted. A child with resources can easily tempt others to take advantage of them. Life changes. Any of the aforementioned individuals have my permission to get professional advice and charge my estate "to keep the kid as the priority."

Mame asked about moving, and I answered, "Custodial parent/ guardian decides, visiting as comfortable, health challenges considered, "kid priority."

Mame said, "What if the child's needs are special or become special unexpectedly?"

"Good thought," I said. "Maybe the lawyer could research that. Severity matters, but let's continue to have the lawyer advise and make changes accordingly. We should also update our wills."

Mame asked, "What do you think about August of '94?

Me: "What about September and trying not to interfere with the school year? I think the earlier conceived, the better. You?"

She nodded.

I continued, "I've got a few ideas. I'd like it to be fun and memorable . . . maybe surprises, not so exciting you won't be able to conceive, but little gestures of thoughtfulness and sensitivity. Isn't that how most guys plan?"

Mame said, "No. Most are 'dumb and done' . . . sometimes age brings refinement. The gifts get better, and guys are better off financially, but this is different. It's nice to hear you have a plan or forethought regarding conception."

I said, "We might want to continue adding a sexual possibility to our friendship."

Mame said, "Maybe. One step at a time. Let's see."

My thoughts went to New York, or a beach house, about Bach, food, baguettes, and of course, the focus: conception.

I'm hoping August will work out any kinks, if any, and we'll conceive with God's blessing and help in September. I'm obsessing. Maybe if I allow myself to obsess, I'll be able to let nature take its course. One thing at a time versus everything all at once leads to overflow, which gets sopped up versus being addressed adequately. *Capisce?*

"Stop! Enjoy the process! I need to focus on the experience with preparation, as much as is pleasurable; when it begins to consume and take control of me, it's too much." Mame said.

My reply, "So, the best I can, as thoughtful as is comfortable, let items have their own lives and times. This is huge and life-changing, but why deliver an obsessed sperm?"

On a long bike ride, I considered the public or private questions. Also, how much input and at what age should the child's opinion be considered? There were no real answers except to be flexible and keep the child's best interests as our guide.

Are we putting off deciding when it is our responsibility? We should discuss it, each taking one side and then the other, and try to be reasonable. Did I send Mame an email about keeping this public or private? How shall we share it with the kid? Discuss or decide?

The next day, she replied: "Willing to discuss but have decided. This is one of those issues that demands agreement and could be a delay or deterrent. 'Public.'" Mame always made sense.

I said, "It's our decision, and giving her/him the truth from the beginning is something s/he can share or not as s/he likes, but we're not serving the kid and setting a good example if we decide to keep it private."

She added, "And the layers of complications are mind-boggling. People don't forget as they exhibit prejudices, but one's circumstances of birth should be a right a parent passes on, honestly."

I came to a similar decision after bike riding 19.6 miles.

I responded: "It's our choice, and we're making it for him or her."

"I'm not ready to march in a parade or suggest this is right for anybody else, especially young kids, but it's right for our child and us," Mame said.

"Next?"

"We'll see." Mame said, "Still willing to proceed? Kid First?"

"Absolutely! Thanks," I replied.

"Thank you!" Mame said.

Journal Entry 34, Will, 49–50, 1994–1995

During the summer of 1994, with the paperwork and preparations in order, conception attempts loomed. We had gone on dates with some benefits to avoid being complete sexual strangers. We had been careful, explored, and got to know each other in ways that we expected would make our plans fruitful and pleasurable. At no point did either call a halt, and we reached compromises and agreements on every issue.

In August, I appeared with two oversized pillows with washable pink velvet cases for our first attempt.

Pink was warmer than blue, and I didn't want to choose to have both when the intention was for Mame's comfort and extending the post-coital possibility by elevating her legs, hoping to encourage a swimmer sperm to find an egg. I lingered inside her until I slipped out.

Then I adjusted the pillows, and we held each other quietly and listened to each other breathe with Bach in the background. I sent flowers the next day.

At the end of the month, Mame wasn't sure one way or the other.

We both looked forward to my plan for September and decided to take advantage of not knowing for sure. On a Friday afternoon, I picked up Mame, with the pillows and a bag, and we drove to one of the beach cottages with a jacuzzi tub at Castle Hill Inn on Ocean Drive, Newport, Rhode Island.

Mame commented, "I'm so glad you're making this fun. I've never experienced being spoiled to this degree. And, I detect a bit of . . . let me ask: Are you enjoying this?"

"Immensely!" I replied. We walked the grounds, returned to the cottage, indulged ourselves with Bach—who I hoped would have approved—in the background from the beginning, and refreshed our intent each time.

We had late-afternoon tea at the Inn's dining room and later heated and enjoyed Mame's eggplant parmigiana. Mame craved frozen custard and pistachio ice cream, so we drove into town to the Newport Creamery.

I rose early and showered on Saturday, and Mame ordered fresh, warm, crisp croissants and an espresso pot of French Roast coffee. The inn made a picnic lunch, which we ate on Ocean Drive, read the papers, did crosswords, read to each other from the books we were reading, and took advantage of our purpose more often than we thought possible.

As darkness descended, the gas fireplace provided an ambiance too encouraging to ignore; we were satisfied with a cheese plate, fruit, and crackers. Sunday morning, after showering before and after, being intimate, and writing, we had reservations for brunch and grinned through Andrea Bocelli singing Puccini's "Nessun dorma," on a portable CD player in the background.

Journal Entry 35, Zuri, 69, 1997

In 1992, Prime Minister John announced, with regret, the separation of Prince Charles and Princess Diana of Wales. In 1996, their divorce was announced. Will wrote about learning of the incident in the Sunday papers: one was about Diana in an accident, and the second wrote of her death on August 27th. PM Tony faced a sad challenge two months after becoming Prime Minister. I thought of my friend Cherie.

Newspapers published a photo of him and Cherie calling on the Queen to extend condolences.

My Palace Friend sent me a request to prepare cotton tatted handkerchiefs with the initials P, C, C, W, and H for men, and one with a D for Diana, plus a matching mulberry silk pillow cover, and one handkerchief with an E for the queen. I kept a supply of extras of every letter in the alphabet for females and males, and requests were often with short notices from local funeral services.

The public knew about the bickering between the two Charleses, Diana's brother and her former husband, and this incensed the queen. The press speculated on the friction. I could only imagine the conversation; thus, no quotation marks.

PF: We have two sons to put before all considerations. Philip, I, the boys, and you both have handkerchiefs to carry on the funeral day. Diana has a handkerchief like ours. Her wedding handkerchief may be shared by whomever her sons marry and then by each female spouse of her progeny, for which I thank whoever of you has it in your possession to bring it to me.

I have sent for tea and will await the settlement of the final arrangements between you both.

Don't let the tea cool.

I will await your agreement in the next room.

To her son,

Charles, knock on the door before you both enter.

Watching the services on the telly, my emotions spilled seeing the boys, William, 15, and Harry, 12, their father, and uncle, walking behind their mother's casket, all carrying the same pocket square pattern as the boys, made for their parents' wedding in 1981. The world watched, but they were alone . . . as I was at 12 . . . alone . . . I was at the pier again as the boat with Zuri-Mama left . . . and I imagined these young men felt the same.

'Tis the eve of a new year. For some, the year has already arrived.

About ninety-five minutes of 1997 remain, and I will follow my pattern and sleep through the change after writing this entry. This is the last of the holidays, and I am reminded how much I prefer the radio to all other forms of news, though the images of the queen delivering her addresses are like hosting her in my quarters. I remember when she walked into a room and stood to greet us, gave us a digest of the year, and wished us good health. Now, she is seated, looking ever so regal for her age, dressed well in an intense color with a tasteful broach. Papers went from a dais to a table where the camera zoomed in while she turned pages to avoid glimpsing her fingers. Usually, she is always gloved, and as I recall, I only once saw a formal portrait with her hands exposed.

I believe Philip was with her, still looking dashingly handsome, tall, and slender.

I wondered about the rumors and his dalliances, which she somehow managed, as many wives and mothers do, especially if they want to keep the family intact. She's had her share of challenges, children, and always being in the public eye.

The times we spend together are a little escape here and there selecting thread for tatting or just a cuppa, careful to whisper, and I, acting as an aide, followed very discreetly by those in her service.

She's a wonderful friend, and we chat sporadically between my visits.

We continue to make bookmarks with quotations on the back and no indication of her as the source of the creation. The bookmarks are donated to those, eldest first, who have served the United Kingdom and are being mailed with thanks but no creator's name. Several of us worked on this project. My, how that all came about: Tatting.

Cherie, my student-contact friend from years ago, shared that she has worked to try to find my Zuri-Mama and my father, about whom Mama said so little, and hinted about him being the man by whom she was employed. As separated as staff and children were in Guernsey, we were even more separated in London. Based on such little information, Cherie could not get to the source of my being, and by this time, I felt Mama was dead.

Were she alive, she'd have found her way to me.

Ah, me. My Grandchild!

Another year is upon us.

Sunshine on my Shoulder

Journal Entry 36, Will, 57–62, 2002–2007

I love my Mum, Lily, and Dad, Gordon. I grew up knowing what they had done for my birth parents and me. And I loved my time with T, and when Z was with us, as we had been for a short time, I remember more profoundly that we three were born on Guernsey, and that common fact allowed us a distinction. We shared . . . differently. . . .

Our conversations included a healthy sexual dimension at all ages whenever the time and subject surfaced. Z and T never married, but they had a friendship that stretched boundaries and definitions. When they slept together, I occasionally intruded when I was cold and young.

Yet as I grew and visited T, he and I would share the single-plus bed he and Z shared. He expanded the mattress with sacks of rags and folded blankets. He wasted nothing.

The meals we ate whenever we were together were fish-based, depending on what T caught. He cooked fish in a bit of water, and when oils and butter or fat became available, he'd smear the fish with one of them for flavor. Garlic was a staple and lasted well into the non-growing season until new cloves were ready. He planted cloves in the autumn, covered with clippings and mowed grass, watered once, and in late spring, we had enough for a year. Parsley and fresh mint, which grew prolifically, enhanced T's "sauce" of lime, lemon, and orange juices after zesting the fruits, removing the seeds, and extracting the inside flesh. The pulp went into a container T used to fertilize the plants and soil. The color mixture was as appetizing as the palette of flavors. We'd had fruit. When cows produced, T whipped up cream.

I never tired of hearing how Z and T lived apart and together, and I was comfortable hearing and sharing their lives individually and as a couple. When I learned how babies were made, I could not imagine

Mom and Dad in that intimacy, but Z and T made it sound cool . . . I doubt any kid imagines adults intimately with any comfort.

Z and T often said, "There are things friends don't ask, and if asked, responses are not required."

I wondered what they did for those stretches when they were apart.

Was it easier for women to be more faithful and men more often excused for going beyond? Z said she was often tempted out of loneliness but never found anyone as worthy of her or her time as "My T."

T tried his best early on after we were separated and discovered his need for male friendship and intimacy evolved without a contest to his feelings for Z.

"I did not need her permission, nor did I seek it, but had she asked me not to, I would have tried my best."

"Did you think it might build resentment?" I asked.

They both shrugged their shoulders.

T said, "We don't know because we didn't need to find out."

Z said, "We trust and love each other and are friends in the broadest and best definition of the word."

T and I slept naked in summer when it was warm. We always said we loved each other and never intruded on our respect for each other. Often in the mornings, I'd be on my side, and T would say, "Enjoy!" We laughed. I'd go pee. Whenever we slept together and could feel our bodies against each other for warmth or through the fabric, it was never a threat of discomfort, and it fed a closeness I have with no other person.

I felt it was healthy, loving, and supportive. The selfishness that makes some men or women sexually forceful with others was never our experience. If anything, it caused me to seek more meaningful relationships.

When I first wondered about my tendencies, T assured me that most kids are uncomfortable sharing that doubt or exploration.

When I did, T and Z agreed, "Be careful," and then explained when I asked for elaboration, and I had to ask. They did not lecture; they weren't the lecturing type.

More and more, as much as I tried to like girls beyond friendship, the naturalness was absent. I loved my sister and her friends, my Mum and Z, and grandmothers, but they were relatives; though much I heard from my guy friends about how nice a girl felt, I took their words for it. My feelings ran contrary, and taking advantage of my interests was something I had to decide for myself first.

We spent Christmas 2001 in Guernsey. In February 2002, I made plans to take Edel to Orlando, Florida, for her 7th birthday in May. The proprietor of St. George's, where T made a suite off the burner room, called and sent an email: T was found "still" making a journal entry.

Breakfast had not been set up; they knew something was amiss With regrets.

I made a wallet-size card, which I had covered in plastic with an image of T, Zuri, Edel, and me on the front and his dates and a few words on the back.

I bought a three-urn plot at a cemetery on Guernsey overlooking the water and wrote that the burial would be private, but whoever wanted to may attend at the funeral home's convenience. A Tea Gathering will be celebrated on 19 August when we'll uncover a marker, and I plan to read the following from memory:

Events strain the ability to express.

A trinity describes T to a T: love, generosity, and humor.

His "two words" were a clever perception.

Whatever he had, if he could find it, it was yours.

Love needs little amplification.

T was not a fan of goodbyes.

Everyone knew when he arrived: subtly, quietly.

While he is busy with "Hellos," we try to reconcile his departure.

Grief reminds us that we share what we love; grief is love-based.

Our trinity can become love, generosity, and sharing.

Thus, others may know the spirits we carry and the essence of our being, the person we want to be.

"Him that I love, I wish to be free—even from me."
—Anne Morrow Lindbergh, author and aviator
(22 Jun 1906–2001)

Colui che amo, desidero essere libero—anche da me.
Al que amo, deseo ser libre, incluso de mí.

PS: This is harder than I thought!

Edel, not yet 7, never asked about our trip.

"Regarding Orlando," I said, "we're still going."

She smiled and, with tears, said, "He'd approve." And I held her for one of our long, infrequent "Sunshine on my shoulders" hugs.

In 2007, when Gordon passed, I focused on his unselfishness.

Both Dads were friends and brothers to each other and others.

Ralph Waldo Emerson wrote, "A friend may well be reckoned the masterpiece of nature."

As I grow, friendship becomes more meaningful.

Regarding losses: pauses need to be longer.

Edel at 7

Journal Entry 37, Carmel, 82, 2007

Dear Edel,

Twelve!

Dear Heart, where does the time go?

I've been rattling my brain all day trying to figure out how to do this, and I think I have what will work for me.

You, my dearest girl, were wanted by so many.

I know you did not have many things other children had, but know you have love.

Seeing you grow and age, as I am aging too quickly, brings me to this.

You know how I feel about journals and diaries: none of anybody's damn business! I have burned each little notebook Will has given me—and I've kept track of people and my relationships with them individually. I thought to have my lawyer deliver this, but he'd probably charge my estate, the SOB! So, I've decided on this path and hope I am not expecting too much for your age; and, if so, perhaps understanding will become more apparent when you re-read this later.

I have written the same letter to Mame and Will and nested the envelopes with yours first, placed into Will's, and both yours and Will's are placed into Mame's, so if either of them chooses not to give this to you, each has that choice. Knowing them as I do, I can bet Mame will wish she had not opened her envelope and will enclose her letter in an open envelope, and Will, will not open his, and let you do that, and open your envelope when you are ready.

"Being your '*cumata*' is one of my greatest joys."

I could not have children, and after my husband died at 47, I threw myself into my work as a nurse, and Mame and Will and I became a triumvirate.

Mame was divorced with no children, and Will wished he could be a father.

As friends to our colleagues, many of whom worked, with us without families to help, we found a lawyer. We set up a foundation among ourselves so that others among us would take any children who may be without parents by choice, so the trauma of grief would be dealt with as best we could without having the child subjected to state and social services.

However, we respected, incorporated, and kept the specific wishes of parents as guidelines as well.

Mame remains a lovely, tall, statuesque woman unwilling to give marriage another chance and grateful she had no children, as she worried about the alcoholic gene's impact on any progeny from her husband at the time, and her mother, whom she loved but never liked. She feared very young children and would never be alone or hold one for fear of harming the child. No one ever did more for others than she.

Will feared marriage. He felt a good relationship would sour when the little annoying things built and became significant intrusions. A child being a pawn or forced to live with a parent because of age— became a complication of life he did not want to experience, nor did he feel compelled to stay together for the child's sake, which may be a rationale for some, but not him.

"Why contribute to one's misfortune when promises, expectations, and trust eroded?" he often said. He wanted to be a father from the first time that he fielded questions about what he wanted to be when he grew up.

I asked Mame and Will if I could share their information with the other, and both agreed, and you were naturally conceived. Though we often laughed regarding your birth story, it worked out as planned. Much of this is not new to you, as they have kept you informed as soon as you could understand. I'm giving my version as I hope you are one kid who never tires of stories where she is the central character.

Your birthday was a Saturday, 20 May 1995. I can see you rolling your eyes in boredom over that repeated reminder, but it gave us a reason to go to Boston after a trying week at school, and your due date was far enough away—or so we thought.

You had other plans!

We had planned to go into the Museum of Fine Arts when it opened Saturday, have lunch in the North End, and then return to Medford, High Street, where my Mom lived in a two-family home on a bus line. My Mom thought Mame should not deal with public transportation, so I planned to drive us into town, park in a lot, and point to Mame, hoping the attendant would find a space if spaces were tight. We stayed in my second-floor apartment, now used as sleeping quarters for my visiting family and nieces and nephews.

Mom did not like noise overhead, so I paid some rent. She occasionally rented to Tuft's faculty guests, those who lived a distance in inclement weather, and visited doctors at the Lawrence Memorial Hospital, where she worked as an office manager for several doctors.

Mame had a restless night but wanted to move on with our plans. Her water broke in the bathroom, and she called me in. I called Mom, who called one of the doctors, and he made a house call—all before your Dad returned with breakfast pastries.

"Should we go back home?" Mame asked.

The doctor squeezed his eyes and jerked his head back.

"You want to deliver en route? You're dilating quickly."

To all, he announced, "I suggest we meet at the hospital as soon as you can get into the car.

"I'll make arrangements.

"Meet me at the main entrance."

"Though this is my first—I think it will be quick . . . my genetics. . . ." Mame added.

A bed, orderlies, nurses, IV, and the doctor met us and scurried Mame into the birthing center. I had worked at the hospital, knew many of the staff, and had most as nursing-program students.

Mame sipped ginger ale and wanted to do something other than be attended to at every twist and turn.

We tried watching **Singin' in the Rain**."

At 11:16, your birth was recorded as 6 pounds 15 ounces. Your Dad wrapped you and showed you to Mame, who kissed your tiny foot and uttered "Perfect" before he helped clean you.

Journal Entry 38, Edel, 12–14, 2007–2009

As soon as we met, I researched his name. Ren means "Lotus" and is of Japanese origin. Ren is a name used by parents who consider unisex or non-gendered-baby names.

We are the same age; we swim together from different schools; he has my Dad as a teacher.

We're both kids who have experienced prejudice and not fitting in, though Ren's culture and distance from his homeland are significant. Ren feels prejudice and the misfit syndrome, and is not having a good year with this intimidation and constant worry about being bullied and standing out.

His parents sense it and wonder about sending him home to his grandparents, maybe returning Mom and him to Japan. His father is stationed at the War College as one of a group from foreign countries.

I remember a National Park incident once when Zuri visited . . . and we were stopped by a GOB, Good Old Boy, dressed in a belly-stretched "uniform," on a National Park trip. Zuri's perception of Americans is more accurate, and the more Dad experiences, the more he says to Zuri, "You're right."

I began searching for a community-service project in grade seven to satisfy my high school graduation requirement a few years off, but the source of my planning-ahead gene was kicking in! I met Ren at swimming classes at Roger Williams University. I live in Portsmouth, and he lives just over the Middletown line. His Dad's orders here could expand to three years.

Making foreign families comfortable and familiar with the language was a program Dad started when he learned most foreign students lost a year of education in their country because their countries did not recognize American education. Though bright and exposed to English, most kids had a tough time adjusting, and it was usually not until after winter break that their familiarity with the language became sufficiently adequate to function in school. Dad devised a two-week volunteer crash course for spouses and children, and I often went along to help.

Ren and I became friends, and the guidance departments at each school approved of us imitating the teachers' "Buddy" Program. It also helped promote regionalization by integrating students from different communities.

Ren missed home and his family and friends. The novelty of being here and learning English didn't last long when kids made fun of his pronunciation, and some were rude and prejudiced. Dad worried about covering uncomfortable topics, especially recent wars, where family members remember, and some had fought against Japan. Dad didn't wait to get to the end of courses before discussing current events; he often began courses backward, not at the beginning of events chronologically but at the present day, so students can appreciate the threads from the past as they saw the rationale for researching the present. He hadn't had a student from Japan. Now, his planning was at the performance stage.

Dad had met Ren's parents before school started and again when Ren felt homesick. His parents had considered sending Ren back to Japan to live with his grandparents; if necessary, his Mom would soon follow.

Ren was aware of their concern and was brought in on the possibilities from the beginning. His parents said the final decision would be his. He had often been separated from his Dad, and having him home this year was one good reason to stay together. He said he would try his hardest to make this work. Swimming helped, as he made friends immediately, and practice didn't allow much time for chatting or bullying.

When our best swimmer, a kid known for bullying, saw Ren swim, he realized Ren would threaten his status.

The coaches and the other kids were excited, but the top kid did not look forward to being toppled. Once, I heard him say to Ren, "Slow down, Slanteye!"

I checked with male friends about what went on in the locker room.

"Oh, we joke around; we're guys, you know?"

Dad suggested I talk to the coach, who sucked in his teeth and said he was afraid of that, but he, too, had issues to consider. He would not go into the locker room alone, but parental volunteers could help.

I said, "I have one guy who would help."

"We need two."

"I wonder if they'd like their Moms to be considered monitors in the locker room!"

The coach's eyes bulged, but I was serious.

I told my friend to spread the word: women would act if there was any more screwing around in the locker room, especially making Ren or anybody else feel bad.

"No!" was the general reaction.

One guy added, "I don't even let my Mom wash my skivvies anymore!"

"Oh? Wow! That part of a Mother's Day gift?" I could not help saying.

Ren proved himself a team player and was put last in the relays so that, even if we were behind, he could put us ahead. When "Slow down, Slanteye," saw that, he apologized for making Ren uncomfortable; they became buds. Classes remained a challenge. I asked Dad how he planned to deal with it.

"I've been thinking about that.

"You know, I start at current events just in case we don't get there by June, and I was thinking of doing a video interview with Ren.

"I would give his parents a list of questions addressing Japanese culture, particularly their esteem and reverence for the emperor.

"In the aftermath of the war, the injuries, people killed, and suffering to this day is a question I'd like American students to answer from a Japanese perspective."

"I would ask students, especially those with Japanese parents or grandparents, to try to address the turmoil Truman faced as president to use the bomb first of all, let alone twice!

"I don't expect to resolve or come to an agreement. I aim to have students see the other side and express that via research and interviews.

"Each student's response will be seen and read by all without names (which will be on the back), and what grade readers think the student deserves.

"And at the end of the year, these will be returned, and the final exam will be: Do you wish to change what you wrote in September?

"Include at least a paragraph on how to improve the process.

"Maybe a trial or debate?

"What do you think?" he finally asked.

"I think we'll see!" I said.

"Smartypants!" he replied and adding, "How about an 'Awful Awful'?"

I said, "You always know how to relieve tension, colds, and disagreements! Nothing like our version of a milkshake frappe."

"Chocolate with jimmies coming up!"

That summer, Ren and his parents went home for a week and brought the grandparents here for the last two weeks in August and the first two weeks of September. I planned to work on Rhode Island rescinding, continuing to celebrate VJ Day! UGH! It's embarrassing!

When we started high school, Ren had to decide if he wanted to continue school here or in Japan and where he wanted to go to college.

He decided to start high school here and spend vacations and three weeks in summer in Japan to retain the language and be in touch with his family and friends. Prospects had it that his dad was being recalled to Japan for service if he did not retire.

Changes loomed, and we agreed to stay friends regardless of where we were. We're not boyfriend and girlfriend, but . . . he's a boy and my friend; I'm a girl and his friend . . . maybe someday. Hold hands? Why? Like in crossing the street? I can do that on my own. We talk. We fast dance. We've seen each other in bathing suits . . . that's enough for now. Maybe someday . . . one of us will need or want more. Boys are just making it out of the "yucky" category and are starting to smell. I don't think they're interested in some of my body changes. Heck, I'm not so sure I am.

Slow dance . . . close . . . no.

As Dad says, "Don't do anything with consequences."

Journal Entry 39, Zuri, 82, 2010

"Alone" on the pier, as the yacht and Zuri-Mama faded from sight. How often has that image been recalled?

I was twelve in 1940. Prince Harry lost his mother at twelve in 1997.

People come into and leave our lives, and we leave theirs. I left T at sixteen in 1945. Every day, Will leaves me. I get the same twinge of panic, but I haven't shared it—yet. Will left for school daily, and then boarded at school, followed by college in the U.S.A., where he now makes a life. The memory of a twelve-year-old is significant.

The Writing Coach said, "You've heard me say how 'hard' writing is.

"This week, I'd like to focus on how writing can reward and what to do when facing writer's block." He speaks, and I take notes.

"My job may look easy, but I've thought all week about how to share this with you (15 minutes), and to let you develop this in class (30 minutes). Then we'll talk (for 45 minutes)."

"'Writer's block' can happen anytime, on any piece, and though it may seem less possible when writing about something like a 'reward'— still, see the block as a gift.

"What is 'writer's block'?"

"The inability to continue writing" was the consensus.

"In the next few minutes, fill in the blank for the following two words: 'I **felt** ________'"

"Can we use '**feel**'?" someone asked.

"I thought I might be asked that.

"If you are considering a recurring issue that isn't resolved to the point of using a past tense, you may express it in the present."

"Has anyone ever experienced 'block'?"

A couple of people weren't sure, but . . . we went on.

"Well, if you haven't experienced it yet, you may, as the writing process continues—or does not continue.

"I'm not seeking to be nosy and won't intrude on what may be very personal. However, if you feel blocked, stop, and listen. Do something else.

"Often, a solution surfaces as you do something else besides write.

"That's when the piece is taking on a life of its own and allowing you to try to continue another way, so listen—hear it out.

"I doubt you'll hear a voice, but you might be nudged into thinking to yourself and coming to a realization . . . something new.

"Try a way you hadn't planned.

"You may explain a feeling as a way of getting to the basis of the story—behind the feeling. Have you reached peace about the adjustment if you have not resolved the feeling?

"If so, what helped resolve the discomfort?

"Thus, my initial use of "**felt**," the past tense of "**feel**."

"This is what I mean about reward in writing, especially how it helps to make you see something you hadn't seen before or in a way you hadn't seen before and allows you to move forward.

"Our discussion after writing is not intended to be intrusive.

"Get to the heart of the matter: How did you get to a feeling of adjustment, or Peace, regarding the issue?

"You may fictionalize it if you like.

"You may also take someone else's experience as an example if done with anonymity."

I wondered.

My mind filled with recurring memories, each a story in my life.

Alone . . . Alone on the pier. . . . Alone on the pier, the yacht and Zuri-Mama . . . fading from sight. 1940 found in the smeuse by

T. . . . 1945 . . . T . . . 1950 . . . Will boarding school . . . every time he leaves . . . 1962, Will, U.S.A. . . . Diana 1997.

The kindness of the girls—the daughters of the mistress of the house who told me not to come back—when their Mum died.

They saved Zuri-Mama's journals and gave them to me.

I had Zuri-Mama all those years we were separated. We shared agony.

I wish I had kept better, more consistent journal entries, but being young, the skimpy facts became important, not the feelings. Yet, I had feelings; I have feelings too; hmmm. I tried to understand how feelings were in me and how they awakened.

[1950] Some events keep reappearing in memory, like watching Zuri-Mama being held at the stern of the boat when I disobeyed the Mistress and reappeared. I could not hear Mama with the wind and the boat noise, but what I saw has returned throughout my life, and I try to find additional details. By remembering the details, adjusting will be more complete.

Mama said the Mistress had an errand for me and added, "Run back as fast as you can." Maybe the details will be lost, but I keep recording the incident as I age, hoping some forgotten detail will emerge, perhaps a better description of the people, especially the woman who gave me the hatbox and ordered me, very quietly, to "Take it to my maid.

"Do not return."

I could not understand the contradiction of the instructions at twelve years old.

Alone on the pier, the yacht and Zuri-Mama faded from sight.

[1945] I brought the hatbox to the house. The bag in which I carried my journals and needles, threads, shuttlecocks, underwear, face cloth, and soap on my back under my shirt.

The maid closing up the house looked at me with bulging eyes. "What are you doing here?"

I did not know what to say.

"Where is your jacket? You have clothes in the pockets, right?"

I nodded.

I began to say "Zur . . . " but could not finish. She put her arm around me and shook her head. She found another jacket, put some things in the pockets, and walked me over to Dolly, who cared for children, where Zuri-Mama taught us. They spoke in whispers. I held back tears.

Dolly gave me a plate with a slice of hard bread smeared with butter, drizzled some tea from her cup over the bread, and pinched a few grains of sugar on top. I swallowed bites . . . as hard as the bites were, swallowing was harder.

I stayed in the hedges until T found me in the shrubbery.

Journal Entry 40, Edel, 15, 2010

I've read Carmel's story of my birth so often that the pages are beginning to curl. Perhaps I'll make a copy and keep the original elsewhere, so the oils from my fingers won't mar it. Everyone has treated me with care, love, and kindness, and answered my questions. I'm fortunate Dad and Mame decided to be honest. My circumstances seemed as usual to me, as do those of other kids to theirs. Everyone in my family has had unexpected trauma, and we don't avoid conversation when we are together.

I will give them a copy of my gratitude for my fifteenth birthday and hope they will keep up their efforts, as I have the rest of my life ahead of me.

I wish all my grandparents could hear and read, and I think they will.

23 January 2010

Dear Dad, Ma-me, (pronounced like the last four letters of edamame), Zuri, Cumata Carmel, Godfather Pro, Willa, T, Gran'pa Gordon [even though some of you are elsewhere, you are also in my memory], Gran'ma Lily, and Uncle Will.

I'm beginning this on Dad's birthday and hope to have it ready for mine. I will add to it and hope it reflects my gratitude without getting mushy.

How I came to be and what I have come to be—I have you in my background as family. How my family will expand as I mature, I can't predict. I have many friends who are as "normal" as I am and some who follow an upbringing that has been their good fortune, perhaps more "normal," but I would not trade mine for theirs.

All my friends at preschool had brothers and sisters, and Dad always asked how many kids I would have. He reminds me all the time. That was before I knew you had to be married first—wrong! My parents weren't, and neither were Dad's. Anyway, I may start with one kid and see how I do . . . and I'm not sure I'll get married, either. Supporting another adult could be challenging, and I want my kid to come first.

Education. After I'm 25, I'll see. Dad always wanted to be a Dad.

I thought it was cool when Grandma Lily let him call her "Mum." I never met her, but I hear stories about her, and I think Aunt Willa has a letter she wrote to grandkids she, Grandma Lily, wouldn't see.

She asked that they be given them on their fifteenth birthday.

Grandma Lily wrote one and asked Aunt Willa to copy it as needed.

Do I get to keep the original? I will try to write once a month and on special days like Zuri's birthday and Mother's Day, and I'll see what else happens before my birthday. I don't want to leave anyone out.

Happy Birthday, Dad!

I'm glad you are my Father, and although you had only one kid, I hope I was enough. You're a cool guy, and Mame always says she will marry you in your next life, and that's okay with me.

After a long bike ride . . . I've been thinking, and we all know that is ominous.

I felt the names were not as respectful as the changes, and I foresaw myself as Gran' E, which I liked even better . . . Eventually.

Dear Dad, Ma-me, Gran' Z, "Cumata" Carmel, Godfather Pro, Aunt Willa, Gran'pa T, Gran'pa G, Gran'ma B, Uncle Will.

I'll continue to add names as my "family and friends" grow and people remain alive in me.

I haven't gone on a "real" date yet, whatever that is, but if it's anything beyond spending time with another . . . I'll wait.

Is someone taking my hand? I can cross the street by myself, thanks.

Is someone brushing up against me? It had better be because of a crowd pushing.

If I want a hug or a kiss, I can ask for one just as another can.

I'm not a prude and can send signals as well as anyone, smile, excuse, welcome, and reject as much as another can. This keeps a relationship balanced.

A greeting, especially within a family, can be spontaneous unless germs and perfume abound. Friends? Possibly, but assumptions are best left to religious experiences! I may never go on a date or ask anyone to go on one, but at 15 and a sophomore in high school, I'm in no hurry to squeeze the rest of my life into a compact mess that could have long-range ramifications. My reputation matters, and I must live with what my conscience allows. I may trust someone to keep "things" between us, but I can't count on it . . . it's like trusting a fart!

Being forced against my "will" is a word I've grown up with; defense "will" is exercised.

I like to laugh, watch TV, read, watch movies, "play," pets, spontaneity, travel, people, languages, friendships, black, purple, exercise, cooking, being lazy, ignoring what doesn't suit me, music, working—I'll add to this, so no period. I want to be taller and more challenged.

In a few months, I'll be old enough to drive! I can't wait. The independence scares me, but I want it. Driving to the pool, to school, not having anyone take me . . . I can only imagine.

No music, no distractions, and think ahead for the driver who isn't thinking. Dad already taught me words I can say depending on who's in the car: bird brain, ass wipe, and shit bird.

I practice them on people who pull out without looking, drivers who don't use directionals until they are in a turn, or not at all, people who "door" bikers, don't fold in mirrors, can't park well, poop along, stay in the left lane when a turn may or may not be 1/4 mile away . . . they all suck! He sometimes shows people their IQ with his middle finger, but he ensures I don't see it.

He drives very defensively, and I also want to drive like that. He keeps buying cars with gears versus automatic to peel off at a light and stay awake shifting. He says he can be kind and polite; if he wants to give someone the right of way, he points to them and waves them on. If they do the same, we are gone. He said women drivers have a reputation, and I have to decide what kind of driver I want to be. I reply, "Really? I've seen men do things that don't make me proud."

"Maybe, but at least they move."

"Next time we're behind one, you start leaning on the horn and yelling, 'Move!' I'm going to add that to the ice creams you owe me."

He conters with "'Wise' was a brand of potato chips, not a description of you!"

I ask, "How old must you be to be 'Wise'?"

Under my breath, I want to add, "There aren't many much older than you," but I know when to hush.

Most parents wish kids a good day, and he does that, but occasionally, he varies it with something to see if I'm listening, like, "May you have the confidence of being freshly showered and looking good."

I may add an "A" for my Alter ego and make everyone nuts.

I do have conversations with myself. Not out loud, but when I'm thinking, thoughts drift in and out, and I don't know where they come from or how long they've been there. They're not voices in my head but thoughts.

It's like if I have ice cream and want another one. "Did you earn two?"

"Do your clothes have that much stretch?"

"Pop-a-button-time, is it?"

Gran'ma Z's birthday is 5 March, and Dad gets cards, and we Skype and chat. Skype has been around since I was eight and has gotten better. I will tell her about this project and expect an email on my birthday.

In fact, this can be an annual thing happening.

Oops! Already.

It's a good thing I started this now. Aunt Willa's birthday is on 6 February. Maybe I should put greetings in chronological order even if I use the same sentence for everyone. Now, I'd best make a list so I don't forget anyone. It's a good thing my list is short. Maybe I'll keep these with the names and hope I'll remember to check them.

Dear _____,
Happy Birthday!
Happy Mother's Day!
Happy Father's Day!
Happy Holiday!
Happy New Year!
Thank you for being my _______.
That's the best gift . . . and thank you for the other "gifts."
Peace and Love,
Edel

23 January

6 February, Aunt W
5 March, Gran'ma Z
May, Mother's Day
20 May, Me
June, Father's Day
Dad and Pro
15 September, Ma-me
16 December, Carmel

OMG, this reads, *Like father, like daughter!*

Oh, crapola . . . I suppose I could write the word I'd rather say; it is my journal and no one's business. I tried it on scrap paper . . . and saw scrap rhymes with crap, and I'm writing poetic rhymes without trying. UGH.

5 February 2010

Dear Aunt Willa,

I am sending this early so you will have it on your birthday since your time is six hours ahead of ours.

Happy Birthday!

Thank you for being my aunt.

You are the first person I am writing to as part of my new plan of sending a gift on my birthday year. Dad will have to wait until next year to get his first as I started it on his birthday; then, ideas kept coming, but I would appreciate a little elaboration as you are the first in this project.

I'm still drawing and wondering about Uncle Will. We can Skype tomorrow or soon after that when you have time.

Peace and Love,
Edel

PS: Dang, I used to look forward to February break. After T died, we went to Orlando, as planned, which helped balance my memory.

Dad told me my Godfather Pro isn't doing well, and Dad will be his executor, which means a few trips to Boston. I'm glad I looked up "executor," and it did not mean what I thought!

Pro told me he wrote me a letter of recommendation for college.

He shared a paper he wrote on President Kennedy that he and Dad used as an exercise in Italian and said, "May you meet many men like him."

I read one line daily, "A man above all men," *un uomo sopra tutti uomini.*

Journal Entry 41, Willa, 65, 2010

Dear Edel,

Thank you for your birthday greeting.

It was beautiful to talk with you and Dad.

Gran'ma Z called also; maybe we can connect all at once one day? She smiled when we talked about Will crying in the house after I reprimanded him for calling our Mum "Mum." Mum took me aside and asked me not to make him cry. I tried to explain my rationale, but everything came out with mucus and tears.

"Is he going to call Dad, 'Dad'"?

And Mum said, "Ask Dad."

When I saw Dad coming up the walk, I dashed to the door, which I could not open, and as soon as he entered, I greeted him with, "Can Will call you 'Dad'?"

And he said, "Why not?"

I ran, saying, "I'm going to tell him!"

I don't feel like an aunt some days, yet I am very grateful for you.

My work keeps me busy; little lives with significant heart issues that so few can deal with. So often, our work isn't enough.

I saw your note just after I had done two surgeries; then I personally handed the babies to their Mums, saying, "See what your love can do." I gripped the father's arm, returned to the bathroom, read your note, and then returned to work.

Approaching fifteen . . . I want to see you and be more a part of your life.

I want to visit various U.S.A. hospitals to see how my work in cardiac neo-natal units works there. Maybe I can do more for more. I've been trying to house people at Menton who come here for their children's surgeries, and perhaps it's time for Dad and me to plan continued use of the house.

I understand you like fashion and art. The medical world could use you, too, especially your imagination and art.

I have written some stories for children so they can know what is going on while they "sleep" under anesthesia, and I try a crude drawing occasionally. Babies have siblings, and often, seeing what they've been through as babies helps them know how special they are. Maybe you can help me illustrate blankets and sleeping clothes that look better than what the hospital provides. Do you think you'd be interested? The writing and crude drawings helped me a little, but better graphics would help the kids and their families.

You were so thoughtful to ask about Uncle Will. Dad always hesitated to ask Mum and Dad much growing up, as it made them bleary-eyed. When Zuri took us out in the stroller, we always prayed to him and left a little space between us for his spirit. The stroller in Guernsey was the best. T found a way to adapt the frame of a discarded baby carriage and housed two stroller seats. I sat in front on the even days because I was born on the 6th, and your Dad sat in front on odd days because he was born on the 23rd. Even our months are odd and even!

The war was still on when we were born, and records were sparse. I think Uncle Will had what we now term HLHF, Hypoplastic Left Heart Syndrome; everything on the left side of the heart is too small and doesn't allow adequate blood flow. Your letter gave me another idea if you're interested.

We'll chat more and make plans.

Know that I love you and am carrying your birthday greetings and re-reading them, especially when my surgeries aren't enough.

Peace and love to you,

Aunt Willa

Journal Entry 42, Zuri, 85, 2013

Never underestimate . . . anyone.

Never overestimate . . . anyone.

Why estimate anyone?

Estimating is guessing.

Let actions speak.

The Coach appeared in a blue pinstripe suit with a blue shirt striped with thinly spaced pink lines, whose colors were repeated in a hand-knit bow tie bordered by a white collar and matching cuffs.

If the writing didn't interest me, I'd just come to see what he wore.

His socks were black, and only through a hard stare could I see Navy blue shoes. Navy blue shoes!

"Anyone have trouble choosing a cliché from last week?"

He had proposed completing "Never underestimate ________."

It had so many possibilities that we wondered if the original could ever be ascertained.

After we all thought we were so clever, and one response led to another, we finally quieted down, and he grinned and wrote on the chalkboard, "anyone."

"I was driving today and wondered what I would learn or realize and why I hadn't thought of that before. I was coming from my volunteer work with prisoners. I was astounded by their cleverness, determination, and purpose, and it reminded me of Colditz, where the Germans held prisoners during World War II.

"What do you think the prisoners were fixated on?"

And he held up his hand, "What consumes most prisoners?"

"Food?"

"Safety?"

"Even then, prisoners had rights. Most were fed, exercised, and had time to find ways to get out. And some did escape. Their intelligence, ingenuity, and cleverness keep them one step ahead of their captors. Anyway, once I inserted 'anyone,' I thought the lesson might be forgotten, so I kept repeating it until I could stop and write it down: Never underestimate anyone. As soon as I did and read it, I crossed out 'under' and replaced it with 'over.' And, as soon as I did that, I crossed it out, left out any adverb, and just let 'estimate' work its magic.

"When we talked about adding anything to 'Never estimate anyone,' we decided the following might help expand the three words:

"Let them show you everything you need or want to know by their actions."

"And you were asked to create a story or find an illustration to exemplify that. Anyone care to share?"

I thought about Zuri-Mama, T, being a friend, and love. They helped make my life enjoyable, and every day, every interaction, was a gift of love.

We barely said the word but often expressed it as being "friends" with each other in the broadest definition. I hoped I was that to them and remained that to others I encountered. It helps keep me who I am and what I express. Why can't political or any kind of leaders do that? Why can't they act individually as examples—instead of being examples of power, be examples of humility, mercy, and friendship? T made me realize a more mature version of Zuri-Mama, blood versus non-blood, but both friends, the definition I keep expanding.

Make a topic with the last sentence as a guide.

"Another's Time," topic

When one meets another, or an "other," versus a stranger, the surprising a effect (influence) becomes an effect (result), and comparisons and questions surface:

What just happened here?

How did it happen?

Compare a player to a piano who knows the instrument so well that s/he can create a performance that astounds—a ball and a catcher's mitt, ying and yang, salt and pepper, and so on. Some people kill that spark of electricity with greed, control, and maybe marriage. Yet some make that marriage, or bond, exemplary. In a relationship, frequency, differences, distance, and challenges do not matter.

I want to use the pronouns "I," "you," and "our."

I understand you.

I know you.

You consume my thoughts—at least temporarily—and I allow the exercise of possibilities. One more prompt: How does one earn the privilege of another's time?

Journal Entry 43, Will, 68, 2013

After the surprise of coincidences, I credit God for acting again. On a visit to T, he had mentioned a folder of "Fred's" papers. Years after T passed I found the folder and read the contents. T kept a record of his attempts to locate his friend, yet he was also leery and cautious about doing so.

The folder contained individual handwritten pages in English, German, and Italian, perhaps to ward off censors. However, it had no identifying name, and the penmanship of the pages was barely readable. There were some typewritten pages as well.

T told me about "Fred" who remained in Guernsey after the war to resettle some folks, ensure men who served there got out safely, and offered fathers' names if women wished for the sake of the record, and if possible, support when Germany was able. Prejudice and anti-German sentiment was substantial. I began posting ads after T's passing in 2002 in Germany, Guernsey, the UK, and the U.S., online and in whatever accessible sources I could find to locate "Fred," or a family descendant. These papers must be as meaningful for someone to read, as they were for "Fred" to write.

"Fred's" sons would be older than I by 7–10 years, but their kids, opps, children may be Edel's generation—though having fathered her at 50, there may be a generation gap on my part. The wife/mother would be older than Z. As time passed, the possibility of finding anyone diminished. Fast forward to Edel's senior project, which began the summer before her junior year (2011), and the writing project that is the opening entry of this book. German military records were scattered and in German. Would descendants want to locate an officer in the Nazi service? Where to start? Churches? German ghettos in foreign countries?

I read what I could in English and my limited Italian and felt more strongly that descendants deserve to read of the agony and anxiety this officer felt.

The high school students in the Guernsey writing project took it on, and as Edel's graduation approached, the effort of the online student sleuths reached fruition.

I placed the following in every free resource and paid for some ads in international newspapers: "Seeking contact information for a German officer who served in Guernsey (UK) 1940–1945+. He had two boys and a wife in Germany.

"He was a large man but had a demeanor of casual elegance, 'sprezzatura.'"

"He was German and familiar with English and Italian. He was probably between 25–30 while in Guernsey, 1940–1945+ (UK).

Any information may be significant; kindly contact this cell number in the U.S.A.: 1–401–849–2053

"I have papers that may settle or fuel discord, but this officer's sentiments deserve to be known by descendants.

"The onus is on you, the responder to this ad, to convince me of the connection before any sharing is considered. Photos, papers, and memory may be used to build a connection based on confidence and truth."

After Edel and I visited Guernsey in 2011, where Edel led a group of teenagers in a writing project, Fate—God—set to act once more. In Edel's haste to greet her junior year of high school, she gave me a copy of the group's effort to find a self-publisher, which took me well into her senior year of 2013. Among the pages was a slim folder Edel was handed by the writing Coach in the last session with a note on the folder:

"Here's what I got online. Can you integrate what helps our work while your Dad looks for a way to publish? Best of Luck, Nice working with you." Coach When we arrived home I remembered she had the folder but had little time to attend to it.

One morning, I found a sticky note, Edel on the folder: "Dad, Would you. . . ." Peace and Love, E

I began my search again for "Fred" and/or descendants. There were teasers here and there, and then one attempt differed.

A few responders soon became boxes of possibilities.

We kept all replies as they came in by name, location, and date and rated them by the possibility of interest 1, most, to 10, least.

Some were professional scammers who doctored photos and made you think they were interested if money was involved. Two kids working on family ancestry and archives from two countries were doing similar work to Edel's. They were one of a grandchild of grandfathers whose parents had served in Guernsey (UK). Before this got more complicated I devised a simple generational "tree."

Generation #1

Zuri, T, "Fred" (Friederich), wife Beau, sister worked at Kew Gardens

Generation #2

Will (formerly Edel) Ben, older son of "Fred" and Beau, and Fred, younger son

My 3rd generation, Edel (b.1995) Ben had two sons Fred had a boy and a girl

Generation #4

Fred's daughter had a daughter, Beau (b.1995), who connects with Edel on their senior project

The father of the now grandfathers (Ben and Fred) had served in the German military. The grandfathers were elderly, had two different last names, and had not spoken or contacted each other since the older boy, Ben, left home after graduating high school in the U.S.A. He had returned to Germany and had changed his name, gone to school, and brought up his family in Germany.

The younger boy, also with a different name, made a life in the U.S. A. in one of the German ghettos.

His mother spent her last years with him and his family.

His mother had given him papers and made him promise not to share anything as the papers would only breed animosity. The children had been reared with this caveat. When their children and grandchildren asked about family, searches ended with, "All documentation was lost during the war."

The younger son shared what he knew, made allowances for the times, and lived as well as he could in the U.S.A. Their mother continued to educate them in English, French, and German so they might find work as she did, translating.

This story exuded honesty and a craving that sent a chill through me. My eyes filled, and I looked up and said, "Thank you" again. We began phone conversations, as he was concerned emails might be seen, copied, or hacked, and who knew what retaliation might occur and continue to haunt him, as his mother had forewarned.

His mother had died in 2000, and he published obituary notices in England and Germany, hoping friends of his mother and his brother would contact him. Now her papers were his. He had seen my ads before and hesitated to respond, fearing the ramifications.

Now, a risk seemed overdue. With his mother gone and not knowing much about his brother, and scant memories from childhood, we pieced together that T and his father were "friends" during the occupation.

T wrote some of Friederich's journal entries in English, Italian, and German. I remember T saying, "He spelled every word I wrote, including accents!"

Friederich wrote some himself in a barely readable script and asked T to hold them until he could send for them safely, as he hoped it would help his family understand how he managed to serve in the German army.

He loved Germany, what it stood for, and the strides it had made historically before Hitler came to power. He knew he had to keep serving because he was separated from his family, and his family would be killed if he defected. No one could imagine the censored letters his German father and English mother shared. She always reminded them, "Your father is trying, as only he can, to make the occupation of Guernsey as reasonable as possible. We love each other, and we love our countries."

When Friederich returned to Germany, the younger boy, who was 7 in 1945, never forgot how gaunt his father looked. "He has spaces between his fingers," he remarked to his mother, who put a finger to her lips.

He told me his parents met when his mother, as an assistant to her professors, taught for them, and was offered a semester in Germany with housing to take any courses when she was not instructing in Italian or French languages, two languages in which she minored.

He took Italian, and at the end of class, he spoke with her.

"Domande?" she asked.

He froze.

"'Question?' I see you took no notes," she added.

"Do you think I'd forget anything you said?"

"They married in London so he could meet her family and returned to Germany. As 1940 approached, my father heard of plans, and he and Mum decided it was safer for us in Germany versus being bombed and chancing evacuation of children. When my father eventually came home after the war, they often whispered after we were in bed, and my mother kept repeating, 'Together is better.'"

"And my father would reply, 'Eventually . . . eventually.'"

"We were never told directly, but we children and my mother were to go to London, despite its condition, to visit her family. From there, arrangements were made to go to the U.S.A. The Germans were hated everywhere, even among themselves; there was danger and distrust.

My father would work on being assigned to the U.S.A., and they would make a new plan once we were together there. He never appeared.

"When we left Germany, it was the last time we saw him. My mother counted on him sending money. When she contacted the military, she was told, 'Officers were only being paid while they served during this time. Pensions would be resumed once funds were allowed to families and veterans discharged or deceased.' My mother carried a 5x7 sepia photo of her and my father the day they married. It was never exposed publically and only shared with family when we celebrated a holiday or birthday, so he could be with us, then she put it away.

"My mother changed our names, and we settled in Germantown, Quincy, Massachusetts. My mother found work, and we were old enough to care for ourselves. My brother sent a note to his friend and got a reply that he did not share, but he did not eat for three days and was tearful and quiet. My mother asked to see the note. He refused.

"My brother was older and assumed he was the head of the family.

"She approached him and brought him to her chest, both heaving quietly.

"He pulled out the note, and she told my brother, 'We're safe. Let's pray Papa is, too.'"

"She wrote to a colleague with whom she had taught in Germany and received a reply. A rowdy group of drunken soldiers stopped my father, and one among them slurred, 'Traitor! Because of two-faced people like you, we lost the war!'

"Bystanders watched. One said, my father pleaded, 'Please, let's talk.

'Please, put the gun away; people around here could get hurt.'"

One of the rowdies said, 'They won't get hurt—but you—'"

"He shot my father. People ran. The rowdy group picked up my father, put him into a car, and drove off. One of the bystanders, a colleague of my mother dabbed her handkerchief with my father's blood and concealed it, hoping to contact my mother somehow.

Whether it would ever be any help, she didn't know. No one ever saw my father again.

"The colleague returned to the bar night after night, hoping to see anyone in the group who picked up my father's body. The colleague tried to get the men to chat individually. A young man was at the bar nearly every night, thinning, sleepless, and troubled. In the men's room, washing his hands, he reminded the colleague of Macbeth . . . 'Wash this blood/Clean from my hand. . . .'" (Act 2, scene 2).

"The colleague asked, 'Where is he?'

"And the drunken young man sobered up immediately; the sclera of his bloodshot eyes a maze of red lines.

'Buried or in water?' the colleague persisted.

"The young man ran out and was never seen again by the colleague.

"The images of the others from that night remain in the colleague's head, though clouded by a veil of drunken stupor that might make an alert person see another person entirely.

"The house we lived in was confiscated, as no one lived there.

"Everything we had was lost.

"Some must have believed he was a traitor, and that story persisted after the fact when he could not be found, explain, or defend himself.

"There is always an attraction to gossip, as it seems to have some truth as its basis. Still, it is usually verbal and affects others strongly, as if they know the story behind the story, giving them an edge of contradiction.

"Maybe my brother believed that, too." Fred, the younger son said and continued.

"I've always hoped something written, even if not my preference, would ease knowing, similar to getting a diagnosis versus wondering what symptoms contribute to the imagination.

"My mother did not believe in anything that tainted my father's reputation, nor did I.

"Perhaps the pages can help explain my father's genius and ability to get opposing sides to work together. Though nothing can justify the violence that took him if, indeed, it happened.

"I've often imagined he staged the entire scene and would eventually make his way to us, but with my mother gone, I'm hoping the papers are his way of returning to us.

"All people like gossip . . . it has an element of 'truth' to most, untold for a reason, which is woven in T's folder here," I said.

"For much of my childhood, I was plagued with nightmares/daymares over thinking while awake. I remember sucking my thumb and being reprimanded, and when asked, 'Why,' I replied, 'It happens, all by itself . . . during the night. I would awake ashamed with my thumb in my mouth, all wet, shriveled, and pruney. And I was only old enough to remember, not just know, by being told stories. 'Stories enrich the story.'"

I shared a segment of the papers regarding the issue of driving and signs.

The Germans wanted signs in German and driving on the right versus the British left, with the steering column on the right. Both sides were firm.

"My Mum always said, 'If he [my dad] could get you to talk, he could change your mind.'"

"After being in Guernsey for a while, the topic continued. Friederich invited both men in charge to tea; Germans could still bake crisp, flakey sweets then. He listened and listened and listened. When they tired of talking, sipping tea, and eating cakes, he told the Brit when the German went to the potty, 'The British are known for their manners and the ability to comfort guests; Guernsey will be a model of occupation if the war ends in our favor.'

"And, if it doesn't, how easy would it be to take the signs down and replace them with the ones saved and claim hospitality was your guide?

"After a sputter, the Brit said, 'And I have my job and am not seen as lacking firmness?'

"Who could criticize you?" Friederich questioned and added, "As for the future behavior of the Germans, when the time comes, and food packages may strike the consciences of those in power, I can tell you that if Germans interfere with the food parcels, they will be shot.

"They'll be given spoons to scoop up any broken containers, but otherwise, the food belongs to you . . . and we are suffering the same as you are regarding food supplies.

"And, for this courtesy to the Germans, we owe you in return, and it is good to have a wild card in your hand in your favor."

"This is only one issue," the Brit retorted.

There are pages of examples of diplomacy and how a man without formal training managed coexistence.

Friederich, the boys' father, wrote, "'I apologize for the military and artillery used when we arrived.

"'I had no part in the plan, which was out of my power.

"'I pray never to be put in a situation where I'm part of hurting and killing people.'"

"This sounds so like my father. I like to think that, with my mother gone, she has learned his fate, and these have come to light so that I may learn about them here and now."

We paused for a minute, and I asked, "Are you considering what I'm thinking?"

Simultaneously, we said, "Brother."

"Have you tried in 60 years?"

"He left; he's older, and the onus is on him. I had obituaries printed and have heard nothing . . . yet.

"And your father would sit you both down and not allow you to leave—or pee—until the impasse was passed."

"R . . . rrright. . . . ," he answered.

"You can always be the man the family needs versus the stubborn resistor, who may not go to his grave comfortably with that weight on his shoulders. Plan the conversation, and once he says, 'Hallo' and you say 'Guten Tag,'—don't stop."

He also worried about sharing these papers. When I spoke with Edel, she said, "They were intended for his sons, and they should decide where they go and with whom they are shared. Families and descendants could be endangered."

"There is a Boston Antheneum," I added.

Edel countered with, "There is a Guernsey Antheneum where the papers and people involved may feel safer."

I wore one of T's shirts that day. And, And, Zuri lives! She played cribbage with your Dad.

There is a character list with most of the details before the novel begins.

For the sake of clarity, the following with more details and is also offered as of 2013:

Will, 68; my generation, #2: sons of Friederich, the German Officer on Guernsey, and Beau, his wife, were the parents of Fred, 75; and Ben, 78, who graduated high school in 1953 and left the U.S.A.

The brothers have not seen/spoken to each other in 60 years as of 2013.

Z and T's generation, #1:

Friederich, the father (b. 1915, d. 1945?) also "Fred," on Guernsey, German Transition [Ambassador] Officer on Guernsey, 1940; wife Beau (b. 1914; m. 1934; died before 2000), parents of two boys.

Back to Will, My generation, #2: Ben, age 5, in 1940 (b. 1935, m. 1960) Generation #3: 2 boys: one, b. 1963, m. 1985; the other, b. 1965, m. 1990; Generation #2: and Fred, age 3, 1940 (b. 1938, wed 1968)

Generation #3: fathered a boy, b. 1970, m. 1993, and a girl b. 1972, m. 1994, who was interested in ancestry and had a Generation #4 for their daughter, Beau (named after grandmother, b. 1995, the same age as Generation #3, [for us, Z, T, and Will/Edel, who was due to graduate in 2013; they made a connection].

The German brothers are grandfathers.

The children of Ben and Fred are the grandchildren of Friederich and Beau.

I fathered Edel at 50 and skipped a comparable generation to these grandchildren; thus, my child is the age of the younger Beau, named for her grandmother, one of T's generation #1, elder Friederich and Beau's grandchildren.

When the U.S.A. was being settled, foreigners from various countries settled together in what became ghettos, which were supportive neighborhoods where religions, schools, customs, languages, foods, bakeries, and traditions helped many to transition to becoming American.

As differences occurred, these areas became objects of prejudice.

Remnants of their origin can be found to some degree even in the 21st century, but what these neighborhoods once served, residents moved on from, and residents today are more homogenized. However, the history of these neighborhoods is indisputable.

One such area was Germantown, in Quincy, Massachusetts.

This is where Beau came after World War II with her sons Ben and Fred.

Fred [Friederich], the younger boy, had anglicized his father's name.

His brother changed his first name to Ben.

Their English mother, Beau, had a sister, their aunt, who worked at Kew Gardens, responding to inquiries from all over the world, . . . the parents thought it wise to correspond indirectly and using two envelopes.

The aunt would then add the proper postage from a sum left to her.

The parents thought this a safer method to stay in touch.

Only the parents corresponded.

Not hearing from the husband/father in weeks, the older boy, Ben wrote to his trusted best friend in Germany using the aunt as the intermediary, as the parents had.

Kew Gardens:
Telephone: 020 8332 5655
Street: Kew Gardens
Postcode: TW9 3AB
City: Richmond
County: Surrey
Country: United Kingdom

Weeks later, he received a reply: "My parents ordered me not to write further and told me to order you not to write again, or we will report you. I had to pay for this stamp with my allowance."

Journal Entry 44, Zuri, 87/88/89, 2015/2016/2017

Age makes changes. Leg spasms plague and interrupt my sleep occasionally. Sharing this with my chiropractor won't happen for nearly a month now—the experience is the worst thus far. I clenched my teeth to a degree close to giving birth. I risked cracking the new night guard as one lifting weights might. I went to the kitchen with duress, ever grateful for living alone, and downed a supplement, a banana, and lots of water. Eventually, the tightness subsided enough for me to return to bed. Still, the lingering strain on the muscles of my left leg, especially the inner thigh, twinged at various times the next day as I went about my regular physical exercises. A minor complaint compared to others with more challenges.

Every time I bring up attempting another National Park trip, Will remains hesitant.

I went to Yosemite alone in April 2017: I took photos, experienced a snowfall, painted, wrote, and had something new to share.

I don't think Will ever got over the incident that got us lifetime passes back when Edel was in elementary school. I asked, "Did you ever get the Good Old Boy's name?" We always referred to him as the GOB.

He replied, "No."

We've never used the passes since the incident.

"Let's try to think something up. We're spending less time together. Does Edel remember any of it? It would be nice to balance out that experience with a positive one."

Will wasn't biting.

After a pause, he spoke. "It was too close for comfort and too heavy on discomfort. I keep shaking my head, saying how right you are about prejudice in this country. I don't think you've been avoiding it—have you?"

"I haven't, but I am not encouraging it, either. That was unnecessary, and I understand how it came about," I said.

Will recalled the questioning verbatim: "'Are you the chauffeur?"

And—"Did you kidnap them? The Nanny and the little girl?'"

He continued, "No one got hurt physically, yet emotional scars last a lifetime. That GOB stretched my patience and his shirt to their limits—and didn't change how his Mama and Daddy brought him up. See, you haven't forgotten."

I hadn't.

I keep learning from the writing coaches.

In the first class of one session, I heard:

"Everything one writes says something about the writer.

"For every piece we write, skip a line, and write what you learned about yourself."

I learned ____ about me.

So often, as I walk and ride public transportation, I see homeless people. I rarely see them reading or writing, and I want to help them. I began collecting calendars, like Zuri Mama, and making alphabets from headlines. When I see free pens and pencils, I take a few. Inexpensive watercolors, crayons, colored pencils . . . what fits into a two-wheeled shopping cart. When I get tea or coffee, I get two, and sometimes we talk. Some who knew how to read or write haven't done either in years. Some never learned. Some get embarrassed, so I face out, and they face a wall and little steps like initials . . . it's a start . . . thanks to Zuri Mama. I carry a string bag with an alphabet of blocks and follow the Easy, Learn, Play pattern: ABC to read, which most remember. Then I take out the keyboard and ask them to repeat C and go to G.

Mirror Lake painting

"Right hand, ready? Thumb on C, middle finger on E, and smallest finger on G. Hit all three at once. Sound good? That's a C major chord. Now listen to the sound when you hit CDE and G; then CEFG. Hear the difference? I show them a page of notes on lines to practice while I attend to someone else. If no one is around, with the left hand, I introduce a C, an octave below, and turn the paper over to see notes, staffs, and measures. Now you can read some music. I have a six-line song/poem. Can you read?" Depending on the answer, I begin a reading lesson, and they put each line to their music. If they get ambitious and the music contributes we can try another stanza beginning with the last line and sing to the first: I call it, Do the Reverse!

"Our Time"
Our Time begins.
Prior labor dims.
Word shadows glow.
Writers will grow.
Interest may rise and fall.
Our Time awaits as do all.

-

Our Time awaits as do all.
Interest may rise and fall.
Writers will grow.
Word shadows glow.
Prior labor dims.
Our Time begins.

And, they come back. I keep folders on them and offer them copies of the pages if they like.

Easy? Easy, Learn, Play, ELP, then onto ESP, Essentials, Specifics, Process.

Another year . . . my age rises . . . hard to imagine. I've been very fortunate with my health.

Still able to spend time in London and Newport.

My interests and projects keep me busy and helped me find a way to support myself and Will and T.

Dear T.

I miss him.

Fifteen years.

I remember Princess Margaret died a week later, and seven weeks after that, the queen's mother at 101, who'd attended her daughter's funeral: a figure in a black hat . . . black coat, shoes . . . black gloves, huddled into herself.

Zuri-Mama said I had "Mani d'oro," or "golden hands," when I learned to tat, sew, write, and write calligraphy, provided venues for income and friendships, especially my Palace Friends, whom I won't compromise on, even in these personal pages. When Will and Edel visit, we go to Guernsey. I'm still doing as I've always done. Willa stayed in touch and asked me to promise to call her first if needed, and I would.

She's busy making a name for herself and women in her profession.

I often wonder if the priest ever recorded my almost-marriage to her father.

Gordon immediately passed after I repeated what the priest said, and Gordon was about to repeat it when he smiled, held my hand, and slipped away. That released the priest from any obligation.

I asked him not to and told him I would never use it to challenge Willa in court, even if necessary. Maybe she and Will will disagree, but they both know their parents' wishes and will respect that. Will already

Yosemite photo snowfall, grass, footbridge

told me that, should there be any challenges—there won't be any. I gave him a wink. Edel is our next generation.

She and Willa have a solid relationship, and Willa always felt like a stand in for Mame, who has been more generous and loving than we could ask for . . . a good friend. Edel and I used to have conversations about missing mothers, and I never knew my birth father. I wonder if I legally, would have a claim to his estate? He didn't claim me. Why would I claim anything of his?

He tried making up for taking advantage of Zuri-Mama by caring for her later in life. Ignoring me, I leave it to God and the afterlife.

Still, I look forward to T. We'll spend time together and time apart.

A man, a friend, needs independence and a life of his own, as I do, and that brings richness to time together and shared.

Not much on church or religion, but if there's an afterlife and a Paradiso, it'll be together, independent, and work. What will that work be?

It's also part of being grateful for the gift of living . . . and more T time—forever.

Journal Entry 45, Edel, 22, Will, 72, 2017+

The student participants in the writing project introduced in the first Journal Entry had questions for the fictional character Will, who guided the publishing phase and joined us in supporting L by not having our names listed. This conversation led to an interview.

Edel, E: What has publishing a book taught you?
Will, W: A book faces Jersey barriers that time may resolve. Separating one's self from writing is an asset. Clarity comes when I am not trying to force it. Because pastries and cookies, like all temptations, are available, it does not mean I have to indulge. Writing has a negative aspect: too much ass time.

E: Was there anything practical you learned structurally that was unexpected?
W: Unexpected. Yes. Other than my thesis, which started out in the typewriter age, technology has brought us a long way. I'm frequently challenged by the editing process. Start at the beginning work your way through repeat, repeat, repeat. However, working with a number of pages how does one make changes and keep the same page numbers?

I haven't thought this out to teach it yet but working with the publisher I thought of a car.

E: A car? Okay go on.
W: Using our usual standard, only until the first yawn?

Cars have multiple gears going forward but only one reverse.

E: Analogy approaching?

W: If you begin at the end and make changes and work your way back to the beginning, then the page numbers remain the same pretty much.

E: Okay.

W: Print out a "hard" copy.

Make your changes and edits.

Then insert them from the last page to the first page.

Then, check where the beginning of chapters or whatever entry division you want to call them, and reformat the pages so each beginning is at the top of a left or right page.

Match the page numbers with the table of contents, and you have new proof to read and edit—and you haven't lost your way or your page numbers.

Often starting at the beginning screw up the pagination every time a revision is made.

E: That makes sense, and it's helpful; you never knew that before?

W: No. I have never worked with so many pages, nor have I worked with a self-publisher or any who helps edit and proofread.

E: I may call for a refresher when I write my next paper. Would you comment on writer's block?

W: The term is a misnomer; at the very least, I call it Writer's Gift—that's a more positive term. I'll elaborate if you're interested.

I, Edel call Dad, aka Will . . . our repartee:

Edel: Hello, Dad.

Will: Who's this?

Edel: That always makes me smile. How long have we been doing that?
Will: Since we had phones! What's up?

E + ME = W E interview:

Edel: I want to interview you. I have questions, and, as you say, "Just because I ask doesn't mean you have to answer."
Will: That sounds reasonable. How do you plan to do it?

E: I'd like to record or videotape it/them. Voices are distinctive, and I'd like to preserve our timbre and resonance as well as I can.

I can edit it, and we may return to them for questions that may take longer to answer.

I'll send you an email. Embed your answers, send me your responses, and I'll send back additional questions/comments your responses stimulate. This could continue for a while, but let's not exhaust it. Keep it interesting, and stop when one of us yawns.
Will: For some questions, I may jot notes, and maybe we'll return to them; others may require longer answers, for which I'll wait to respond.

E: Pre-questions question? What has/will happen to the Journals?
Will: Willa and I both have copies of each. I have the originals of Z and T, and she has the original sources of Mum, Lily, and Dad, Gordon. I'm not sure if Willa still keeps a journal. You know I do, and you'll get mine. You could ask her about her journals. Eventually, a school or library may find them interesting. You and I should write on the first page who may have access to them.

1. **E: How long did the publishing phase take?**
   W: A year.

2. **E: What else did you discover?**
   W: The book told me better alternatives if I did other things and carried it with me in my head.

3. **E: Like exercising, riding, walking . . .**
   W: listening to books, gardening, cooking. . . .

4. **In the process of writing, what impressed/surprised you? What did you discover/learn?**
   a. The book often "told" me how it wanted to be written. Every delay and unproductive hour made an improvement I hadn't expected.
   b. With time, more truth—the range of the truth of fiction— keeps surfacing.

Yes, there are and were people who denied then and deny now that the Holocaust happened. From my interviews, research, and evidence, I believe the Holocaust happened.

People (Jews) did not resist. They did resist. More will surface.

People (Jews) believed what they were told. I think they acted as expected to save their lives.

People (Jews) had hope.

People (Germans) lied.

Rudolph Vrba, formerly Walter Rosenburg, #44070, and Fred Wetzler escaped Auschwitz in 1944 and produced "The Auschwitz Report."

(**The Escape Artist**, Johnathan Freedland). People did not believe it: Roosevelt, Churchill, and Pius XII (who could not write the word "Jews" when he pleaded for help).

Individual copies were handed out and made with carbon on a typewriter had an impact, but some Jews believed they were being relocated, even standing in the cold naked after neatly stacking their clothes and shoes for easier retrieval after the "baths" and being given a piece of soap before entering the crematorium, where the Zyklon B tablets killed them.

People, in general, don't believe they are going to die.

What some individuals believe is the truth may not be true. Time eventually, and often, not always, produces truth, though some people act on beliefs to the best of their considerations at the time.

Intelligence must be believed before it becomes knowledge—when action is taken on that intelligence.

    c. People are resilient.

    d. The definitions of words change over the years.

Terms that had meanings, upon which assumptions were made in 1940–1945, have been broadened since then: *intimate, relationship, friendship, living with, common law, friend, partner, wife, husband, attracted to, sex as an exercise versus a reflection of love or marriage, blood versus legal* status; I address this a bit with T, Fred, and Guion. This is one reason why dictionaries continue to publish new editions.

5. **Unanswered questions**? Amplify, **Colditz, Prisoners of the Castle,** Ben Macintyre

6. Topics you wish you could have done more about, like reparations

7. Comment on: Legacy? Hope? Despair? Humanity?

8. **Kurt Gödel's loophole: A contradiction in the U.S.A. Constitution cited by Gödel in 1947 on how a democracy**

can be legally turned into a dictatorship. Citation in resources while in draft form only—not final copy.

9. Maybe Bigger Questions?:
   a. What does it mean to be human?
   b. How do we want to live?
   c. Who will we be to each other?

10. **I won't ask you to narrow this to one, but for whatever reasons, what are your top three books?**

W: For various reasons . . . if you are interested—

E: **I'm interested, but don't make this a lecture; I know lecturing isn't your favorite, and I bet I could name them.**
W: **Go, girl!**

E: **Ironman, *La Commedia*; I can't remember the third book, but I can give you the reason: Lee, the Asian servant . . . James Dean movie—**
W: **East of Eden.** John Steinbeck.

E: **Yes! But I also remember something about the embodiment of evil that . . . I can't recall.**
W: My favorite—and least favorite literary characters—are coincidentally in the same book. Nudging Lee is Naburo Nakatani from *Ironman*.

E: **Right! Back to *Eden*—she walked out on her kids. I wondered how many fathers—**
W: No lecture—remember? All three highlight *classical, contemporary,* and *characters*, three "c" words.

E: I can't write as fast as you think.

W: Awww, add one more "c" word, and tie them together . . . coincidentally.

E: And, Dante's book begins with—STOP! We need to move on. Dare I ask? Oh! Wait! . . . that Langston Hughes poem title that was a treasure hunt . . . how many found the title?

W: All, and without sharing the title, "I Dream a World." What was as interesting was the process and how each found the answer.

Back to Dante.

W: You know . . . I could get along with just the first and last cantos, one and one hundred of Dante; Steinbeck's, I could extract the Lee pages where he speaks and is spoken about . . . but intact, the book that makes me grin and teary, excels in characters . . . What's this?

E: Oh, a little prediction I pulled from a passing cloud!

    [I slide a 3x5 card with the title **Ironman** on it.] You know I carry Naburo's words from his last meeting with the Angry Management Group. Is there anyone who defines Mercy better?

W: You know me too well! When you read it, I remember you mentioning changing the names, as the characters were kids with whom you went to school.

E: Care to elaborate? "Whenever you think you've had your share, there's more."

W: Sounds like something I wish I had said.

W: No two stories are the same. More and more, I value one versus a collection. A single rose says more than an armful, the scent of which could trigger a migraine.

E: What of the strength in numbers?

W: Counts in voting; politics; but, if we each saw what we add as individuals. . . . The government amasses people with labels, yet each of us is a stitch in the fabric of a quilt.

E: And others?

W: If each of us were isolated, others wouldn't matter, but we are social, and if things don't concern us directly, we have friends or know others who are fellow citizens. When we say "American," that includes pride and shame, and we take that all on, and we are a part of that when we swear loyalty and become citizens . . . and even noncitizens—we share the country and air and place in which we live. We're not the only country with pride and shame woven into our history, but too often, people are mistreated. The Fourth of July is a day, not every day, but every day should be used to rectify unjust, unequal, and mistreated. *Capisce?*

E: Isn't that the same in every country? We learn its language, live its culture, food, etc.

W: But, when a country is number one, it is looked to as an example; it has no worldly objectives, and despite its shameful pages of history, we, as citizens, need to correct what is wrong—and there is plenty—and forge ahead carefully, trying not to make old mistakes or new ones.

E: So we learn from the past, live in the present, and look to the future. For example?

W: This is intricate, and I'm trying to sort out the facts. Technology is making more history available; owning our errors isn't something we do proudly, but as a people and as a society, that's tough for individuals and tough as a nation. People live in limited lifetimes, and waiting for a better balance doesn't work. It's wrong.

E: Individuals can get therapy or talk to a psychologist. What can a country do?

W: I'm not a fan of reparations in a financial sense; money gives descendants claims on the backs of ancestors. There are better ways to honor those ancestors, our predecessors. When people become citizens, they swear loyalty to the new country, but their hearts, language, and traditions remain in their former countries, During World War II, the Japanese were put into camps. The Nazis learned from us and thought that one drop of blood made a person a Negro—I'm using the term in use then; I still prefer the solid yet melodious sound of the word—was too restrictive. Still, they taught us about concentration camps and labeled people "enemy aliens."

E: The Japanese?

W: The spotlight was on the Japanese as they were easily visible, like a person of color. But, on the edges of that spotlight were the Italians and Germans, who were not so visible but were also classified as "enemy aliens." They were restricted and had curfews and conditions.

Conversations from Italians in California seeped out about being in camps in Missoula, Montana, especially from February to June 1942.

The idea of the camps was a good one in one sense: to keep people safe from the mobs who were a danger to the "enemy aliens," but how the country put them into the camps was as bad as what the Nazis did. Their spirits were killed, and some committed suicide because their reputations were tainted, which, for Italians, was a cultural affront some could not wait to see corrected. Even in literature, Willa Cather in **My Ántonia**. Her father committed suicide—he missed his Bohemian homeland.

If we had put people into our camps with careful records of seized property to be returned after the war, had troops for order, and provided medical and religious support, people would have better understood the government acting on their safety vs. acting on the country's prejudices. We botched a chance that a little care could have helped.

E: So only West Coast Italians went to camps? Why not Italians on the East Coast, like Boston and New York, where they are entrenched?

W: Interesting, eh? I started hearing some of that when I listened to clusters of men on the corners who gathered in parks, played cards, and were very careful about non-Italians who overheard. I never asked questions about whatever I heard, but Pro and I had some fascinating discussions that were primarily oral—but *history* nonetheless. I never pressed my presence, and frequently, as I walked by, I would hear "*Zito!*" and a guy quietly put his finger to his lips. Despite a few words in Italian and the culture I was exposed to in the Italian section of London, I was not one of them.

Despite all my studies, I was an outsider; even those limited in language and writing had a cultural advantage that I did not. But I could express what some of them could not, so the balance was there to their advantage, which was all I was seeking to make others aware of their plight.

E: You know why East Coast Italians weren't put into camps?

W: I have my thoughts. Even if it is oral history, evidence may prove why.

E: This sounds like a sequel . . . you're not thinking of "bailing out" anytime soon, are you?

W: Not that I know of. I'll work on it as long as I'm able. I have considered asking my lawyer to be my literary heir if you're too busy or uninterested. I don't want this to burden you at this stage of your life.

It's all in my files, which I'll share with you when you have time if you are interested. It might be a good opportunity for us to explore this more thoroughly, make a plan, and see if you want to spend a couple of summers bringing this to fruition.

E: Fiction or nonfiction?

W: You'd be the author. You're creative; a novel might be more fun, less frustrating, and less fact-dependent, so one wouldn't lose credibility. Lug it around. Let's chat later.

E: How could this country better its future?

W: Oversimplification here, but ask the electorate to vote Yes or No on a Constitutional Convention. The result becomes a mandate from the people. No is no. Done. Yes, it means creating a committee with a plan and timeline within a year—the electorate votes upon the 202?-Constitution.

Committee members must disregard party loyalty, commit to loyalty to the mandate, and act expeditiously. Those who demonstrate commitment to the party are replaced. Each committee may dismiss and replace the next person on the list. Each state has a committee of three. The country has a committee of three. All elected officials voted onto committees may remain in public office and be able to function on committees. This requires the cooperation of the media. Every daily newspaper and every news-reporting program agrees to a three-minute update on what happened in the last twenty-four hours. Each paper and news presentation agrees to keep the public informed. Each news agency and reporting program has one representative.

I don't have all the kinks worked out, but I'm flexible.

Professional mediators will rule.

E: Pardon me if I cough!

W: I get it. You think I have a plan for everything.

E: You think? Where would I have gotten that? Hmm?

W: Guilty. I guess. But . . . I know you won't let me go on longer than your interest allows . . . but I'm on the front line of the future . . . my future . . . elsewhere . . . and maybe I have a trajectory in my DNA. However, I'm still intact now, functioning on all cylinders—which could change at any time.

Epilogue

D**ear Reader,**

How do we survive the challenges of life and build lives?

Does your life have a theme? Main idea; underlying meaning.

Our Time: how we spend our lives, our time, will, as a quality, a characteristic.

Humans are resilient. We face challenges and can make life work.

Often, the choices over which we have the least control help strengthen us. Adjusting to life is a skill we continue to learn and hone all our lives. Often, friends, family, others, and faith help, but our inner "soul" is responsible for our acts and motivation. Often, we question and judge ourselves. We realize adjusting is worth our time.

In the time of our lives, life reveals itself to us with the gift of mystery for each day and each moment.

When we think we've had our share of challenges, we discover we have more to learn. May the characters with whom you have shared time help you recognize the power within you to live as best you can with persistence, effort, and gratitude. May this book, its characters, and events, inspire you.

Thank you.

Peace,
Edel, Will, and Len

Post-Reading Study Guide

1. With which character(s) did you feel a connection?

2. Who would you like to know more about?

3. Take a virtual tour of locations. Which would you like/plan to visit?

4. Interview people who have recollections about the period. How would you integrate them into the book?

5. What questions would you ask the author and characters?

6. Did the book inspire you to write?

7. Comment on the format.

8. How would you rate interest (1, least, to 10, most) and readability?

9. Was your time worth reading/listening?

10. What would make this a better "read"?

About the Author

Len DeAngelis
(Leonard A. DeAngelis)

Photo: Monica DeAngelis, 11 November 2023.

Birth: Boston, Massachusetts, U.S.A., 23 January 1942, attended Boston Public Schools: Paul Revere, Eliot, Michaelangelo, Robert Gould Shaw, Roslindale High, 1959; State College Boston, B.S. in Ed., '63; Boston College, M.A., '65; USNR-R; Middletown Teacher of the Year, '89; Rhode Island Teacher of the Year, '90; Disney's American Teacher Award, '90; English Department Chair, MHS, '94– '00; Stopover Services Board, '01-'06, Secretary ('02-'03), President ('03-'04); Rhode Island Council of Teachers of English Board, '94-present; Salve Regina University, Circle of Scholars Instructor, '02-present; Leadership Council, 2020–2023 Edward L. King Senior Center, Instructor, 2000–2010; Art League of Rhode Island, Corresponding Secretary, '03-'06, Nancy Gaucher-Thomas Award, '05, president, '06-'07; Governor's Scenes of Rhode Island, exhibitor, 2008; Rhode Island Watercolor Society, artist member, 2008; Rhode Island Ambassador, The Portrait Society of America, 2010-present; Newport Athletic Club, Member of the Month, March 2015; Education for Service Award, 2018, University of Massachusetts, Boston; Resident, walker, and bike rider of Newport, Rhode Island, 02840 since 1970; Swims and works out at The Boys and Girls Club of Newport, and The YMCA, Middletown, Rhode Island, 02842; Greater Tiverton Community Chorus, 2014-present). ARIA, Association of Rhode Island Authors 2024.

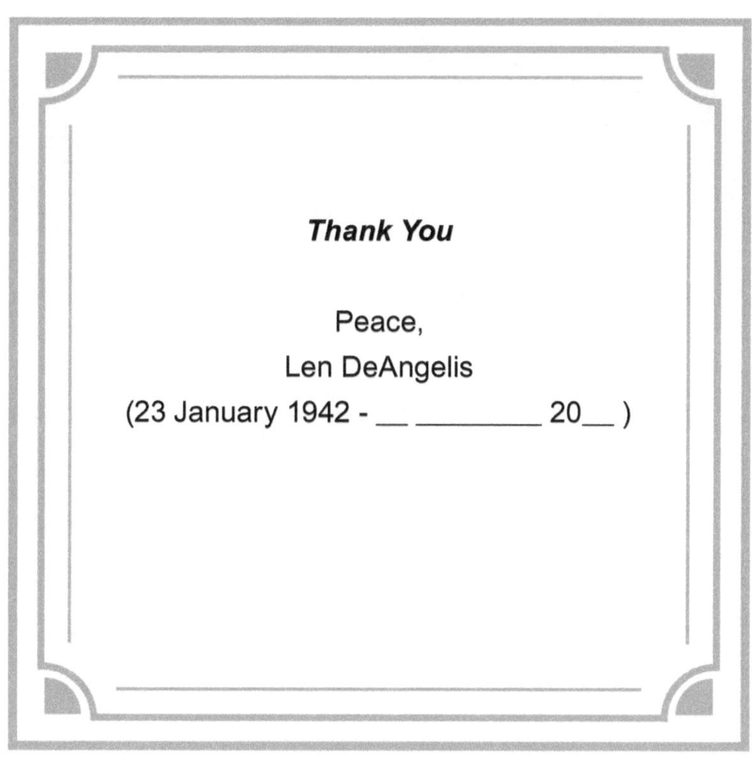

Thank You

Peace,
Len DeAngelis
(23 January 1942 - __ __________ 20__)